"I love books that have some humor; I think it gives some flavor to the story. And this story has a wonderful one. The story line had some unique ideas, the dialogue was amazing, the characters deep and so real I swear they seem alive, and the action so well written that it kept me under its spell until the end. Five stars for this outstanding book, you shouldn't miss it."
—*Booked Up Reviews*

"The tension between June and Harry through the first part of the book prevents the novel from being too predictable, while the cat-and-mouse game keeps the tension high. Filled with magic, pack politics and a few surprises, *Pack and Coven* is a face-paced, sensual urban fantasy that will appeal to readers looking for a story as well as some steam."
—*Library Journal Xpress Reviews*

"Harry and June are likable characters. The idea behind the world building was not something I recall coming across in previous shapeshifter books, which is kind of a remarkable feat. It is a book about a reluctant alpha who doesn't want to be a pack leader, with a non virginal heroine, a May-December romance complete with a car chase, dog jokes and a tea room."
—*Dear Author*

Pack & Coven

JODY WALLACE

CARINA PRESS™

ISBN-13: 978-0-373-77808-9

PACK & COVEN

Recycling programs for this product may not exist in your area.

www.CarinaPress.com

Printed in U.S.A.

Acknowledgments

I'd like to thank Gina Bernal, Angela James and the rest of the staff at Carina Press for working with me on this novel. More thanks to Rae Ann Parker and Monica McCabe for the research trips to tearooms, Cathy Pegau for the biology lessons and brainstorming/critiquing awesomeness, and West Virginia for being wild and wonderful. Last, I'd like to thank my recliner for being my loyal companion and offering me such unfailing support on this writing journey. I'd never replace you with a treadmill writing desk, my dear. Never, ever.

CHAPTER ONE

"Sorry, sweetie, we're out of porterhouses." Harry's gray-haired waitress slid a stemmed water glass onto the table in front of him and flipped her receipt book to the next page.

Out of porterhouses? How could Miss Sandie's Tea Room run out of steaks when he was the only customer who ordered them?

Harry stared at the frilly, blue-checkered menu as if another werewolf-friendly item were going to appear among the scones and scotch eggs. Miss Sandie's was his customary lunch spot, but he'd rather fire up the grill himself than settle for a fruit plate.

Which was saying a lot. Harry hadn't gotten a culinary gene, just a furry one.

"Are you sure, Annette? Did Sandie order T-bones?" He sniffed the air but couldn't detect much beyond the fresh flowers on his table and apple-pie odor that saturated the dining room. He didn't have the greatest nose in wolfdom, but it wasn't as dull as a human's.

"Your friends from earlier cleaned us out." Annette slipped into the chair across from him, clearly intent on a chat. The café wasn't busy at this hour. "Sandie doesn't mind keeping you in steaks, Harry, but this isn't a greasy spoon."

"Which friends?" He peered around the pastry cabinet next to his chair, but a table of female diners blocked his view of the café.

"Your lady friends." Annette smoothed a wrinkle out of the tablecloth. "I use the term *lady* loosely, you understand. No ladies I know behave like that."

He didn't like the sound of that. Harry had a number of lady friends, and none would give Annette a sour face. Or order steak at a tea room. He liked his women sweet, talented in the kitchen and one hundred percent human. He also liked them roughly his own age, which left Miss Sandie and her staff out of the running. Too bad. Miss Sandie in particular had a great sense of humor, an open mind, a big heart, and was one of the best cooks he'd ever known.

The question was, why would Annette connect some random, steak-eating women to him? "My friends, huh. Did they mention me by name or something?"

Annette tapped her pen on her receipt book. "They said they knew you. They looked familiar, but I haven't met every single person in town."

"Maybe they weren't from around here." Millington, West Virginia, wasn't big, but it was close enough to Wheeling that they did get tourist traffic. It was possible some of the independent shifters he'd known in New York City were visiting.

"Could be." She leaned toward him. "I certainly

don't know anyone in Millington who thinks dog collars make good fashion accessories."

"Not even pink ones?"

Annette rolled her eyes, so Harry changed the subject. He'd been in Wheeling all morning buying supplies for his garage, and he was starving. "What are the specials today?"

"Same as every Thursday, kiddo," Annette teased, but she told him anyway.

While she talked, Harry cursed inwardly. These "friends" sounded like local pack members. He frequented the tea room and befriended humans as part of his strategy of pack avoidance. If the pack invaded his sanctuary, he'd be severely put out. It had taken years to cultivate Sandie and her staff, trading discounted automotive repairs for steaks cooked the way he liked them, friendly faces and the occasional heated bunco session.

This was his place. His. Why did they have to ruin it? Couldn't they just leave him alone?

He could just hear the alpha female, Bianca's, coaxing tones—*Bert agreed to accept you, Harry. Wolves aren't made to live by themselves, Harry. Join the pack, Harry.*

The pack could kiss his hairy butt. Contrary to popular werewolf belief, shifters could be as human as the next human if they wanted. Pack life was a choice, not a necessity.

A choice Harry didn't plan to make.

"Earth to Harry." Annette tapped his menu with her pen. "What do you want for lunch?"

"Ham-and-cheese croissant—heavy on the cheese, heavier on the ham—a side of scrambled eggs with that tomato sauce, a plate of scones, a selection of marmalades and a strawberry-and-walnut salad. Oh, and fruit tea."

"Hungry boy." Annette stuck her pen in her up-swept hairdo. "You remind me of Junior."

"He doing okay at school?"

"He was home at Christmas. He looked thin."

"I'm sure you remedied that." Harry handed over the menu and winked. Annette ran a close second to Sandie as his favorite person in Millington, and that was saying something, because Sandie was his favorite person outside Millington too. "If any of my so-called friends come back, tell them you're out of steak and save the porterhouse for me."

The bell above the door tinkled a merry tune. She rose and slipped her receipt book in her apron pocket. "Why don't you tell them yourself?"

"What do you mean?" He swiveled in his chair and watched local pack members Bianca, Violet and Susan stroll through the front door. Their spike-heeled boots and skintight clothes were as out of place in Miss Sandie's Tea Room as Annette and Sandie would have been in a biker bar.

Bianca's chin lifted as she scented the air, and her gaze fell unerringly on Harry. "There you are."

He did his best to conceal his flinch and regretted

the fact he'd already given Annette the menu because he couldn't duck behind it.

"I'll get your tea," Annette said before she left. "If your friends order anything, let them know that around here we tip the wait staff."

The three shifters swaggered through the tea room, attracting a good deal of attention. The ladies at the next table bent their heads together, whispering. Thanks to his sharper-than-human ears, Harry could hear them.

"Those are the ones I was telling you about," the blonde said. Her name was Donna Manns, and Harry had gone out with her years ago. "They're dating that lowlife Bert Macabee whose gang got caught robbing the Webster place."

Hold on, this was news. The pack alpha had gotten his ass arrested? Donna was married to a cop now. She'd know what she was talking about.

"All three were dating him at the same time?" one of the ladies gasped, horror and delight in her voice. "Did they know about each other?"

"Apparently," Donna said with relish. "The one with black hair, Bianca Macabee, she's married to him. Those people down the river are like a cult. My husband says they're nudists or survivalists or something. I guess they do things different. Well, they can't break the law. Macabee's going to be sent to prison."

Harry cleared his throat. When the ladies turned, he nodded politely. Bianca liked to pick fights. If the news were true, she'd be especially belligerent right now. The ladies realized Bianca had closed in, so they hushed—the better to hear whatever she planned to say to Harry.

"Harry," Bianca said, lingering over the *R*s. "We've been looking for you all day."

Bianca might be a wolf, but when she talked—at least when she was in a good mood—she purred. She didn't sound belligerent. Donna must be wrong about Bert, or Bianca wouldn't be smiling. The pack had a good lawyer.

"I just got back from a purchasing trip," he answered, relaxing a little. "I'm having lunch."

"They have excellent steaks," Bianca remarked. "I may have to bring my friends here."

Harry didn't want the pack haunting Miss Sandie's. Moreover, he didn't want Sandie and the others associating him with the shifters. Not that humans knew about shifters, but the local pack had a bad reputation in these parts. They maintained a few lucrative businesses—bar, bike shop, convenience store—but they liked to bully the humans.

And, apparently, rob them.

"They don't usually have steaks," Harry lied. "What can I do for you? Is your truck giving you trouble?"

"Now, Harry, there's no need to be all business. We've known each other for years."

Yeah, years of him distancing himself from pack politics. He and the local group had coexisted in uneasy accord after Bert satisfied himself Harry wasn't going to make a play for the territory.

That didn't stop other pack members—mostly women—from imploring him to join. They'd get in big trouble if they slept with a wolf outside the pack, and for whatever reason women regarded Harry as desirable.

A burden he valiantly bore.

Bianca slid into the chair across from him while Violet and Susan hovered behind her. The lace-topped table only seated two. Over Bianca's shoulder, Harry saw Annette peek through the round window of the kitchen door. She probably wouldn't come back out while Bianca and company were here.

So much for his tasty beverage. Damn, he was thirsty too.

He did have water. He sighed and crunched ice, wishing it were Sandie's fruit tea. "Why are you looking for me?"

"You know what we want." Under the table, Bianca's boot nudged his calf, inching upward. Her black hair was pulled into a sleek tail, and her dark eyes were made darker by makeup. "We want you to come to our party."

Pack wolves hosted annual ceremonies to renew bonds. Their annual was next month, but he'd rather gnaw his own foot off than show up for a party like that. Snacks or no snacks.

"I sent my regrets." Harry crossed his legs under the table, kicking her boot aside. "I have plans that night."

"Doing what, playing bunco with the grannies?" Violet asked with a snide laugh.

Bianca chuckled a moment but then snapped her fingers, silencing the other female. "How many times have you missed our party? I won't take no for an answer."

Independents frequently left the vicinity during annual ceremonies to avoid being sucked in. Harry was no exception.

"Sorry. I'll be out of town." He kicked her foot away again, and his knee banged the underside of the table. Silverware rattled. The eavesdropping ladies at the next table jumped in their seats.

"Right, your yearly vacation. Since you're so predictable, we switched the date for you. The party's tonight." Bianca smiled, her teeth straight, white and not at all canine.

"Tonight?" She had to be lying. Bonding ceremonies took weeks to plan. You couldn't just whip one up because you felt like it. "It's not the full moon."

"Full enough." She studied him. "I thought you didn't care about lunar cycles."

"I don't, but I know you do."

The Millington wolves were classic conservatives in the larger world of shifters. They lived in packs ruled by an alpha male and female and preferred a home base as close to the edge of civilization as possible. Ceremonies were tied to cycles of the moon. It had been proven by shifter scientists that werewolves were no more connected to the moon than any other primate, but conservatives regarded that factoid like certain human groups regarded evolution.

Shifters had some unique biological constraints. Moon madness wasn't one of them. The moon controlled the tides, yes, but howling at it was optional.

Bianca thunked her elbows on the table. "Harry," she said, in a different voice, one that almost seemed rational. "You may have heard. Things have changed."

Was she talking about Bert? Harry played dumb. "I haven't heard anything."

"Don't lie to me." She jerked her head toward the eavesdroppers. "What Blondie said is true. Bert and a few others are headed to the pen. There's no way our lawyer can get him off this time, and we already made the party plans. You know what that means."

Packs required two alphas to function. With Bert out of the territory and in prison, he wouldn't be able to serve as a fulcrum. He'd also be cut off from his shifter nature unless there was a pack in the pen he could join.

Harry doubted it. Most shifters weren't stupid enough to get nabbed by human law enforcement.

But Bert's arrest meant the Millington pack was under the gun. With the pack bond ceremony initiated weeks ago, they had to go through with the rest or the bond would dissolve and leave them permanently toothless. And they couldn't have a pack ceremony without two alphas.

Harry had no idea what unlucky shifter was about to get a boost in pack hierarchy, but he could hardly be more of a sleaze than Bert.

"Sorry about Bert. I know you were married to him

a long time." In most packs, the male and female alphas were partners legally too.

"Gosh, thanks. We had no idea he was into that stuff." Bianca smiled. "We're so upset."

Why did he not believe her? "I'm sure you'll have enough people at the party without me."

"That's just it." She adjusted the silverware in front of her before continuing. "We can't have it without you. You're the guest of honor."

Silence reigned as Harry stared at Bianca in horror. To his surprise, what with her being an actual pack alpha, she looked away first.

"You're joking," he said flatly. Every wolf in Millington, hell, probably on the continent, knew Harry didn't want to follow a leader—or be one.

"I'm not." Bianca looked as serious as he'd ever seen her, and the woman had a microscopic sense of humor. "I'm begging. You know what we've got to choose from, and they haven't got…what you've got."

"It's called brains." Harry's voice was more of a growl than intended. "All sorts of people have them."

When he'd moved to the area and discovered the pack was conservative, he'd considered returning to the city, but he was tired of concrete and skyscrapers. Even liberals liked to run free on occasion, and that was hard to do in New York.

"I'll ask you nicely," she began, before he cut her off.

"I'm not coming." If he had to, he'd drive to the closest airport after lunch and book a flight for Vegas.

Without their alpha, pack wolves couldn't leave their territories for extended periods of time. Two days, max. They certainly couldn't stray long enough to track him as far as Nevada, and Millington was short on alphas at the moment.

"I wish you hadn't said that." Bianca vibrated with an intensity that let him know how grim his situation was. Harry had no doubt about her meaning. Because he wasn't part of a pack, he was no match for pack wolves physically.

Mentally, he hoped, was another story.

"This is a free country, Bianca. Join the century. You can't make people do whatever you want." Good God, he hated conservative wolves. They thought they could ignore anything that conflicted with pack law, including free will. No way in hairy hell was he going to join the Millington pack, much less be its alpha.

"Can I not?" Her eyes flashed pale blue with anger, with the onset of her alpha strength.

Harry shrugged, fury building in his own chest. Other packs had pressured him to join, but nobody had threatened to shanghai him. He just wanted to fix cars, eat steaks and make love to pretty women. Why couldn't they accept he was different?

"I guess we have until tonight to change your mind," Bianca said.

"Find another guest of honor." If they weren't a bunch of damn crooks, they wouldn't have this problem. Harry's sympathy was nonexistent, and he was angry enough that Bianca's alpha side didn't influence him.

"You're the one we want. We voted."

While the touch of democracy in the pack surprised him, it didn't sway him.

"Import somebody." A wolf had to carry the alpha gene in order to serve, but that didn't mean candidates were so impossible to find that any pack would have to resort to him. There were plenty of alpha wannabes willing to jump ship. They were probably panting at the gates if news of Bert's arrest had circulated.

As long it wasn't one of the degenerates from the pack where Harry had been born, Bianca could hardly do worse than Bert Macabee.

She shook her head. "I'm not interested. The current crop is all idiots."

"Like Bert isn't." Harry tried not to growl. Not a good time for his primitive side to claw its way to the surface. Humans dealt with testosterone too, but when they got pissed, they didn't sprout fur and fangs. "Make a few calls up north. You can't throw a stick up there without hitting some guy who, uh, likes to party. You don't want me."

"Yes, we do," Bianca insisted.

"Why?" He might have the right DNA, but there was nothing else right about him.

Her lips tightened. "We voted."

"As a United States citizen, I have a vote too. It's no. If you don't mind, I prefer to eat alone," he lied.

Wolves could handle many things alone, but they rarely preferred it.

"We've got time. We'll wait."

Harry had several choices. He could make a break for it, but he'd never escape the pack under his own steam. Fighting was also out. They'd wipe the floor with him. Plus, he didn't want to subject the people in the tea room to a wolf-style throwdown.

Failing that—and it would fail—he could involve the police. They might not issue a restraining order against three hot chicks who wanted him to party, but Harry could contrive to get himself thrown in jail. Punch a cop or something. He didn't particularly want a criminal record, so he'd save that as his last resort.

For independents like Harry, human laws and shifter wits were their only recourse if they squabbled with a pack. It happened. Packs existed everywhere, under various guises. Some packs were worse than others when it came to trampling a wolf's right to independence, and there was no appeals committee. The packs couldn't cooperate long enough to agree on anything except Humans Must Not Find Out. Revealing the secret was the only thing a wolf would be punished for by the shifter world at large.

They certainly weren't punished for abusing those who were weaker, not if their alphas ignored it. Or did it themselves. Packs worked together to cover up their secrets…by any means necessary.

Harry's best choice seemed to be humoring Bianca long enough to locate a small vehicle with a large en-

gine. Maybe that Porsche he'd almost finished. If he
remained in pack territory, they could find him as easily as Bianca had today.

Discretion, valor, cowardice—who cared as long
as it worked and nobody got hurt?

"So are we settled?" Her tone had a tinge of sympathy. "You had to know you couldn't avoid our party
forever."

"I don't see why not," he answered in a low voice
he knew she could still hear. "There's no rule that says
everyone has to come to these parties."

"There should be. It would save time."

Packers and indies rarely saw the appeal of the other's lifestyle. Too bad packers were the majority. Too
bad indies had nowhere to go that was free of some
pack's influence. "You're disturbing the other diners.
I'll be at my shop by three. Meet me there."

"I don't think so."

He contemplated his empty glass and wondered
how long he'd last if he got into a spoon-and-doily
fight with three adult pack members. Ten, fifteen seconds. Twenty if he upended the table and they yelled
at him for spilling food on their boots. How the hell
was he going to get out of this?

He raised his hands, palms up. "What's the matter?
You don't trust me?"

"Would you trust me if the situations were re-
versed?"

A small hand belonging to a small woman landed

on his shoulder. He recognized the scent—his friend Sandie. Where had she come from?

"Are you harassing one of my customers, Mrs. Macabee?"

His rescuer was five feet tall and old as the hills, but her intervention flooded Harry with reassurance. It was one thing for packers to strut around in black leather, ride through town on choppers, harass people in tea rooms, vandalize public property, evade taxes and traffic in stolen goods. Humans did those things too.

Humans were less inclined to drag grown men out of tea rooms because they wanted to "party." Bianca's strategy had just become conspicuous.

"I'm extending a polite invitation," she said to Sandie in a sharper voice than her normal purr. Unless Harry was mistaken, anger had constricted her vocal cords with the beginning of a shift. The trick was not allowing it to go further than that. "Don't get your drawers in a wad."

Hot-tempered Violet looked equally angry. He didn't see any sprouts of hair, which was good. Susan seemed as impassive as always.

"Let the poor man eat." Sandie plonked a heavy plate on the table. Steam rose from the eggs in fragrant clouds, and he had not one but two big, fat croissants full of ham. "If he says he'll meet you at three, he'll meet you at three. Not a minute sooner."

Harry hid a smirk. The person he trusted most in

this world had his back. And his eggs. It might not cow Bianca, but it sure gave him a laugh.

Too bad Bianca wasn't impressed. "I don't think you know who you're talking to, old woman."

Harry quit grinning. Bianca wouldn't dare wolf out, but hearing the threat in her voice directed at Sandie angered him in a different way. Nobody bullied his friends without going through him. Which he knew Bianca would be happy to do.

Sandie, though, wasn't impressed either. She had an answer for everything, which was especially handy if your internet was down.

"I don't think you know who *you're* talking to, dear." She wriggled her fingers in the steam rising from the eggs. Though she had age spots, her fingers were straight and agile. Parsley sprinkled from her hand onto Harry's food. "This is my restaurant. If you don't leave my customers alone, I'll call the police."

Then she dusted her hands dismissively, flicking parsley onto Bianca's side of the small table.

Pressure built in Harry's ears as if he were driving up a mountain in a fast car. When Sandie bumped his arm with her hip, his ears popped.

Bianca pointed at him with a daggerlike fingernail. "If you aren't waiting for me at three, I'll find you. My friends are keeping an eye out, watching the roads to make sure you get to the party tonight."

Which meant she'd assigned sentries to shut down the territory.

"I'm not going anywhere." *Damn.* His best plan of

escape, shredded like a bag of cheese. Had she gone as far as a regional lockdown? Resentment churned inside him, twisting his nerve endings until he was afraid his hair might stand on end.

To Harry, there was no worse fate than joining a pack. Not one.

"If I can't find you…" Her voice trailed off ominously as she rose, and the women sauntered out the door. They'd doubtless lie in wait, unwilling to give him a chance to slip through their fingers. He could only linger for so long before his own behavior became conspicuous.

Sandie clucked her tongue. "Girls today, I swan. They have no manners."

"I have to agree," said Donna from the next table. "That's pure low-class. A girl shouldn't have to chase a man to catch him."

Sandie smiled at the woman. "I can recall a few times you might have chased Timothy."

She'd chased Harry too. He kept his mouth zipped shut.

"That was different." Donna flushed, and the other two women at the table laughed. "Oh, hush, all of you!"

As the lunch companions began arguing what constituted chasing, Sandie returned her attention to Harry. "If you want to leave out the back, that's fine with me."

Her hand patted his hair, combing through it as if he had tangles, which he didn't because it was too short.

Sandie wasn't huggy, and he appreciated the gesture. Some of his anxiety eased. As a shifter, he liked a lot of contact, particularly from people in his inner circle.

"Thanks." She never let customers in her kitchen, something about recipe espionage. "I'm sorry they barged in here like that. I don't know them well. I just work on their vehicles. I have zero interest in their party."

For a moment Sandie didn't answer. It would suck rocks if she cold-shouldered him because of Bianca. Not that Sandie was judgmental, but it would bother him if she thought poorly of him. In addition to that, the grannies, as Violet had called them, were his primary social network. No werewolf, not even indies, handled complete isolation without consequences.

And, really, he adored the grannies. He watched his language for the grannies. The day he'd slipped into Miss Sandie's Tea Room eight years ago had been like coming to a home he hadn't known he had. Sandie had plunked herself down at his table to ask how he liked his sandwich, and that had been that. He'd been a goner. His relationship with her and her friends was more fulfilling than the indies he'd palled around with in New York. Tastier too. He'd never been happier and less inclined to travel—which didn't mean he wanted the option of travel taken away by a pack bond.

Once a wolf bonded with a pack, he or she was stuck as a packer, usually for life.

And pack life wouldn't include, couldn't include, Sandie and the grannies.

Finally she patted his shoulder and sighed. "I've been telling you to find a nice girl and settle down, haven't I? Then ones like that won't hunt you down."

Harry reached out and snugged the old lady to his side. He knew she had a larger personal space than he did, but sometimes he couldn't help himself. "How could I? You're the only woman I want."

"Nonsense." She smacked his hand away, but when he glanced at her face, she was blushing. She had bright blue eyes, a snippy nose and hair like white cotton candy. She must have been remarkably pretty in her day. "I'm old enough to be your grandmother."

"Haven't you heard of May-December romances?" he teased. He loved her scent—cake and fruit tea.

"Player." She extracted herself from his grasp. "Are we still on for tonight?"

"I may have to miss this week." Several of them drove to the closest town with a theater once a month for popcorn and cinema. Or cinema criticism, which is what it turned into.

"If you change your mind," Sandie said, "I can pick you up at seven."

"I'll let you know." Harry was pretty sure he could find a way out of Bianca's trap, but it wasn't something he could discuss with Sandie. He suddenly wished he could, wished he could tell her everything so she could help him fix it.

But no. She was human, he was shifter, and they could only take a friendship so far.

She watched him for a minute as if she were reading his mind. "Is something the matter?"

"Nah. I'm just too popular for my own good." He shoved food into his mouth to end the conversation. If he couldn't figure this thing with Bianca out, what was he going to tell Sandie?

Goodbye?

Instead he said, "Good eggs."

"Don't talk with your mouth full, Mr. Popular."

"Mmf," he responded, not watching when she left.

No reason to think about goodbyes until he considered his situation from all angles. The pack's traditional ways were confining. Prehistoric. Bert hadn't encouraged male alphas of any stripe to hang around. He didn't want a challenge. Harry had been an exception. Now Bert was gone, and if the pack couldn't find somebody fast they were in trouble.

Not Harry's problem. After seeing his mother humiliated and abused during his pack upbringing, he'd vowed never to be a packer. He fulfilled his shifter drive for interaction in other ways. Like tea rooms. And bunco. And movie night, dammit.

In fact, he had no idea why anyone would choose pack over independence. Why commit to one group, one set of faces, one geographic location, when there was a whole world to see and billions of people in it? He wasn't a mutant—he liked a stable home base— but he could travel. Only last summer, he, Sandie, Annette and her husband, Pete, had rented a condo at the beach for two weeks and helped a conservation group flag sea-turtle nests. Packers couldn't do that unless they lived at the beach already.

His inclinations, his will, were the only things he had to heed. Pack bonds compelled you to obey your alphas. No way was Harry tying himself to that kind of existence. He'd promised his mother before she'd died, and he'd promised himself.

He just wasn't sure how to avoid it this time without getting himself tossed in jail.

CHAPTER TWO

FOR THE FIRST time since he'd met Sandie, Harry regretted setting up shop in Millington.

It had seemed the perfect choice for a shifter looking for a little room to run. The town sprawled in a valley between two West Virginia mountain peaks. Townies had used every available square foot of space before the mountains on either side grew too steep. Some buildings perched on the slopes like goats.

Miss Sandie's Tea Room was uptown, with the old brick buildings along Main Street. New developments like the Wal-Mart and hospital were downtown on River Street, which tended to flood in the spring. Only three automotive bridges crossed the Beacon River for miles in either direction, and they were all in or near Millington.

Bianca's sentries would have all routes out of the county watched. Packs the size of Millington's had experience with runners and claim jumpers, so trapping a single indie would be child's play, even if they didn't notify other territories.

Certain packs were notorious for impressment, but who would have thought, in this day and age, a pack would force an indie to bond as alpha? A regular packer, maybe, but alpha? Ludicrous. Once absorbed by the pack, he'd have little choice but to cooperate. The bond's hive mind would see to it. If he severed the bond without transferring to another pack, his shifting ability would be forfeit…among other things.

Was it worth it to give up his abilities? He'd never be in this position again if he survived the severance, but that choice had killed his mother. A choice she'd made to save him. He couldn't tarnish her sacrifice.

After he'd finished eating what he hoped wasn't his last meal as a free man, Annette bustled Harry through the fascinating odors of the kitchen before he could so much as peek into any ovens. Sandie, to his disappointment, was nowhere in sight. He thought about borrowing her car, but it was on its last legs. Tires. Rims. Whatever. Blowing out the motor in a high-speed chase with Millington's wolf pack wasn't the way to gently suggest it was time for Sandie to give up the Caddy.

He didn't know anyone else to ask, and he wouldn't steal a car unless he had to. Bad karma, to steal from friends. He hated the thought of leaving forever. This place suited him. Everything about it satisfied his shifter need for a foundation while leaving him free. The geography suited him. The level of industry suited him. The people suited him.

Except for the pack. Maybe he should have stayed in New York.

Harry shifted, clothes and all, when he reached a

private area a couple hundred yards up the mountain. He was good for a few more shifts before he got form stuck, a pain in ass at the best of times and a really bad idea today. While it was tempting to run like the wind in the opposite direction, the pack would be on him before he got out of Millington. He might be fast, but they could sense alphas like him from miles away. Yet another annoying skill shifters picked up with a pack bond.

His best chance was that Porsche. Now he had to get to the car in one piece.

Adrenaline pumping, he loped through the woods to his shop, three miles up the state highway that led in and out of the valley. He veered off his normal route but didn't scent any recent wolf spore, which surprised him. He figured he'd have to dodge lookouts all the way to his garage. Wary, he returned to the game trail he'd worn between his place and Sandie's so he could pick up speed.

Soon he arrived on the outskirts of his property. According to his nose, Bianca had been here. He could scent his cats, small game, the metallic taint of his garage and something, someone else.

Intruder. The thick hair along his spine ruffled as he growled deep in his chest.

A two-leg. Traces of the person existed in the forested area of his property, where his private trail to town began.

Might be human.

Might be a shifter in human form.

With some difficulty, he resisted the urge to mark his perimeter. He could handle this situation better in human form. It could be innocent. A tourist with car trouble searching for a mechanic.

Except the scent was near the edge of the woods on private property marked by no-trespassing signs.

He had to find out who was here and get to the Porsche. If—no—*when* he made it out of pack territory, he'd call his part-time assistant, Chip, and discuss business contingency plans. Within reason, because Chip didn't know about his furry side.

Harry slunk into a stand of pine and changed. Though it sapped his energy, it was otherwise quick and painless. The media definitely had that wrong. He'd learned to transmute his clothes and possessions fifteen years ago after studying with a shaman in Manitoba. Cost an arm, a leg and free car repairs to anyone bearing the shaman's token, but it had paid off time and again.

Slipping his pocket knife into his hand, Harry broke cover and approached the back of his house. His cabin and garage were nestled away from the main road far enough that passersby couldn't see them, just the signpost.

He didn't like this. While he hadn't believed Bianca would give him until three, it would be hard to access the Porsche if she'd planted guards. Since he wasn't pack, he could only locate other shifters in normal ways.

He peered around the property, listening, scenting.

Nothing out of the ordinary. In human form, he'd lost the hint of the trespasser. He rounded the side of his house and noticed a tiny, stubbed-off car in the gravel parking lot of his garage.

His prowler drove a Smart car. Or was it a tourist? It wasn't a vehicle he'd pick for cross-country travel. Not enough horsepower and nowhere to put your luggage or your beer cooler.

He sighted a flash of pink near the car, a glint of sunlight on pale hair.

As quietly as possible, Harry unlocked the side entrance of the garage. The smell of gasoline crinkled his nose, but he ignored it and peeked through the front windows of the office.

The flash of pink turned out to be the dress of someone he knew well. Somebody whose scent he should have recognized instantly. Somebody who had an important place to be this time of day, and it wasn't his garage.

Harry rolled up the bay door closest to the supermini, and his guest started at the sudden noise. She held her hands over her heart. In them was a large, shiny purse.

"Sandie?" he called out, pocketing his knife. "What are you doing here?"

"I'm not Sandie." Quick as a cat, she removed a compact from her purse and dabbed powder on her nose. "Are you Harry?"

"Of course I'm Harry." He approached her cautiously, a little concerned about her mental state. In the years he'd known her, Sandie had shown zero signs of dementia. Why in the world was she pretending she wasn't herself and driving that ridiculous car? "Are you all right? Do you need me to call somebody for you?"

"I'm not Sandie." She waved a hand up and down her body, inviting him to take a closer look.

Harry blinked, and the woman blurred. When his vision cleared, she still looked like Sandie, with one major difference.

She was a good fifty years younger.

This Sandie was all pink and white and girly. Her eyes were the same blue, but her curly hair was blond. Her nose was the same snip, but her skin was plush and dewy as a peach. She was a little taller, a little rounder. As pretty a lady as any he'd ever laid eyes on.

"Do you need glasses? Sandie is my grandmother."

"I don't need glasses." How could he have thought this sweet young thing was an elderly woman? Harry edged closer, squinting. Had Sandie been wearing that dress in the tea room today? He was no expert on women's clothing.

She slipped her compact back into her purse. "A girl could feel very insulted at being mistaken for her nana."

"I didn't know Sandie had kids, much less grand-kids."

"Surprise." She held out her arms, her giant purse swinging. "Now that the introductions are through, there's something we need to discuss."

"Is there?" Even though he was intrigued by this woman, his metaphorical hackles had yet to settle. Genetics didn't explain why he'd seen her as Sandie, why she smelled like Sandie and, most of all, why he didn't know Sandie had grandkids. Harry stalked up to her and placed his hands on her shoulders.

"What are you doing?" She shoved her pocketbook between them like a shield.

"You really look like Sandie. You could be twins, give or take a few decades. Is this a prank?"

With a funny smile—or a smile that would have looked funny on Sandie—she allowed his overfamiliarity. Harry soaked in her details, using as much of his shifter self as he could summon without wolfing out. Her skin was unlined, her lips plump and rosy, and her ears small. Her pale eyebrows feathered up as if surprised, but it was how the hairs grew.

She was a ringer for Sandie from afar, but not from anear. There were differences. Her nose had a scrunch to it that…

No, wait, she *was* scrunching her nose.

"Good gravy," she said, sounding exactly like her grandmother. "Nana didn't warn me you were slow. This is going to be harder than I thought."

Leaning forward, Harry whuffed in her scent, and his mouth started to water. She was more than pretty. She was edible. Cake, fruit tea and a little bit of… What was that? He could barely tell over the smell of gas.

"Excuse me. I think that's enough." She shoved

her purse into his chest and hopped backward. Harry advanced, she retreated, until she bumped into her car. Because it was so ridiculously small, the impact shook the vehicle.

"You're excused. Now hold still." He whuffed again now that she couldn't escape and finally put his finger on it. Amber. Sandie didn't smell like amber, but this woman did. That's why he hadn't recognized her mark on his property.

"You are a very pushy person," she said, breathing a little faster. "You shouldn't go around grabbing people you just met."

"Probably not." Good thing she didn't know he'd like to do more than grab her. He'd heard of lust at first sight. This was more like lust at first sniff.

It was also damned inconvenient.

She pushed him again. "You're not being very nice."

Harry scratched behind his ear and stepped back. "Why didn't Sandie tell me about you?" Despite the fact none of this was relevant to his current crisis, he felt more than a little hurt.

"I don't know. She told me about you." She opened her handbag, pulled out a rubber glove and snapped it on. Then she extended her hand for a shake. "I'm June. Nice to finally meet you."

Harry eyeballed the glove a moment before accepting her greeting. As Sandie's granddaughter, he'd cut her some slack. Humans didn't have shifter constitutions, and some got freaky about germs. Sandie carried antibacterial wipes everywhere.

June had a grip as firm as her grandmother's.

"Nice to meet you too," Harry said, his curiosity aroused. What else did he not know about Sandie? He hid stuff from her, but that was different. He wasn't human. "Does Sandie have a big family?"

"No." June rubbed her palm against her cotton dress. "My mother was Nana's only child, and I was my mother's only child."

"I'm an only child too," he told her. And an orphan, but she didn't need to hear that part.

Her eyes widened. "I didn't know that about you."

"Why would you? We just met." If June could cook like her grandmother, his lust at first sniff could easily turn into more. Damn, she was pretty. "Is there a Mr. June?"

She blinked up at him, her cheeks pinkening. "What difference does that make?"

"Just checking." Harry rocked back on his heels. There was no Mr. June, he'd bet his toolbox. He'd also bet she knew exactly why he'd asked. "So tell me, why were you poking your nose all over my property?"

"I didn't think you'd mind," June said, "since I was looking for stuff to help you."

"Help me?" Harry glanced at her car and back at her. "I figure Sandie sent you here so I could help you."

"Why would I need your help?"

"Obviously to pick out a decent car." Not that he could advise her right now. In fact, he shouldn't even be flirting with her. He needed to head for the west coast ASAP. He'd grab a few things and put extra food out for the cats. Sandie could check on them later, and Chip could handle the business. Every indie worth his pelt had steps in place in the event he had to disappear.

Hopefully, June would be here when he got back, and there'd still be no Mr. June.

"My car," she told him, "is the least of your worries."

"I don't know about that." He sniffed. "I think you've got a gas leak."

"I don't, but that's not why I'm here." June opened her pocketbook again—really more of a suitcase than a purse—and withdrew two prongs of evergreen. They looked as if they'd been clipped from the white cedar near the back of his property.

"Then, Miss June, what are you doing here? Stealing my plants?"

It was possible Sandie intended to set them up. Interesting. She'd never done that before. In fact, she'd always tsked his choice of girlfriends. If Sandie thought they'd suit, he was definitely willing to...

He was definitely being stupid. The pack could show up at any moment, howling for him. This wasn't a safe place for a pretty female human who smelled like cake.

The pretty human watched him with eyes much older and wiser than her years.

"What am I doing here?" she mused. "It's hard to explain."

"It will have to wait." Harry tore his gaze from her

and checked his watch. *Damn.* Two-fifteen. "Sorry to cut you off. I'm late for an appointment out of town."

"I know about your appointment." With her un-gloved hand June started waving the cedar up and down as if dousing for water. "It's not out of town."

Had Sandie told her about Bianca? Great. Now June probably thought he was a player. Which he could be. But there was no reason for June to know that.

Oh, hell, that didn't matter. "Sandie doesn't know about this appointment. Kinda like I didn't know she had grandkids. Ask her to check on my cats tomor-row, would you? Right now, I have to run. Nice meet-ing you."

Harry dismissed her, but she just stood there, wav-ing her twigs.

"Bye," he tried again.

"Harry," she finally said, "I don't know how else to say this. I gather you have a little pack problem and I'm here to help you solve it."

CHAPTER THREE

JUNE'S HEART BEAT so fast and hard she feared Harry would hear it. What she was doing was dicey, and her coven hadn't exactly approved it. Her coven wouldn't have approved anything that tossed one of their members into pack politics. But she'd realized, when the idea of losing him struck her like a pie in the face, she had to try anyway. And she had to do it immediately.

She wouldn't let him be forced into the Millington pack. That wasn't fair to anyone, much less Harry. He was perfect the way he was.

Nearly perfect. He had kind of a potty mouth.

"A problem?" His bushy brows arched. "I wouldn't call it that. It's this woman who wants me to come to a party. I RSVP'd no."

"A pack bond ceremony, to be exact." June let the cedar fall to her side. She couldn't purify his property and hide their tracks while tiptoeing around her kind's sacred covenant about keeping shifters in the dark. "I understand why the alpha wants you—" Did she ever! "—but most indies don't make good packers."

"Ububobu whu?" Harry stuttered.

"I can help you, but you have to swear on your pelt you'll never tell anybody what I did."

Quicker than she thought possible, considering he wasn't pack, Harry invaded her personal space, grabbed her shoulders again and pinned her against her car.

"What do you know?"

She could barely make out the words through his growl. His whiskey-colored eyes sparked pale blue with the onset of the shift. His tousled hair glinted blue-black in the sun. Oh Goddess, his scent was wild and musky, his hands strong. Being this close to him when he was riled was much more erotic than she'd expected.

She always had to be careful about getting close to Harry. His senses were keen, and some of her secrets had to remain secret.

Like the fact he'd been right the first time he'd called her name. Well, not right—her real name was June—but she'd been wearing her Sandie camouflage for years. She'd considered keeping it after the encounter in the tea room, but it took too much power to maintain. She needed all the magic she could squeeze out of herself to help Harry, so all she'd kept was a minimum facade of humanity.

"I know enough," she told him. Summoning a spike of power, she channeled it into the cedar and poked his stomach. He jumped back with a yelp as if he'd been stung, which technically he had.

"What the hell was that?" He jerked up his shirt to

check, and she nearly whistled. Shifters were physically fit in two-legged form, yeah, but his abs were especially delicious. With her libido dampener forfeit like her Sandie mask, all that black, silky hair on his chest, trailing down his midriff, weakened her knees.

"Sorry. Cedar has sharp needles." If she came out of this with Harry ignorant about magic, her coven might not go completely off on her. They'd still be furious, but the covenant would be intact and so would Harry.

Now she just needed to stuff an angry werewolf into a tiny car and transport him to safety before she ran out of juice—and before anybody figured out what she was doing.

He circled her, prowling, his brows lowered. She had no fear he'd hurt her but kept her front to him anyway.

"So you know about shifters," he said.

"I do."

"What are you?"

"A person who knows?"

"How many humans know?"

Good, he assumed she was human. "Not many. And we're not about to broadcast it."

"Sandie?"

She shrugged.

He continued to stalk around her, making her a little dizzy. "What do you think you can do to help me?"

"I can help you hide." Covens used magic to shield themselves from shifters' senses, and she hoped to employ a variation of the spell on him. Or, more precisely, her car. They'd be safe inside while she fashioned a stronger disguise geared to Harry's alpha chemistry. Afterward they'd toddle off while the pack dashed around like chickens missing their heads.

Easy peasy.

While she'd rather hide him in her house, people might check there. And she didn't hate the idea of a road trip with Harry.

"I already have a plan," he growled.

That didn't surprise her. Harry was no cream puff. But neither was Bianca. "They cut the fuel lines on all your cars."

"They what?" He ran to the garage and checked under a gray sports car, a minivan. "Son of a…gun. Even my truck?"

"And the motorcycle." Indies had been forced into packs before. Millington wasn't one of the worst offenders, but they'd know how to handle a wolf like Harry.

"What about the—"

"They got the loaner too. They're not as dumb as you think," she couldn't resist chiding. Independence was all well and good, but a wolf had to be mindful. If he'd made himself less tempting, Bianca wouldn't be so hot to add him to the pack. Harry should have behaved antisocially. Disguised himself so he didn't seem powerful.

And virile. And sexy.

Wow. Right. Without the libido dampener, it was

going to be a bigger struggle than usual to keep her hands to herself.

"They're dumb if they think—" he began, but stopped himself. "Tell me your plan."

"I fed your cats, packed your shaving kit and gathered everything we need." She hoped. "We should hurry. They could be here any minute."

He faced her, hands on his hips. "Did you wash my dishes and vacuum?"

"Your house didn't really need it," she joked.

He didn't smile. Being threatened with a life sentence in Bianca's pack would put anyone in a bad mood.

June shifted her weight to the other foot. "I'll drive, okay?"

"I'm not riding in that…thing."

"Don't be silly. They'll never notice you in this car. It's the perfect disguise." And the only car small enough to extend her test spell around, but she couldn't tell him that.

"It won't even pull twenty up some of these mountains. If you know about shifters, you know they can outrun that."

"They won't be chasing us, so it won't matter."

"How did you get here so fast?"

"I live close by."

"Why have I never met you before?"

"I don't…get out much." She kept her answers as truthful as possible. Some shifters could smell dishonesty, and he was skirting the edge of her secrets.

If he realized she was Sandie, it would be impossible to hide the existence of magic from him.

"Is that so?"

"We need to get going." It would take time and energy to cast the car's disguise spell. She hadn't tried to mask a wolf before. Too bad she'd burned through a lot of her magic reserves earlier today.

If she'd known she'd be going on the lam with Harry, she'd never have cheated on her gardening or prepared a batch of healing salve, both of which involved a sizeable magical outlay.

If she'd known she'd be going on the lam with Harry, she'd have worn more practical clothing than her pink shirtwaist.

At the same time, she didn't hate the fact she looked pretty the first time she officially met him.

Stop that. Bad June. Not going to happen.

"So Sandie knows about me? About…all of this?" he asked again. "Why didn't she tell me? I thought we were friends."

"Can we discuss this on the road?" Tentatively, she reached out her gloved hand and tugged him. He wouldn't budge. She hated to use magic when she needed it to cloak the car, but his stubbornness was putting them in danger. She rustled in her bag, pulled out some dried lavender and crushed it in her fist.

He sniffed. "Lavender?"

"It won't hurt you." She funneled a tweak of power through it and flicked the scraps on his bare arm.

He whuffed out a sigh as the magic calmed him.

Lavender didn't work that well on humans, but on shifters it was marvelous. "Why did you do that?"

"It's good luck before traveling." Well, it was good for her if the werewolf in her car wasn't fuming. "Plus, it smells nice."

"Are you saying I stink?" His lips quirked in a welcome twitch of humor. Excellent, the spell must have worked. "Is that a species-ist comment?"

"Of course not. You smell fine." In fact he smelled meltingly masculine.

And there she went again, getting sidetracked by his sexiness. Poopy doop, maybe she shouldn't have dropped so many of her customary barriers. She ought to save a teeny bit of power and cast that libido dampener before he noticed she had a thing for him.

The deep thrum of powerful motors on the highway reached the garage, and they both stiffened.

"Quick, Harry, get in the car." If it was the pack, she barely had time to cast the spell before the motorcycles reached his garage. She had her components organized in the passenger's seat.

"I'm driving."

Dang it, he was supposed to be compliant! June pried him away from the driver's side. "It's my car. I'm driving."

"This may get tricky," Harry argued. "I'm driving."

Not the time for his alpha gene to kick in. She plucked a piece of lavender off her dress and flicked it at him.

"Hurry up," she urged with a touch of magic.

He nodded and stepped away from the car. Thank Goddess.

"Going somewhere, Harry?"

Bianca, completely nude and surrounded by wolves like some ancient deity, stepped out from behind the garage.

Blast. June had bespelled the female alpha to be true to what she'd told Harry and not show up until three. Must have been bum parsley if Bianca had already shaken the compulsion. Magic was wonderful, but limited when it came to harming or controlling others. Now how was she going to get Harry out of this?

"Been skinny dipping, Bianca?" He averted his gaze from the statuesque woman. June didn't.

Bianca stroked the head of a wolf, a pale beauty who was likely female due to its smaller size. "I thought you'd be more interested in our party if I showed you what you'd be missing. I hear you have an eye for the ladies."

Harry grunted. "The nice ones."

"Who's your friend?" Bianca ruffled the ears of the wolf, who pressed against its alpha in obvious affection.

"Nobody," he answered.

Bianca's eyes glinted as she inspected June and June inspected her. Bianca made no move to cover herself.

Well. This was awkward.

"I'm June," she said. "Gosh, you're a very…genuine person, aren't you?"

"You could say that," Bianca agreed.

Bianca was pack. Alpha. Her senses would be stronger than Harry's, as would the shifters on four legs. June shoved her gloved hand into her purse, slipped off the latex and dug a fingernail into the special talc in her compact. Channeling power through the herbs that augmented the talc, she increased her I'm-a-human glamour.

Beside her, Harry rubbed his temples, likely feeling discomfort as the relaxation spells warred with fight-or-flight.

"Are these your dogs or are you a dog walker?" June asked Bianca. She had to be close to people in order to affect them. Approaching Bianca was problematic, but the important thing was getting Harry out of here.

"They aren't dogs. They're wolves." Bianca regarded her with a frown, head cocked to one side. The chopper contingent of Bianca's dishonor guard seemed to be idling halfway down Harry's long driveway, blocking anyone from coming or going.

Well, burn the bread and spoil the milk. June would have to brute force their way out of this. And first, she had to touch Bianca.

In her natural form, June's blond hair and youthful appearance often caused people to assume she wasn't intelligent. Her talc spell included rosemary to encourage this impression, and she hoped Bianca would fall for it. She hated improvising spells almost as much as she hated eating at fast-food restaurants.

She smiled, fluttering her eyelashes. "Can I pet your wolf dogs?"

"They're not safe."

Not true. They were safe as long as they thought she was oblivious. Shifters were canny about protecting their secret. The pack would have come in human form if they'd known Harry wasn't alone. Acting like barbarians, yes, but two-legged barbarians—in clothing.

She had to give Bianca props for bluffing through this.

"You must be from that nudist colony on the Hartsell River. In town you're supposed to put on clothes." June giggled as she felt around in her purse for the lavender. Hopefully there'd be enough. If she could find her cayenne mix, it would help, but she'd lost the pesky vial days ago. One of the disadvantages to overstuffing a supply kit. "I have one of those fold-up raincoats you can put on."

"How civilized of you," Bianca said. "June's very civilized, Harry. I hope you weren't planning on inviting her to our party. She won't like it."

June reached the edge of the milling wolves and hoped her talc spell would hold. It wasn't strong enough to fool a shifter who touched her for long—hence the rubber gloves. When wolf fur brushed her legs, her nylons decreased the skin contact.

"Nice doggies," she said.

One of the wolves growled.

Her fingers encountered something crinkly. The lavender. She squeezed a few leaves with her power and stroked the growling wolf with her other hand, sending peace and harmony through it. Her bare skin increased the purity of the charm. The wolf plopped down and panted.

"Good doggy."

"I said don't touch them," Bianca instructed, somewhat amused. "They bite."

"I'm sure they don't." June crouched down with a fistful of lavender and spelled it, her magic welling like an underground spring. In a singsong voice, she said, "They're good doggies. Aren't they? Yes, they are. Good boy. Good girl."

She caressed each wolf with a touch of lavender magic. None shied away, which meant they weren't agitated. Several snuffled her. She spelled them before they had a chance to sort through the complexities of her scent.

"I hope you're not angling for an invitation," Bianca said. June could feel the alpha's annoyance. Her amusement had waned.

"I'm busy tonight, but thanks." June tousled another ruff, pushing magic. The wolf rolled onto its back, offering its belly for a scratch. She needed to end this. Fast. Shifters weren't usually killers, not with the advances in forensic science, but people tended to disappear when they veered close to the truth. "That's a good boy. I love animals."

Their coats were rough but pleasant. They didn't smell like dogs—one of the easiest ways to tell weres apart from canids. Thank Goddess she'd packed a lot

of lavender. She flipped leaves at the wolves as dis-
creetly as possible. The calming effect was temporary,
and from the sound of it she and Harry had several
motorcycles to get through.

And Bianca. Two-legs were harder to control than
four.

Big, strong hands dragged her to her feet. "June,
that's a really bad idea."

Harry was proving exceptionally hard to control,
as well.

"But I like dogs." She smiled and hoped he understood. For good measure, she lavendered him again, allowing their bare flesh to connect. "And they like me."

For a moment, they locked gazes. Recognition
flashed in his face before the lavender took hold,
amped by the contact. He let her go and yawned.

With great daring, she extended her hand to Bianca.
"By the way, it's nice to meet you. Thank you for letting me pet your puppies."

Bianca arched a thin brow. "I didn't let you."

June stood there with her hand out. If she pretended
to stumble, she could toss lavender at Bianca. Would
it work? It was weird enough that she, a presumed
human, was nonchalant about Bianca's nudity. If she
started throwing twigs, it might break Bianca's patience.

She returned to her purse. "Let me see if I can
find you that raincoat. This has to be embarrassing
for you." She could stick the lavender to the inside of
the coat, and voila!

"Not really," Bianca said. "Harry, your girlfriend is going to have to leave now."

"But I just got here," June protested.

"She's right." Beside her, Harry sighed, his voice resigned. "There's nothing anyone can do now. Tell your grandmother I said… Tell her I said thank you for everything."

Drat, she'd mellowed him so he'd cooperate with *her*, not Bianca. Perhaps the triple hit of lavender had been a bit much.

Instead of the raincoat, her questing fingers landed on the glass vial of cayenne mix.

Bingo.

She wrapped more lavender around the vial and pulled the whole thing out. "Oh, this isn't the raincoat."

Bianca solved part of the problem by advancing until her prominent breasts were almost touching June. The woman glared down her proud nose in true alpha style, dominance rippling off her. The wolves, already pacified, dropped to the ground. Harry remained standing, which surprised June, but there was no time to dwell on it.

Bianca's rude maneuver would have worked on a human female, provided that female weren't already scuttling away from the naked person.

June wasn't a human female, but she needed to pretend she was.

"My goodness," she squeaked, backing up. She slipped the purse strap up her arm and cupped her hands protectively at her chest, frantically twisting the vial.

"It's time for you to go," Bianca said.

The lid stuck. Cayenne tended to grit in the threads, especially primed cayenne. *Crap.*

"Gosh. I only wanted Harry to, uh, check my tires," she lied, hoping Bianca couldn't smell it. "I can't drive around on unsafe tires."

The metal lid screeched against glass as June broke through the corrosion.

"What are you doing? Give me that." Bianca reached for the wad of leaves and vial. Because her reserves were half-drained and her normal protections gone, June struggled against the pressure to obey Bianca's command.

"You're v-very rude," she stammered. The metal top flipped toward the ground. Bianca snatched for it, breaking the compulsion on June.

June poured powder into her hands. Cayenne had no capability of its own but could be used to store magic. She had combined hers with poppies for a super-duper forget-me blend.

Cayenne also had side effects. The red grains scorched her skin. Her eyes began to water.

"Oh, Christ, don't cry." Bianca offered the cap with a grimace. "Just leave."

Instead, June shoved Harry out of the way. With a deep breath, she forced magic into the lavender and cayenne, which blew it into a swirling cloud around Bianca and the pack.

Each and every one of them sank to the ground, unconscious.

"Did I just see what I think I saw?" Harry said.

"Nope." A buzz of referred pain from the cayenne muffled June's hearing. Tiny blisters formed everywhere the cayenne touched. No time. Still had the motorcyclists to deal with. Goddess, she hoped the shifters forgot this so the coven didn't have to wipe them. She would be in enough hot water when they realized she was the reason Harry had escaped.

"Get in the passenger's side," she yelled. She couldn't grab him or he'd get burned by cayenne. Maybe knocked unconscious, and it would be a trial stuffing his big body into her car.

Harry complied. They slammed the doors of her microcar simultaneously. The concealment spell components she'd arranged on the seat scattered all over the interior.

"Gather all that up, we need it." She gestured at the assorted twigs, berries and packets. Again, Harry complied without question.

June turned the key and revved the motor. Her hands ached so much it was hard to concentrate. She gunned down the driveway, jouncing through ruts, wondering how she was going to break through the bruiser barricade that awaited them.

They reached it too soon. Five choppers. *Bugger.* The bikes were bigger than her car. None of the shifters wore helmets, and they all looked mean.

She didn't have time to activate the car's disguise

spell. She slammed on the brakes, the car skidding in the gravel like a top. Rocks sprayed the shifters.

"I don't know what you did back there, but we can't fight them." Harry placed the last of her supplies on the dash. "You need to stay out of this, June."

"Sorry, my friend." With one blistered finger and some degree of regret, she touched Harry's hand and knocked him out.

When she jumped out of the car, the shifters were pissed.

"Are you nuts, lady?" one yelled. "You could have hit us."

"You chipped my chrome," another complained.

"Please move your bikes. I have an emergency." An emergency getting away from them.

"Sure," the biggest guy said. "Just leave Harry here."

"Oh, I couldn't do that." Since the guards couldn't see the garage, they'd have no idea what June had done. She walked up to the shifter and smiled.

He smiled back. It wasn't as if shifters disliked small, blonde human women.

She reached toward him. "Night-night."

He slumped over his bike like a half-empty sack of corn. Luckily he'd put down his kickstand while he and the others waited out the confrontation.

"What did you do?" one of the remaining shifters exclaimed.

Now she had to rush. She got two before the rest

wised up and avoided her. One grabbed her from behind with the strength of five men.

As if that would help. She smacked his hand.

Pain erupted as blisters on her fingers burst. She yelped, but the cayenne and poppies worked. Four down, one to go.

The last, a fellow she knew, backed away. "You got knock-out drops or something?"

"Something." Lionel wouldn't recognize her like this, so she couldn't play the friend card. "How about you move your bike out of the way?"

"Forget it." The scruffy guy circled her. *Flippin' flapjacks.* No way could she out-agile him, no way could she lay a hand on him if he didn't want her to. Not without different supplies than she currently possessed. But he had no way to get close to her, either, and no experience dealing with a member of a coven.

Not that he'd remember.

"Did you kill them?" he snapped.

"Of course not. I don't hurt people." Except herself. She jittered her hands, trying to shake the pain. Her arms throbbed up to her shoulders, which is why cayenne was an emergency resource only. "Lionel, you need to let us by."

His glower deepened. "How'd you know my name?"

"I know a lot of things. I know we're at an impasse."

"You better back off. We will hunt you down and make you suffer," he threatened.

She didn't really believe him. He'd never been the violent type.

"That's not neighborly." If she could grab him, none of the shifters would remember her. Probably. Her cayenne-poppy blend hadn't been tested on actual shifters. This was some field trial.

She edged toward her car. He cut her off. As they played cat and mouse—or wolf and witch—she considered the bikes, lined across the road. Just enough room for her car to squeeze past. Good thing she hadn't driven the Caddy.

"Please don't hurt me," she begged, allowing tears to drip from her eyes. Considering her blisters, it wasn't hard to fake a sob. "I went to Harry's and this strange woman and her dogs attacked us. I'm taking Harry to the hospital. He got hurt."

"I don't believe you."

She sniffled. "Why not?"

"There's no way you could have gotten Harry away from…" His teeth flashed, sharpening. "You little snake! Did you hurt Bianca?"

His fingers curled into claws, and he swiped at her in frustration.

With a gulp, she stepped into the blow.

His nails ripped her sleeve and sliced her forearm. Pain shocked through her, and she tamped it down with effort.

Lionel reared back, eyes wide. "I didn't mean to—"

She leaped forward, knocking him out with an extra zing. He'd be lucky to remember what he had for breakfast when he woke up.

But ow! First the cayenne, now a flesh wound. Lionel hadn't put his heart into the blow, but it hurt like mad. Blood streamed down her hand. She whipped up her cotton skirt and staunched the flow.

Enough blood was on the ground that the wolves would be able to isolate it. Lightheaded from pain and panic, June yanked open Harry's door and dragged out her purse. The cedar was still viable, so she used it to alter the blood evidence. Carefully, carefully. She couldn't remove it, but she could remove what made it identifiable. A breeze whisked around her legs, chilly despite her nylons. She was approaching the end of her power. If she reached it, there'd be no hiding Harry from Bianca.

All her efforts would have been wasted. He'd be converted into a pack wolf, lost to himself, lost to her, before she could say *bibbity bobbidy boo.*

Tossing the twig into the woods, she jumped into the car. With a tug, she adjusted her bloody skirt to wrap her injured arm. *Think. Think. Bandage or drive?* She didn't know how long the cayenne would knock everyone out. She needed to put some distance between them so the pack wolves wouldn't immediately sense Harry in all his alpha goodness.

June cranked the car into gear, nudging past the end motorcycle. Maneuvering was tricky with one arm wrapped in her dress, so she unwrapped it. Blood oozed immediately. Jeepers, it was worse than she thought.

No time. She pushed the pedal to the metal, or, rather, the floor mat, and screeched onto the highway. First she headed west into town, laying rubber at Harry's driveway as a lure. After fifty yards, she U-turned and sped east. East was toward the pack's base and away from the coven's, but she might get stopped by the cops if she whizzed through town at a blazing fifty-eight miles per hour. She didn't want to explain her or her passenger's current state to Millington's finest.

Her vision fuzzed and cleared. The road climbed out of Millington's valley, and the car slowed to forty. Thirty. She groped behind the seats for tissues, antibacterial wipes, a shopping bag. Found Harry's clothes and slapped a shirt around her cut. She tightened it and nearly fainted from the pain.

She had to get yarrow into the wound and white willow into herself. Tunnel vision encroached. She pulled off the highway in a pocket of gravel next to a drop-off. The river gushed at the bottom. As good a spot as any. Far enough, but not too far to lose cell reception if she had to call the coven.

The spell she'd planned would work best if they stayed near where she'd harvested the plants. Personal disguise spells, which had to be keyed to personal chemistry, were very fiddly, so she'd had the idea to blanket the car itself first. The coven did that with their houses and hideouts so they could drop their masks inside and take a break. The idea was to mask the Smart car as uninteresting.

Magical improv was rarely smart. It didn't conserve a witch's power and often missed the target. But what else could she do? She needed time to devise Harry's exclusive camo before they fled the territory, and this was the most expedient way to get that time.

Nobody would look for him in a Smart car, but they might in her house. Her friendship with Harry wasn't clandestine or anything, and most folks in Millington accepted it at face value as long as there was nothing hinky going on.

Which there never had been, thank you very much.

Her purse was next to his feet. She hauled it into her lap, cursing as her movements slowed, turned fumbly. Beside her, Harry began to stir.

"Where are we?"

"We got away. I need to stop the bleeding." She dumped her purse all over her blood-spattered skirts. Yarrow, white willow, burn cream. Nausea surged, a product of blood odor and low reserves. Okay, ginger too. She sorted her supplies with shaky fingers. There was too much. She was too flustered.

Hey, a folded-up raincoat. She stared at it for several seconds before Harry took her arm.

He peeked under the T-shirt and whistled. "Jeez, June. How did that happen?"

"Lionel," she answered.

"I'll kill that bastard," Harry growled, posture stiffening.

"No need to swear. He didn't mean to." If he'd meant to, he could have taken her arm off. She breathed quickly, in and out through her teeth so the coppery whang of blood wouldn't upset her stomach.

"You need to go to the hospital." Command shaded Harry's voice. Did he realize how much his alpha gene came out when he was upset? His potency bore down on her, and she hoped he wouldn't lean harder. She was too feeble to resist.

At least the adrenaline and panic had pushed the lust out of her system. Small favors.

"It looks worse than it is." There. She crammed white willow and ginger into her mouth, and as she chewed she trickled a tiny bit of power into it.

Goddess, she loved magic. Instant relief. She found the burn cream and smeared it on her hands. Not too many blisters. The cream, imbued with healing enchantment, flattened the bumps.

"I don't remember what happened." Harry frowned. "You did something to them. To me."

June closed her eyes. She could lie, try to keep him in the dark. Or she could confess a bare minimum of facts and make him promise never to tell the coven he knew.

This was Harry. She could trust him. He was her best friend, even if he didn't realize it.

"Yes," she agreed, the truth popping out like bread from a toaster. "You can do magic, I can do magic. Simple as pie."

His frown deepened. "I don't do magic."

"You just don't call it that." Most of the contents of her purse slid off her lap onto the floor. But not the yarrow. "Would you unwrap my arm?"

He did, and she sprinkled the dried greens on it.

How much power to use? The blood had slowed to a trickle. At full strength, she could heal it as if it had never been there. She tapped her nearly empty well so the wound remained open but the blood ceased.

Harry's nostrils flared and his eyes paled as he soaked in the situation—and her. He looked furious and curious at the same time. When you were a man who could change into a wolf, the existence of other magics probably wasn't earth-shattering.

If he figured out she was Sandie, though, that might get complicated.

"We don't have time for this," she said, pulling away.

"For what?"

"Anything." Was that the grumble of a Harley she heard on the far range of her hearing?

"Make time." He lowered his chin. "Talk. Now."

She did. Because she wanted to, not because he made her.

"I'm going to cast a spell that will make the pack overlook this car, and we're going to park here until I feel better." Or until she broke down and phoned the coven to ask for an itty-bitty rescue.

She really hoped to avoid that. She'd pushed boundaries before, but this took the cake. Which was a funny way to put it, since cakes were a Millington coven specialty.

"This spell thing will work?" he asked, dubious.

"I think so." She pushed her hair out of her face and wished she could tell Harry everything. Ask for a hug to calm her nerves. As far as he was concerned, they didn't know each other. "I'm obviously not at my best."

"If I'm hidden inside the car, keep driving," he suggested. "The pack's territory extends about a hundred miles in either direction. Once I'm out of state, I'm practically in the clear."

"We need to stay put." Remaining stationary aided this type of concealment spell, and she wasn't sure she'd be able to drive after she cast it. "The spell will drain my magic and make me woozy. I can't drive. There's, um, probably a book in back if you get bored."

"We can't have you wrecking the car." Harry smirked, and despite the dire situation, she grinned back. She'd never been able to resist his smile. It had nothing to do with his alpha gene, either.

They gazed into one another's eyes, the rest of the world on hold, until he said, "Looks like I'll be driving after all."

June quit smiling.

CHAPTER FOUR

AFTER SHE DID some mumbo jumbo with the trash from her floor, June sort of passed out.

Harry waited a minute. "June?"

Her eyelids fluttered. She mumbled something about cake.

"I'm going to drive now."

Her forehead wrinkled. "Haaah," she sighed.

That wasn't a no. Harry jumped out of the car and relocated her soft little body to the passenger's seat—only to find the stupid car wouldn't do sixty-five, downhill, without rattling. No sign of the pack, but he heard the roar of a Harley on a mountain road that paralleled the highway in spots.

Dusk fell quickly in these parts. Already the long shadows of trees covered the pavement. With a drop-off on one side and a forested incline on the other, the highway was their only option. So they buzzed like a giant beetle up and down the hills.

Not a beetle. He shouldn't insult VWs that way.

Harry tried dialing Sandie on his cell, but reception here was crap. June lolled beside him, seat belt holding her erect. Her pink dress was smeared with blood. The odor twitched his nose like a memory, like something he should recognize.

He was a little off kilter. *Give it time.*

Too bad he didn't have any and couldn't make any. He couldn't outrun Bianca's border guards in this cheese box. They'd be stationed in a grid pattern threading out from Cranberry Jetty, an unincorporated bump in the road nine miles ahead. Gas station, park visitor's center, intersection and a bridge to the north, which led to the pack's commune. There weren't a lot of roads to choose from in this terrain, and pack wolves had a wide range for sensing alphas— any alpha.

If he couldn't blast through Cranberry Jetty in a car that could exceed a hundred, he wasn't sure how this would go. The trip had taken on a nightmarish quality that reminded him of the night he and his mother had fled the pack where he'd been born. Since he'd been ten, too young to be pack-bound, his mother had been the only one to suffer the severance process.

She'd suffered. She'd suffered, and then she'd died.

No, he didn't want to think about that night.

June whispered something about Tolkien, or maybe it was told-you. Or toffee. The sound cut off when her head flopped forward. It looked uncomfortable, so he tilted her back. Her blond curls were as soft as down. In sleep, she looked young, maybe twenty-one, twenty-two.

He refused to consider she might be younger for two reasons. One, she was attractive to him in a very adult way. He hoped Sandie wouldn't kill him if he seduced her granddaughter once this Bianca thing was done.

Two, Sandie wouldn't have sent a teenager into a pack situation. He was surprised Sandie had sent her granddaughter at all.

Unless, of course, June could do magic. Which was ridiculous.

Yet they'd escaped. How? He didn't remember much after Bianca had shown up. His forgetfulness had been caused by something. June had sprinkled leaves on her arm before it stopped bleeding, which might have been coincidence. As for this camouflage thing, he didn't feel any different.

But there was no denying June had the drop on shifters. Sandie was a wily one, all right. She'd known about Harry the whole time she'd been grilling his porterhouses and beating his ass at bunco. He'd been her pet wolf, and she'd never said a word.

He'd be saying a word to her when he saw her again. He might even curse. What was she thinking, sending June into the middle of a pack dispute armed with twigs and a giant purse? A gun would have been handier, along with a fast car. What would the pack do if they found out Sandie and June had made them?

He might feel betrayed that Sandie had been keeping secrets from him, but she was still his friend. He cared about her more than he'd cared about anyone since his mother died. Now there was June to consider. He wouldn't be able to protect them if he couldn't save himself.

The car whined as he pressed it harder. Those noises weren't healthy. He'd never worked on a micro, but this model had a three-cylinder engine. The little sucker wasn't even a hybrid. Just tiny. Why anybody would buy a powerless matchbox in an area like Millington, he had no idea.

None of this made sense. None of it. The only available person with answers was snoozing in the passenger's seat, mumbling about dessert.

A sign for the visitor's center appeared. One mile to go and no evidence of the pack. They must be spinning their wheels searching Millington, confident the barricades would trap Harry in town.

His and June's luck wouldn't hold forever. He should scout Cranberry Jetty before they tried to blast through it. Harry applied the brakes, and the car squealed like an airplane decelerating.

Another gravel overlook lay before the sign. The narrow highway was dotted with areas like this anywhere there was car space. For fishermen, hunters, tourists, swimmers, hikers, werewolves trying to decide how to break through a barricade, parking areas had myriad uses. Harry angled the micro onto the shoulder, and it thunked ominously when it dropped off the pavement.

Rolling down the window, he paused for a moment to listen. He sorted through June's breathing, awakening night creatures, the rush of the river. Mice in the leaves. The whoosh of diving bats. Mosquitoes. Wind.

There. A truck coughing to life. Choppers from

the…east. Pack members weren't the only motorcycle aficionados in Mill County, but they did love their hogs. Should he turn back to Millington, into the maws of the shifters he knew were there, or wait it out?

June murmured something else and rubbed fitfully at her wound, bandaged in strips of his T-shirt. The blood on her skirt had darkened to brown. Her lashes fluttered on her cheeks.

Harry popped the automatic locks. He was about to ease the handle and step outside for a clearer listen when a small hand on his arm stopped him.

"Don't get out," June whispered. "Told you."

She'd mentioned something about the spell only working if he stayed in the car, which was useful if he believed in magic. Her kind of magic. Shifting from human to wolf might be magic, but it didn't prove the existence of other supernatural beings. Next thing, she'd try to convince him vampires and aliens were real.

He stroked her hand. Her slender fingers were coated with grease that smelled like aloe and mint. She hadn't put her rubber gloves back on, a lost cause after what they'd been through. For a moment he had déjà vu—not from the smell, but from the shape and size of her hand.

He blinked and the recollection was gone.

"I'll just be a minute," he told her. "I can't hear. I need to stand in the middle of the road."

"No. Safe."

The hum of choppers increased. Several, going

about forty. The engines roared as they ascended the half-mile incline from Cranberry Jetty.

It wouldn't do any good to get out now. Wouldn't do him any good to shift and take off through the trees, either, even if he were willing to leave June behind.

Several bikes crested the rise and barreled toward the overlook. Harry tensed. If it was the pack, they'd have to pry him out of the car, peel back the top like a can of sardines. He could take a single pack wolf but not several.

He'd sure as hell try. Presumably they wouldn't rip their future alpha to shreds. He wouldn't die, werewolves being extremely hardy, and when he was alpha he'd make their lives miserable.

No. He wouldn't even consider being alpha. That was the epitome of miserable to him. Being alpha was like being thrust into parenthood unprepared. Not regular parenthood, which had a certain appeal, but the crushing responsibility of the largest, hairiest, most fractious family imaginable.

A family whose evils you were sworn to conceal from the world.

The choppers slowed. Harry cursed under his breath. They coasted to a stop next to the car, so he started rolling up the window.

That's when one shifter Harry'd seen already today stared into his face without so much as a glimmer of recognition.

Violet, Bianca's lieutenant.

"It's not him," he heard Violet announce into her

helmet microphone over the chug of engines. Harry paused with the window halfway up. "Charles, do you smell anything?"

"Not unless he's on the river. He didn't get this far."

They didn't see him. They couldn't smell him. Couldn't sense him. He was sitting in a car fifteen feet away from them. *Holy shit.*

"Another team checked the river. No trace." Unless Harry missed his guess, Violet was chewing gum. She nodded at him, clearly assuming he couldn't hear their conversation. A human wouldn't.

It appeared his half-conscious companion was a magician. Either that or the pack was so thrown by this stupid car, they failed to believe he was driving it.

"If we don't find Harry, I'm not sticking around for one of those dirtbag wannabes," Charles threatened. "We didn't send out a call, and they're showing up anyway. How did they find out? We worked too hard to wind up with another Bert."

"Lower your hackles. That won't happen." Violet chewed for a moment. "The ceremony doesn't have to be tonight. We'll find him. We're on lockdown now."

Harry forced himself not to curse again. Lockdown was an alert to bordering territories that a pack had a runner.

Hard to escape if the neighbors were looking for you too. Good thing he had a secret weapon. June. If Violet didn't recognize him in this car, wolves outside Millington wouldn't either.

"I want this over with." Charles revved his motor.

"It's not good for a pack to have a single alpha. She needs a mate."

"You think Bianca can't handle it?" Violet growled.

Charles's helmet dipped in capitulation. "I didn't mean that."

The Millington pack's dilemma had obviously hit the grapevine if the wannabes were circling. They might end up with a hidebound ass like Bert and they might not. Didn't matter to Harry. He wanted no part. He'd stay away for a month, just in case, and cross his fingers the new alpha would ignore him when he came back.

"I'll let it pass," Violet said at last. "We're going to freak out the lovebirds if we don't move."

"What kind of car is that, anyway?" another shifter added. "Looks like a penny racer."

"It's better for the environment," Violet answered with a lippy smack. The choppers snarled to life and squealed down the highway.

"That was incredible," Harry said. "They looked right at me."

A smile ghosted across June's lips. "Told you."

If he'd informed a human he could turn into a wolf, the human wouldn't have believed him until he proved it—and then the human would have looked for trick cameras.

Harry didn't see any cameras.

"We should go." He turned the key in the ignition, and the car's engine sputtered. It had a little trouble catching.

"Can't," June mumbled. "Told you that too. God-dess, I'm beat."

"Why can't we?" With her hoodoo, nobody would stop them. Once they reached Staunton, he'd breathe easier. In this car it might take four freaking hours, but that was better than countless years of being pack. Then he and June could hole up somewhere until it was safe to return. That condo on the beach. It had a grill. And a hot tub. And a lot of privacy. "You like the beach?"

Her hand tightened on his forearm. "Stay."

"I'm not a dog," he said. "I don't heel, either."

She hadn't opened her eyes this whole time, but she did now, long enough to wink. "Arf."

"We're going." Harry bumped the car onto the curb and took off. They puttered through Cranberry Jetty, past Bianca's guards, without a hitch. And onward, into the night.

They passed clusters of pack vehicles on the road, on the sides of the road, and nobody gave chase. They all stared at June's car, which was understandable, but made no move to follow.

When Harry parked at an overlook to check her wound, a four-leg emerged from the forest. The wolf paced through the glow of the headlights, laughing into Harry's face with canine humor.

If he were alpha and found out one of his wolves had let himself be seen by humans, that wolf would have gotten into major trouble. Probably a youngling. They created the most messes for the pack to clean up and had the least control over their urges. Their wolves. Their rage.

He knew that better than anyone besides his mother.

With a grim smile, Harry restarted the engine and continued their escape. It had been three hours since the garage. Bianca must be desperate if she was sending younglings to work the grid. If another pack caught her runner, she'd owe them huge favors.

How long would June's spell last anyway? Harry needed to take a piss. In action movies, nobody ever had to stop to pee. Stop and bandage wounds, yes, but they'd done that. Stop and reload a gun, but they didn't have one. Stop and have sex, but June hadn't offered. Stop and get gas—which was becoming as necessary as peeing.

No Business was the next town with a gas station.

"June, wake up." He touched her shoulder.

"Nuh." She batted at his hand.

How long did she need to recharge? He could shift from two to four legs a couple times a day if he spaced it out. If he were sick or injured, swapping forms took care of it. It was the rare shifter who had a scar. He only knew of one, and the bastard deserved it.

"June." This time he patted her cheek. Her skin was soft and peachy. Her breath tickled his fingers. "We have to get gas."

She turned her head to the other side. Harry stroked her hair, flicking out a few pieces of grass. "Wake up, honey."

When she shrugged him off, he flipped out his

phone and checked roaming. No service. *Jesus.* He'd gotten through to Sandie's house a couple times with no answer. Had she gone ahead with movie night? Surely not. Harry was beginning to worry. If the pack had hurt her, he wasn't sure what he'd do, but it might involve becoming their alpha so he could beat every one of their sorry asses.

He just hoped he'd retain enough righteous anger to do so. A pack bond adjusted a shifter's perception, bringing it in line with pack lifestyle. That might not include defending a human who'd gotten in the pack's way.

He wouldn't lose himself entirely, but he wouldn't be the same Harry.

If he turned pack, Sandie wouldn't be his friend anymore. June would be off limits too. He'd never finish teaching the grannies to play Texas Hold'em. His cats would desert him. The beach would be out of the question. He'd have to give up his shop since a pack alpha wouldn't have time to maintain one. He'd probably have to marry Bianca. And those were just the small things.

Damn it all to hairy human hell.

"Wake up, June," he commanded in an angrier voice than he intended.

"What, huh?" Her head weaved back and forth and she blinked. "What?"

"I need to get gas."

"Why? I have half a tank." June leaned her head on the window, yawning. They neared the bottom of the valley at a white-hot sixty-eight miles per hour, the car jittering like a youngling on a first hunt.

"Not anymore," he told her. "We're in No Business."

That woke her up. "What? I told you to stay. This is too far."

"Too far for what?" Harry slowed. The air smelled like rain.

"Too far for the spell." June grabbed his forearm, as if a little thing like her could overpower him.

"Don't worry. I stayed in the car."

"I used local components. Turn this car around right now, sir," she said, sounding just like her grandmother.

"We're close to the border. Everything's fine."

As soon as he uttered those fateful words, Harry spotted some trucks surrounding the No Business gas station. Each one boasted several large persons in the bed. Many were dressed in camouflage.

Shifters. Shifters he didn't immediately recognize.

They all turned to watch the Smart car limp toward them. Who were they?

Two wolves bolted across the road, one chasing the other, and Harry slammed on the brakes. June was flung against her seat belt, her hands striking the dash. He heard something pop. The car fishtailed—astounding when there was no back end—and skidded into the city's brick welcome sign.

With a horrible crunch, bricks scattered every direction. The car rebounded with a stomach-lurching jounce. An airbag slammed into Harry, shoving him into his seat.

"Shit!" He fought the tough vinyl of the bag. The front end seemed to have completely crumpled though the doors remained intact. A brick slid down the cracked windshield like a skier. "Are you okay, June?"

"I'm alive." Her voice was tight with pain. "What'd you do that for? My poor car. It's less than six weeks old."

"I didn't want to hit the…never mind." He should have ignored the wolves. The four-legs would have dodged the car. He batted the airbag into his lap. "You're not okay."

June rubbed her wrist. "It's sprained. I can fix it."

"You didn't have an airbag. You could have been hurt a lot worse."

"I disabled this side. Long story." She glanced at him, her blue eyes wide. "I told you to stay in Millington. Goddess, now what are we supposed to do?"

"You didn't tell me in a way I could understand," he growled in a low voice.

His anger wasn't directed at her. Their audience had noticed the crash, and a truck with Virginia tags had bounced onto the highway to head their way.

Virginia was split into two territories—the Roanoke pack claimed the majority, with D.C. at the top. What were the chances those shifters were from D.C.?

"Is the car spell still working?" he whispered.

"I don't know, I don't know. I swan, why couldn't I have sprained my bad wrist?" June started scrambling in her purse. "Where's my compact? Harry, where's my compact?"

"Don't say my name." He checked under his seat, under the floor mat. He found some white twists of paper he assumed contained herbs, a raincoat wadded into a packet, some silverware and a tube of lipstick.

The monster truck closed in on them. If it held wannabe alpha candidates, he and June would be fine. They wouldn't want the competition.

If it held neighbors helping with the lockdown, they were screwed.

"Here it is." June whipped open a gold compact and clawed the powder, hissing as her wrist bent. She rubbed streaks of talc on her nose.

Harry twisted away from the window, pretending to check June for wounds. If these shifters had his photo from the lockdown report, he couldn't let them see his face.

"You and the missus okay in there?" asked the driver in a rumbling voice. In the background, thunder growled in counterpoint.

Harry waved a hand but didn't speak. Bricks from the sign thunked to the ground, and a piece of the car clanked into the gravel. June's eyes were closed, her lips moving.

A familiar pressure built in Harry's ears. He'd trekked up and down several mountains in the past hours.

"If you owned a good, American-made car, you folks would be in better shape," the driver commented. Had Harry met him before? He thought he recognized the voice, as well as the authority in it. Alpha.

Candidate?

"Gavin," said the speaker, "get down there and see if you can help."

Cold dread borne of long-ago trauma settled in Harry's gut. He knew a Gavin from when he'd been a child in the Roanoke pack, and that guy had been the sorriest son of a dog who'd ever shifted into fur.

The name was either coincidence or the worst kind of fate.

"Don't need help." Harry pitched his voice high and waved again. If they were who he feared, there might be no escape. How the hell was he going to get June out of this if they realized who he was?

"Son, do I know you?" The truck door creaked. Boots hit the pavement.

June's eyes flew open. Harry's ears popped. And then she gave him an order he was only too happy to obey.

"Kiss me."

CHAPTER FIVE

WHILE SHE'D OFTEN wanted to kiss Harry during her unguarded moments, this wasn't how June imagined it would happen.

But he didn't hesitate. He grabbed her by the back of the head, his fingers plowing through her hair, and pressed his lips to hers.

She'd thought he'd be bristly. He was a wolf, right? His lips and skin were almost as smooth as hers, a mere hint of whisker to make things exciting.

Their lips parted. Touched again and lingered. June rubbed the talc from her nose and fingers into his skin. She hadn't napped enough to replenish all her power, but she had some.

Then he angled his head, tilted hers where he wanted it and parted her lips with demanding pressure. Their tongues met in a hot, wet tangle that quickly consumed her. The desire she shunted aside for eight years blasted her like heat from an oven.

"God, you're sexy," he whispered. His long fingers dropped from her head to release her seat belt. He pulled her toward him, but she got stuck on the center console.

"Nothing like a near miss to make you appreciate life," the shifter outside Harry's window commented. "I take it this means you folks are still breathing?"

Phooey. The shifters. They weren't Millington wolves, but they would recognize Harry as a shifter as soon as he got out of the car. Alphas broadcast signals. It was part of what made them alphas. June had to shut those signals off.

She lifted her fingers, the ones with talc under the nails, and shoved them into Harry's mouth.

He spluttered, but she kissed his cheek, hoping he'd understand. She didn't have time to hone her talc mix to Harry's chemistry. Goddess, she hated adlibbing. For this to have a chance of working, the talc and its ingredients needed to be in his body. The burn cream on her hand was bitter, but this wasn't supposed to be delicious.

Actually, kissing Harry was supposed to be delicious. Delicious and sinful and everything a witch with half a brain would avoid.

So it just figured.

"Swallow," she whispered.

He did. She did, as well. He nibbled on another fingertip, licking off the talc.

He caught on fast. She opened her magic and pushed her disguise spell into both of them.

Weakness threatened as her power rushed forth. The spell must have done something—a dud wouldn't have taken as much out of her.

Maybe she'd pushed too hard. She struggled to remain upright. Witches could add guarana to spells to offset the droop that came with depletion, but there'd been no time.

Harry abruptly stopped kissing her fingers to shake his head. It was dark inside the car but they could see one another's faces, hear the laughter of the shifters. Harry gave her a tense grin and tugged her into his lap.

The emergency brake jabbed her heinie. The steering wheel had retracted into the console when the airbag deployed, leaving room in the driver's seat for both of them.

Fighting the urge to curl up and sleep, she pushed Harry's face into her neck and peered at the old shifter awaiting an answer. A pure white beard and moustache surrounded his face, and his head hair had given in to the recessive gene not even shifters were able to avoid. He looked like Santa Claus, if Santa wore flannel and denim instead of red and white.

Should she know him? She didn't get out of Millington much, and covens mostly concentrated on shifters inside their territories as part of their monitoring function.

"I've never been in an accident before," she gushed in her best dumb-blonde voice, careful not to lie. "That was so scary."

Santa peered into their car. She heard him sniff. "Did something cut you in the wreck, missy? Your skirt's bloody."

"No, yes, well," she stammered. "I ran into something sharp."

"I can't believe this toy car kept you safe." The others hopped out of the truck bed and started prowling around while June and Harry huddled in the seat. She didn't know what she and Harry were going to do, but whatever it was, it would be easier if the shifters went away.

"Your front end is totally destroyed," one of them said.

Her poor car. Best not to think about that. She had good insurance.

June wriggled closer to Harry, careful not to bend her aching wrist. For a moment, she enjoyed the sensation of his muscular body wrapped protectively around hers. Even surrounded by nosy werewolves, his solidity reassured her.

Ironic. He was in more danger than she was.

Speaking of danger, the only way to find out if her spell had worked was to let the shifters see him. Postponing the inevitable would raise the suspicions of individuals already inclined to be suspicious.

"Honey," she said to Harry, "we should get out. What if the car blows up?"

He nipped her neck. She wasn't sure if it was in play or warning, but it sent shivers through her. June hugged him and kissed the warm skin next to his ear before she fumbled for the door latch.

Santa helpfully ripped the door off its hinges. It was about to fall off anyway. He set it to the side, leaning it against the crumpled front.

"Miss?" Santa held out his hand. She wasn't wearing gloves, but a human wouldn't refuse. She allowed him to help her. When she saw how flat the front of her car was, her knees buckled.

Danger came in all forms, even for witches and weres.

Harry caught her. "Watch that first step, babe. It's a doozy."

June remained between the two men after Harry released her. Nobody gasped. Nobody offered any secret shifter handshakes. So far, so good.

Santa had a pack alpha's air of command. That was odd. A pack alpha wouldn't have come to offer himself to Bianca as a candidate, and this large of a group wouldn't be welcome in the neighbor's backyard.

So why were they in Millington territory?

"As you can see," Harry said, "we're fine."

"You two need a ride?" Santa asked.

Harry shook his head. "We'll wait for the police so we can file a report."

June inhaled a deep breath to calm her nerves. The air was crisp, threatening rain, and clouds obscured the moon and stars.

"Millington tags," a shifter behind the car commented.

"It just so happens we're headed to Millington," Santa said. "You sure we can't give you a ride?"

Santa seemed nice enough, but she and Harry didn't need to get mixed up with whatever these guys had going on. Were they Roanoke? She'd read something about Roanoke in a regional newsletter recently, re-

ported by the Wytheville coven. What had it been…
territorial squabbles? Trouble with indies? They might
be claim jumping part of Millington's territory in the
chaos created by Bert's arrest.

Talk about a mess.

June sidled up to Harry and nudged herself under
his arm. The closer she stayed to him, the better. He
could hold her upright, and the proximity of her own
glamour could enhance his if she hadn't gotten it right.

"That's so nice of you to offer," she gushed. "We
should take our chances with the cops. It's the right
thing to do. We need to pay to replace the sign."

"You drove right into the sign like you were aiming
for it," a shifter commented. He was a stocky, brown-
haired man with a cruel look about him and a scar
down one cheek. To June he tasted alpha, as well. Not
recessive, but a full-blown natural. His eyes gleamed
with meanness. "Did something spook you or are you
just a shitty driver?"

Beside her, Harry tensed—either because the
shifter was challenging him or because the shifter
was a prick. Maybe both.

"A giant…possum ran across the road," June said,
drawing the attention to herself. "Looked like it had
mange."

"Possum?" Several shifters guffawed. "Did you
hear that? A giant possum."

"I hear there's a wolf problem in these parts," the
younger alpha said. "You sure you didn't see wolves?"

"Wolves?" June widened her eyes. "West Virginia only has coyotes."

"I'm sure it was a possum with mange." The man's sharp gaze raked her body. "Or spring fever. That's going around." He licked his lips.

"Knock it off, Gavin," Santa warned.

Harry slipped his arm around her, which gave June a perverse thrill. "It was just some dogs," he said. "Don't worry about it."

Gavin approached Harry and June, his nostrils flaring. "Have we met?"

Harry's fingers tightened on her arm. "No."

She'd never heard so much hostility contained in a single word. June huddled closer to him. The talc spell only hid genetics. If Gavin knew Harry, they were in trouble.

"You sure? You look familiar."

"I doubt it." His unfriendliness was understandable—strangers surrounded them in a remote area. Nonetheless, the pack alpha was regarding Harry with a thoughtful gaze. The shifters would sense her anxiety too, if she weren't careful.

"He does look familiar," another shifter agreed. "You famous or something?"

Harry shrugged. "I get that a lot."

"And you," Gavin said to June, "are someone I'd like to be familiar with."

Harry lowered his chin. "She's with me."

His possessiveness was unmistakable, and June's stomach fluttered.

"Gav, I said give it a rest," Santa barked. "They've been through enough."

Gavin grinned, his teeth sharper than they ought to be in the presence of two humans. His pack alpha sure didn't have much control over him.

Thunder rumbled overhead as a spring rainstorm worked itself into being. A fat drop landed on June's nose. Good thing she and Harry had swallowed the talc or it would have been rinsed off their skin.

"Thunder boomer," Santa observed, making up his mind. "You folks can't wait here in a storm. Leave your name and number in the car and I'll carry you to Millington."

June felt the pull of Santa's command and clenched her teeth. "I can call a friend who lives around here," she tried. There was an extension agent for the coven nearby.

"They want to stay, let them stay," Gavin said. "We have places to go, people to find, bodies to hide." He laughed, but no one else did.

June hoped she and Harry were displaying only the unease that would be normal in this situation. She ignored the comment about bodies since everyone else did. The other comment was more enlightening—people to find. Bianca could have called a lockdown. These guys might be searching for Harry. Which didn't explain why they didn't recognize him, as lockdowns generally came by email, with photos.

How tech-savvy was Bianca? Would she send pictures to cell phones or just computers?

"We can't take time out to play Good Samaritan." Gavin thrust his chin at the driver's door. "Vultures gathering. Clock ticking."

Santa turned on Gavin and growled. June could barely hear it, but recognized it. The pack alpha compelling his subordinate to back down. "There's always time to play Good Samaritan. If you understood that, I could…never mind. The others can finish our project, and we'll give these people a ride to Millington."

"You go ahead. I'm not done here," Gavin said, not as subdued as he should have been. June bet the creep was a huge thorn in the Roanoke pack. Bert Macabee would never have let someone challenge him that way.

Santa punched his finger at the truck bed. "They have Cathy. They don't need you. All of you, get in the back of the truck."

"As long as we get to ride the girl." When Gavin bared his teeth in another smile, the scar tightened one corner of his mouth more than the other. "I mean, ride *with* the girl. We'll keep her comfortable."

"Er," June said, "no thank you."

"She's not getting in the back of your truck," Harry stated flatly.

"Of course she's not." Santa clapped Harry on the shoulder and turned his back on Gavin, dismissing him. From the look on Gavin's face, that might not have been Santa's best move. "You and the missus are in the cab with me. I'm Douglas Householder."

"This isn't necessary." Harry's boots rasped in the gravel as he braced his feet.

"I insist," Douglas said.

The rain picked up. Lightning split the dark sky. June grabbed her purse and a few things from the back. She could tell where this was headed. She'd wanted Harry to turn back to Millington anyway.

Just not in the company of shifters who might be searching for him…and who seemed scarier than Bianca.

"Screw it. I want to get to Jetty before midnight. I have a party to crash." Gavin leaped into the truck bed, casting Douglas an angry glance.

"I thought you were going to Millington?" June asked. "If it's out of your way, you really don't have to take us." She shoved various items she didn't want to leave behind into her purse. The sides bulged, distorting the reflection of the street lights in the patent leather.

"We're headed in that general direction. We have a lot of acquaintances in the area." Douglas opened the door of his cab. "Hop in."

Beside her, Harry grunted as the urge to obey struck them both. Blast his stubborn hide! He needed to comply or he'd give himself away. Pack alphas could manipulate humans in addition to shifters. They only had trouble with other alphas.

Like Gavin.

And Harry.

She gave Harry a shove, and he lurched forward. The old man's benign appearance was misleading if he exerted himself to control strangers. This trip couldn't be over soon enough.

June slid into the cab after Harry, careful not to touch Douglas. He seemed shrewd enough, but Gavin was a piece of work. She didn't envy Douglas that battle for dominance—a battle that seemed to be a stalemate, at best.

Another thought occurred to her. Perhaps this was Douglas's way of solving his problem—fob Gavin off on Bianca. Alpha vacancies attracted candidates from everywhere. Heck, some sent out promotional materials and videos. *The Bachelorette*—wolf style. While Bianca's vacancy was short notice, it would still have attracted wannabes.

It didn't explain why so much of the pack had come instead of Gavin alone. Roanoke wasn't far. If Bianca didn't pick him, he could return to his original pack before severance hit, provided they still wanted someone that unpleasant around.

It was too confusing. Neither she nor her group were experts on shifter politics. That would be a New York or Alaska coven.

Harry scooched against the far door and shot June a piercing glance. "Come here," he said as he dragged her against him.

In their high-stress situation, he was exerting too much alpha himself. What was she going to do with the man? Did he have a pack wish?

Douglas noticed too and studied them with a lot of

curiosity. Humans weren't weak, but it wouldn't do to rouse his interest.

June snuggled into Harry's embrace, propping her injured wrist on her large purse. Water droplets beaded on the shiny surface. "Mr. Householder, we can't thank you enough. Can we give you some gas money?"

"Don't insult me," Douglas said. "Happy to help."

"Yeah, thanks," Harry managed. "I just hope we don't get hassled by the cops for abandoning the scene of an accident."

"We were the only ones hurt." Under cover of her purse, June pinched him. "They'll think we went for help."

"I'll put in a word for you with the police," Douglas added. "Don't worry about it, son. Your lady looks like she could use a trip to the ER."

"You try telling her that," Harry said, some of his tension easing.

June didn't argue. With one wrist sprained and the other wrapped in a bloody T-shirt, she was in a sad state. Her nylons were ripped; her skirt was a mess. And she had no idea what kind of impression Harry was giving Douglas. Due to the talc spell—since it was hers—he might seem effeminate and dim as well as stubborn.

Hmm. No wonder Douglas figured the two of them couldn't fend for themselves.

The other shifters settled into the truck bed. He cranked the vehicle into gear, and they bounced onto the pavement, leaving her sweet little car next to the crumbled welcome sign. When the cops ran the tags, it would show up as registered to Sandie Travis of Millington, West Virginia.

She'd deal with that after the full moon. She needed to get Harry out of this bonding ceremony first. Burning through her magic so fast hadn't been part of the plan.

After Douglas conferred with a curly-haired woman who looked as if she'd be more at home baking cookies than hunting werewolves, they set out. The adrenaline of their encounter gurgled out of June's system like water from a bath.

When was the last time she'd sapped her magic twice in a row? This was like being back in training. Her innards felt as hollow as a doughnut. She might be the strongest in her coven, maybe the region, but no witch she knew could withstand what she'd dealt with today. She ought to feel proud. Instead she wished she'd managed more than she had.

Well, the adlibbing had thrown her off. So inexact. Give her a recipe any day.

"I am so tired," she told Harry, unable to conceal a gigantic yawn. "How about you?"

"I'm good." His thumb stroked the skin above her T-shirt bandage. "How long would you like to sleep?"

Was he asking how much time she'd need before she could cast spells? June yawned again, her vision swimming at the edges.

"I could sleep for thirty hours," she said.

He spread his legs farther apart and leaned back,

adjusting his posture for comfort. His stiffness eased as he held her in a way he'd never held Sandie. Of course, as Sandie, she'd kept her distance from him out of necessity. "That much, huh?"

"It's been a rough day."

He dropped a kiss on her forehead. Another on her cheek. His lips tickled her skin. "Want me to kiss it and make it better?"

If they weren't pretending to be a couple, she'd push him away. Instead she tilted her face up. For the masquerade, of course.

Their lips brushed. Harry tasted her, tracing the seam of her lips until she parted for him. The slow stroke of his tongue roused her even though their situation was as precarious as a soufflé. She shouldn't feel so thrilled that his interest in her, as June, seemed to be piqued, because nothing could come of it. Nothing.

Reluctantly she broke off the kiss and rested her head against his shoulder. "Thanks. That helped."

"You're one tough little gal," Douglas commented. "Most ladies I know would be howling and whining after a wreck like that."

"Believe me, I'll whine later," she assured him. Harry's arms tightened around her. "It doesn't seem fair to inflict it on you when you're being so nice to us."

The big truck climbed out of the valley faster than the Smart car had come into it. At this rate, they'd be in Millington in an hour. The shifters in the bed huddled under a tarp as rain slashed around them.

"They're getting soaked back there," she commented to Douglas over the flap of wipers.

"It'll cool their jets." His window was cracked open, and he sniffed. "The rain won't last long."

"Too bad your truck doesn't have a camper shell."

"It does. I took it off." Douglas smiled. "Where were you folks headed?"

"Vacation," June said at the same time Harry said, "Business."

"He was working, I was vacationing." She smiled. Yawned again. She longed to take another nap but it seemed unwise to leave Harry alone with the Roanoke pack. A faulty spell could fizzle on and off like a spotty internet connection.

"You don't have much luggage." Douglas glanced at her purse. It looked like a pocketbook, but this brand of supply case was specially made by a coven in Maine to be lightweight, sturdy, fashionable and capacious. Lots of inner pockets, zippers, plastic liners and the like, for all a witch's necessities.

"I knew we forgot something," Harry deadpanned.

"He's so silly. I got his shaving kit." One more yawn and her epiglottis was going to fall out. "We were going to a beach house in…"

June yawned. Again.

"Virginia Beach," Harry supplied.

"Mmm-hmm." Douglas clearly didn't believe them. They should quit while they were behind. June made a show of rubbing her eyes before she rested her head on Harry's shoulder. For several minutes no one spoke. Harry's familiar odor comforted her while the roar of truck tires on wet pavement lulled her into a trance. Her eyelids drooped.

She came to with a jerk when Douglas asked a question.

"I apologize. I can't seem to stay awake," she confessed.

She had almost fallen asleep again—it took about five seconds—when Douglas repeated, "I don't think I caught your names."

"My name is June," she said, because it was as safe as anything, "and this is Warren." Warren was Harry's middle name. The Roanoke wolves wouldn't know that.

"Sorry to meet you in unhappy circumstances," he replied. "In the back are my son Gavin and his friends."

"He's your son?" Their physical appearance, not to mention their attitudes, were very different.

"That he is." Douglas sighed, a universal parenting *what are ya gonna do.* "He favors his mother."

So Gavin, a natural alpha, was the son of Roanoke's pack alpha. Was his mother the female alpha? That had to be tricky.

Gavin in general had to be tricky.

Alphas were rare creatures. Recessives had the potential to become alphas if pressed into service, but the recessiveness allowed them to remain in packs without turmoil. Natural alphas like Gavin and Harry turned indie or pack-hopped if they couldn't bide their time. Considering shifter longevity, that could be a very long time.

Waiting for your dad, maybe your mom, to hie off to the great beyond—June couldn't imagine. It explained why Gavin was thoroughly unpleasant. More than unpleasant. She felt no sympathy. For all she knew, Harry was independent for a similar reason, and it hadn't turned him belligerent. She knew his parents died when he was young but nothing else about his family.

Kinda hard to get a man's backstory when he couldn't tell you he was a wolf.

Seconds later, or so it felt to June, the truck halted in Cranberry Jetty. The rain had stopped and a fat moon plus a million stars shed light on the dark landscape.

"I'm dropping off the boys," Douglas explained. He pulled over at the visitor's center. A truck lurked in the shadows of the wooden building.

"Did I sleep?" She surreptitiously wiped her mouth to see if she'd drooled.

"For about an hour," Harry said. "You snore."

"Don't be teasing your lady after the hard day she's had," Douglas chided. "Miss June, you didn't make a peep."

The clock on the dash glowed nine-thirty. Her body ached, and she checked her magic reservoir. She could stay alert now but didn't have enough power to soothe a sloth, much less cast a spell.

Gavin and his friends hopped out of the back, and he rapped on Harry's window. Reluctant, Harry rolled it partway down and leaned back.

"Where are you taking them?" Gavin asked Douglas.

If he wanted to talk to his father, why hadn't he approached the other window? Gavin exuded the same aggressive cockiness despite his drenching. Harry's arm muscles bunched.

"Wherever they want to go," Douglas replied.

"Don't be long, Pop. We have work to do." Gavin turned his attention to June, his gaze pinning her in place as forcefully as grabby hands. He fingered the side of his mouth with the scar. "I'll see you around, chickie."

"I doubt that," she said, but he laughed and ambled toward the truck.

Who was driving it? Could they see Harry? She squinted, but it was too far.

"Do you and your son visit Millington often?" she asked Douglas. If he hoped to leave Gavin here permanently, he might mention it. "We could take you out to lunch as a thank-you."

"Gav's dealing with some issues," Douglas said with a laugh that didn't sound amused. "But no, we haven't visited in a long time. My job doesn't allow me to travel."

That was putting it lightly.

"Doesn't sound like a job I'd like," Harry observed. June pressed her foot against his, hard.

Douglas chuckled, and this time his amusement did seem natural. "It's worth it, son. I'll take a rain check on the meal. We have a busy schedule before we head back to Roanoke."

"What are you doing in town?" Harry asked.

June wanted to hit him. Or kiss him so he'd quit talking. Whatever worked.

"We're doing a geographical survey and helping someone choose a new business partner."

If they were searching for Harry, that vaguely described their activities near the border. It also described offering Gavin as an alpha candidate.

"You're a good friend," June told him, hoping Harry would quit pushing his luck. She hoped in vain.

"What kind of business are you in?" he asked.

June pressed his foot again. He'd always been a devil, had Harry. She loved that about him, but right now he needed to can it.

"A little of this, a little of that." Douglas obviously didn't intend to offer more. "Where can I drop you two?"

"How about a motel?" Harry suggested to June, waggling his eyebrows. "We can pretend we're already on vacation."

The only motels in town were owned by folks who'd recognize him. It was best if they disappeared off the grid. "I want to sleep in my own bed tonight."

Douglas wasn't a local. He'd have no way of connecting her house with Harry, and the sooner they were inside its protective spells, the better. She wouldn't be able to cast protections on another location for hours, and she and Harry needed to talk.

He'd touched her skin enough in the past couple hours that he was going to figure out her secret the next time he saw Sandie anyway. She needed to tell him the truth and warn him to keep his yap shut.

She wouldn't tell him everything, though. The secret that the covens kept hidden from shifters remained verboten.

In Millington, she directed Douglas to drop them off at her place. Harry didn't say a word until Douglas turned a careful circle in the driveway, avoiding the Caddy under the awning, and departed down the gravel incline. She'd kept the Smart car in the garage under a cover, which was why Harry had never seen it. She'd known he wouldn't approve and didn't want to hear it.

"You live with Sandie." His statement wasn't a question. "I've been here a hundred times, and I haven't seen you or smelled you. Were you using your disguise spell?"

"What do you think?" She unlocked the deadbolt, and he followed her into the house.

"I think there are things you're not telling me, and it needs to stop—now. There's too much at stake. If Gavin Householder is involved, people could wind up dead. I don't want one of them to be your grandmother. Or you."

One crisis at a time. She had a confession to make before she and Harry could deal with anything else, including Roanoke's homicidal heir-apparent.

As soon as he closed the door behind them, Harry called out, "Sandie?"

"You're wasting your breath." June kicked off her shoes.

"She hasn't picked up the phone in hours. Movie night never lasts this long." Harry disappeared into the kitchen. She heard his footsteps traverse the small house, doors opening and closing. She waited in the living room, decorated in the style an eighty-year-old tea shop owner might like, for him to return.

He burst in with a panicked expression. She and Harry were close, and she hoped he wasn't dismayed by the truth.

Or angry. He wasn't a man who liked to be fooled.

"Where is she?" He grabbed her shoulders, his eyes pale blue. Either he wasn't bothering to hide his nature or he'd never been this emotional around her. "Sandie threatened to call the cops on Bianca, and I smelled pack outside. They know that she knows me. She could be in trouble."

"Please calm down." June took a deep breath and released it. She didn't have enough magic to don her Sandie spell, so Harry would have to take her confession on faith. "She's fine. Mostly."

"What do you mean?" His grip tightened, not painfully but keeping her in place. "Did she leave you a message? Why didn't she leave me a message?"

She felt the compulsion to answer him and fought it so she could choose the perfect words.

"June, this is serious. Where is Sandie? If she told

you about me, then you know she's like family to me." His nostrils flared as his breathing quickened. "Do you understand what I'm saying? If anything has happened to her, I need to know."

She wet her lips, more nervous than she'd imagined she would be if she ever had the opportunity to tell Harry the truth. Kissing him the second time might have been a bad idea.

"Sandie's not here because...well, she is here." Goddess, she hoped he wasn't too peeved.

"Explain."

How could she tell him about Sandie without telling him everything? In order to conserve magic today, she'd dropped two of the three facades her kind often adopted around shifters. She'd kept her humanness but dropped the face witches donned to hide their longevity—and the libido dampener. Not every witch needed that last spell, but she usually dosed herself, considering her affection for Harry. If he'd realized his "elderly" friend had feelings for him that weren't platonic, there was no telling what he'd have done. Besides, it was better if no sharp-nosed wolves ever noticed any sexual urges from witches.

Better for the witches. That was a bad, bad trail of crumbs to follow.

But after today it was cruel, and impossible, to lie to Harry anymore. He would just have to deal with the ramifications.

June threw back her shoulders and looked him straight in the eyes. "I'm Sandie."

He lowered his head until he was close enough to kiss. "Don't screw around, June."

His vehemence destroyed her composure. She began to babble. "My grandmother's name was Sandie, but she's dead. You would have liked her, except she couldn't cook. My mom's alive. She can cook. She's on her second pass-through. This is my first. My first time to tell anybody too, and I could get in so much trouble for this, but…"

"But what?" Harry prompted, his tone icy. He stepped away from her as if he couldn't bear to be in her space any longer.

"Oh, Harry." June's throat tightened. "Please don't hate me. I'm the Sandie you know. I have been all along."

CHAPTER SIX

HARRY SHOULD HAVE trusted his instincts this afternoon. He'd known it was Sandie in his parking lot. Not even the bloom of youth had been able to mask the woman he'd met eight years ago.

Since then she'd twisted facts, danced around the truth, made a mockery of their friendship. He'd never be able to repay her for helping him escape Bianca and that son of a dog Gavin Householder, but he saw no reason she couldn't have been honest from the get-go.

The woman formerly known as Sandie stared up at him with huge blue eyes. Her lips trembled, and she looked tearful.

Sandie didn't cry. Not even when the movie was a weepie and he himself was surreptitiously dabbing his eyes.

Of course, to his knowledge Sandie had never faced a ravening pack of wolves, raced through the West Virginia mountains and survived a car crash, all while sporting wounds and, apparently, a magic shortage.

Or had she?

The house he'd been in so many times smelled of lemon, herbs and food. Now that he'd met "June," he could sense her sweet amber essence underlying everything. It had always been there, in the house, swirling around him.

It just hadn't been on Sandie. Good God, could his life get any weirder? Magic. Witches. Enemies from the past he'd hoped never to see again.

His favorite granny, his best friend, turning out to be a sweet young thing with hair like sunshine.

He tried to find his Sandie in June's face. "Why did you trick me?"

"Two reasons." She ducked her head and pretended to scratch her nose, but she swiped her eyes.

Shit, she *was* crying. Harry felt like a heel. At the same time, he was angry and crestfallen. He didn't care about appearances. Never had. He didn't care how old she was or how oddball she was or how paranoid she was about recipe espionage. They were friends. Didn't she trust him?

"The reasons are?" he prompted a bit more gently.

She sniffed and raised her head. "One, would you have allowed an eighty-year-old woman to get involved today?"

"I would have done what Sandie said."

"You would not have."

"I would too. If Sandie gives me an order—"

"Oh, please. You're as stubborn as a mule when you think something's a bad idea."

Sandie might have mentioned that a time or two, in the exact same exasperated way. He tried again. "If you hadn't been a stranger to me, it would have gone more smoothly."

"I'm not a stranger." She dropped her gigantic purse on the coffee table. What was in there, bricks? "This is my real face and body."

"This could be the disguise," he argued, sort of hoping it wasn't. Otherwise, the things that had crossed his mind while he'd been cuddling her nicely rounded self in Douglas's truck were more perverted than his usual fantasies about women.

"It's not." She gestured—at what, he didn't know. "This is me. Everything I was, I still am. Except wrinkled and gray."

Harry considered her confession. "So you were a liar before and you're still a liar."

"Oh, that's enough," she snapped, sounding exactly like Sandie. Again.

Sounding exactly like herself.

But his mind went back to those kisses and how his heart had raced faster while she'd been in his arms than it had when the car had toppled the No Business welcome sign.

Good God, he'd made out with Sandie, and it had been insanely hot. In fact, he wouldn't mind doing it again. If this were true, if she weren't an elderly human, what else would change between them?

"This is a lot to take in," he said gruffly. "I wish you'd told me a long time ago."

He'd never thought about romancing Sandie. Yes, he loved her, and would do anything for her, but he loved her as a friend. As family. Never mind that he turned down dates with younger women for Sandie's movie nights or beach trips or even chores she needed done. Never mind that he preferred her company over anyone else's. Never mind that he'd been happier in Millington than anywhere in his life.

What would he have done if he'd known that underneath the gray hair and wrinkles she was the coziest armful in the western hemisphere?

For one, he might have played his cards differently on poker night.

The cozy armful rubbed her wrist. "Should I be offended you never told me you were a werewolf?"

"I couldn't tell you that," Harry protested, knowing how stupid he sounded. "It's sacred."

"Just like I couldn't tell you I was pretending to be old."

"Ah." He raised a finger. "But you knew I was a shifter. I had no idea you were a witch."

She sighed. "We prefer the term wyse, but we gave up that fight a long time ago. Pop culture dictates terminology whether you want it to or not."

"Wyse ass," he muttered.

"No, like wise women, but we're not all women."

"Probably not all wise, either." He was going to lose this one. He could feel it already. She was as stubborn as she thought he was, particularly when it was possible she might have a point.

"The more important reason I came to you as myself," June continued, speaking over his mutters, "is that maintaining another face takes lots of power. I needed the power to help you."

He stepped closer to her. "Why do you make yourself look old anyway?"

"The same reason you don't let people see you shift. Privacy."

That wasn't the whole story. Folks could be private when they looked like June as easily as when they looked like Sandie, despite the fact her current appearance would attract a lot of horny guys.

"Is there anything else you haven't told me?"

She blinked. "Yep."

"Are you going to tell me?"

"Some of it," she said. "I know you can smell dishonesty, so you might as well quit sniffing me."

"Are you the only witch around here?" He needed to touch her, to reassure himself this was happening. That she was real. He fingered one of her blond curls, pulling it until it was straight. Sandie's hair had been curly too, but white, and she never wore it down.

"There are others." The pace of her breathing increased, her breasts rising and falling. "I'm not going to tell you who. It's bad enough I came out to you."

He had a pretty good idea. He knew the crowd she ran with. It was amusing to think the grannies were all hot witches in disguise, but he doubted any would be hotter than June.

Man, this freaked him out in so many ways. So why wasn't one of those ways how much he still wanted to seduce her?

"You can't let on to anyone that you know about magic," she said. "You have to play dumb."

"Why? Is it against your rules to help people like you helped me today?"

She smiled. "We try to be more subtle. What can I say? Bianca jumped you in my tea room, and I had to act fast. It's not like we can enforce world peace or stop wars." Her gaze grew distant. "Not big ones, anyway. Our powers are limited."

"So what now? I need to leave town." As if Bianca's plans weren't enough, the presence of Gavin Householder cinched it. Since he and his mother had fled Roanoke when he was only ten, Douglas and Gavin hadn't recognized him. However, if Gavin realized Harry Smith, staunch indie, was John Lapin, son of Christine Lapin, he didn't want to estimate his chances of survival. Or June's. "You should come with me."

"We can't leave that easily if Bianca put the border territories on lockdown."

"That is a complication." He put his hands on his hips and didn't miss when her attention snagged on his chest, where his gesture stretched his T-shirt.

This pleased him. Despite everything, even the untimely appearance of one of the few people in the world he wished were dead, he was very attracted to June.

It didn't seem to matter to his body that June was… Sandie. His Sandie, who'd never had the hots for him before. He could sense gut emotions like lust, fear and dishonesty; he'd have noticed. Then again, he hadn't noticed his bunco buddies were witches.

He sniffed. And smiled.

Either way, she was into him now. Even if he didn't act on it, he was going to enjoy harassing her about it. It was what friends did.

His friend. His Sandie. His best friend Sandie was a pink-and-white angel who'd kissed him as if she meant it.

She dragged her gaze from his chest and returned to his face. "It's not that complicated. You can hide here. There's a spell on my house like the one I put on the car. Shifters can't sense you as long as they don't come inside."

As he'd seen the car spell in action, that was heartening. But it didn't feel like the right decision or she'd have brought him here in the first place. "Can you get out of work tomorrow?"

"I'll have to," she said. "I should be with you in case anything happens."

"For how long, a couple days?" If they stayed, they'd have to amuse themselves somehow, trapped inside. He had some ideas.

"After I rest up, we can leave town." June cradled her wrist. "You mentioned Gavin several times. Do you know him?"

Harry considered how much he could tell her, how much was relevant. "I did a long time ago. He didn't recognize me, so it doesn't matter."

She watched him with a frown. "It will matter if Bianca picks him. He seemed a lot like Bert."

Harry recalled Violet's conversation with Charles. "I don't think they want another Bert. I doubt she'll pick him." If indies like his friends in New York knew to avoid Roanoke, packers would know about the situation there too.

They had to know what was going on in order to cover it up.

"Isn't it unusual," she mused, "for a werewolf to have a scar?"

"Not that rare," he lied. Only the strongest shifters could maintain tattoos or piercings between forms because the change healed injuries. Harry didn't know whether Gavin maintained the scar to intimidate people or because he couldn't rid himself of it, but he did know how the bastard had gotten it.

June blinked several times as she considered his words. The gesture struck him, suddenly, as familiar. Sandie always did that.

Everything about her was familiar except her age. And his reaction to her.

"Do you know Douglas too?" she asked.

"Douglas isn't a bad man, but he's weak. Gavin's mother is the only thing that keeps Gavin from going feral." Probably the only thing that kept him from murdering dear ole dad and stepping up himself—Gavin wasn't Oedipal.

With his own mother.

"That's when you lose control and shift during anger, isn't it?"

"The wolf is a privilege, not a weapon." Whether they wanted to or not, shifters lived as men in this age of computers and cameras. Secrecy was paramount. Lack of control was a taint that was not tolerated.

"I thought that resulted in banishment."

"It does." When Harry and his mother had been with Roanoke, Gavin and his buddies had never crossed that line in front of anyone who could prove it.

Or anyone who could defend herself.

Except the once. His mother hadn't tried to prove anything after giving Gavin that scar. She'd just taken Harry and run.

"How do you know these things about the House-holders?"

Old frustrations stirred inside him. Harry shook his head—shook it off. It hurt to rip off scabs, and the edges were softening. "I don't want to get into it. We have to decide what to do, and I vote we run."

"You already wrecked one of my cars." She heaved a sigh. "My Caddy won't take your kind of abuse."

"Free repairs for six months," Harry offered. "When does my disguise wear off?"

"I can't say precisely," she said, nibbling her bottom lip. "For me it lasts until the talc and herbs work through my system. The spell wasn't meant for you so it's unpredictable." Her lip darkened as her teeth brought the blood closer to the surface.

"When will you have the strength to renew me?"

"I don't know." Now she licked her lips, and Harry wondered how he could be getting turned on at a time like this.

Adrenaline rush? Avoidance? Animal attraction?

"I need definites." He needed a cold shower.

She frowned. "Don't be so pushy. As long as I get some sleep, we'll be okay."

He ran his fingers through his hair, trying to toggle his brain back on course. It seemed to have bopped past their dangerous situation and fixated on what June would do if he kissed her. "Can you get your friends to cast the spells we need?"

"I don't want to involve them if I can avoid it." She reddened. "We're not supposed to let anyone know about us. If they find out how much I told you, I'll be censured."

The thought of June being punished for helping him got his mind off sex. Some. "Annette likes me. She'd help, right?"

Her mouth opened and closed. "Who said anything about Annette?"

"So Annette's a witch, huh?" he asked, satisfied he'd guessed correctly. He wondered if Annette's family knew. "If you're a Playboy bunny, what does she look like, a supermodel?"

"I don't look like a…" Her cheeks flushed more, and she grabbed his arm, tugging it in frustration. "You swore on your pelt you'd never tell anybody. This has to be our secret."

"I didn't swear, you just told me to swear."

"Harry," she pleaded, "don't tease. This is serious. You know how pack wolves can get voted out—get their bond severed? That could happen to me. We don't lose our abilities like wolves do, but it's grueling to lose your…friends."

What she was describing sounded like a version of a shifter's social drive. Maybe witches needed a network to feel whole like wolves did. He rubbed his thumb across her knuckles. "Come on. You know I won't tell."

"So we'll stay here?"

He dropped her hand and paced to the bay window overlooking the driveway. It was steep, gravel and narrow. Behind the house was forest and mountainside, and to the right was a rocky incline to another road.

Not a great hideout. He didn't want to be pinned here with wolves searching for him, one of them Gavin Householder. When he'd been younger, he'd dreamed of vengeance. Seeing Gavin again after forty years revived those urges, but Harry wasn't foolhardy.

If there was one thing he knew, it was that vengeance would be hollow if he didn't survive to enjoy it. Now June was involved too, her safety at stake. He'd listen to his instincts.

"We will not stay here. We'll head west while my disguise is still working. That Caddy can fly. We'll be a blur." The roads to the west were flatter, with more interstates. They could make better time once they got out of the mountains.

"We should stay until the morning." Her protest sounded weak. "I need a chance to recoup."

He returned to her side and cupped her face, her skin like satin. "Sleep all you want. I'll drive. I'm made of stamina, honey. Next thing you know, we'll be in Indiana."

Her nostrils flared, and her cheeks flushed. "I—"

"If you don't want to come," he said softly, "I can go alone. In your Caddy." He had no intention of leaving her behind now that Gavin had noticed her.

"If your spell wears off, you'll never make it. You're a natural alpha. You broadcast whether you want to or not."

"Then it's settled. You're coming." When Harry wanted something, his alpha side did tend to come to the fore. It helped him be persuasive, but humans weren't influenced as much as a shifter would be. June was, as she always had been, swayed by his common sense. "Are you hungry? We missed dinner."

"I could eat," she said uncertainly. "Harry, I don't think running is a good idea."

"Sure it is." He headed for the kitchen. She followed. No reason to drive on an empty stomach.

She took a deep breath and slid between him and the fridge. Her breasts rubbed against him and he stayed where he was. Hey, she'd initiated the contact. He stared down at her, her scent teasing his nostrils, her body teasing something else.

She placed both hands on his chest. "Listen to me."

"I'm hardly ignoring you." He was extremely conscious of her at this particular moment.

"I know you aren't, but we both know you're stronger than I am."

He frowned. "What's that supposed to mean?"

"You're alpha. Force of character is in your blood. You make up your mind, and you take people along for the ride." She closed her eyes. "You don't always mean to."

"It doesn't work on humans that much." He only wished it worked so well on shifters. Then he could convince the packers to leave him the hell alone.

"Hush. If you talk I can't concentrate." She hadn't opened her eyes. Her fingers flexed on his chest, like a cat stretching. "I want to agree with you. I want to go with you. But we need to stay here until I rest. I need to be able to cast bigger spells."

"Why? Do you need a better disguise?" He hoped she stayed June instead of turning back into Sandie. He'd have too much trouble putting her true appearance out of his mind.

"Your spell won't keep anyone from recognizing you if they know your face. Bianca will have blanketed the neighboring territories with your photo as part of the lockdown."

"That didn't help Douglas's bunch after your voodoo. Why would it help anyone else?"

"I've been thinking about that. What if they hadn't seen the photos? They had to have left Roanoke hours ago, before Bianca called the lockdown." Her lashes fluttered, but she didn't open her eyes. "It's possible they came for other reasons."

"If you mean so Gavin can try for pack alpha," Harry guessed, "he wouldn't need Douglas. The applicant and anyone who wanted to immigrate with him would show up and hope they got picked. They'd have, I don't know, two days to convince the pack here to take them on before severance hit. Douglas and the others have to be here for the search. That's why they were clustered near the border."

"You don't think they're claim jumping?"

"The Roanoke territory's already so large they can't monitor it like they should." They sure as hell hadn't monitored Gavin after he'd come of age and begun terrorizing various packers on the fringes, like Harry's mom. His dad had died when Harry was three, leaving him and his mother adrift in pack hierarchy and vulnerable to Gavin's cruelty. When Harry had tried to protect her from the abuse, Gavin had almost killed them both.

Harry grimaced, glad June wasn't paying attention to his face. He hadn't thought this much about his mom in years.

"I didn't think Roanoke's area was unusually big."

"It's not, but like I said before, Douglas Householder is weak. Everyone knows it." Weak and blind to things even Bert Macabee would have controlled. "He wouldn't want more territory, but he would respond to a lockdown. He'd like it if Bianca's pack owed him favors."

"Then we got lucky." June blew out a breath, ruffling the curls on her forehead. "We can't guarantee we'll stay lucky. I need all my supplies, I need to be at full strength, and I need sleep. Real sleep. Not in a car. We're safe from Bianca here until the morning."

"Okay, okay. Let me think." Gavin and Douglas hadn't recognized him as John Lapin or Harry Smith. They hadn't even recognized him as a shifter. But June said Millington packers would know him if they caught him outside the house.

Damn Bianca. What the hell was she thinking? If he could figure out why she was fixated on him, he'd do everything it took to de-fixate her. He'd marry a human. Run his business into the ground. Turn vegan. Prove himself unworthy of leading a pack of shifters.

Millington's female alpha wasn't so dumb she wanted him for the sex she thought they'd be having. She was too serious to let lust rule pack decisions. Something else was going on here, and he was damned if he could figure it out.

"Why me?" he said out loud. "Why does Bianca want me?"

June, still not looking at him, gave a small chuckle. "Why wouldn't she?"

"Because I'm not interested in anything she and the pack have to offer."

June's eyes flew open, and their bright blue color nearly incited him to plant one on her. "Maybe that's the point."

"What is?"

"Would you say she's a powerful alpha?"

Bianca had force of character in spades. "She held

her own against Bert. Some might say more than held her own."

"You're a challenge," June said. "You defy her and she can't let it go. You alphas, having to prove yourselves all the time."

"Are you saying if I roll over she'll lose interest?" Harry raised an eyebrow. It was easier than ruining his business or giving up meat, but… "I'd be pack and it'd be too late."

"No." June rubbed her sprained wrist, her body shifting against his. He dropped his hands to rest on her rounded hips. "I don't know what I'm saying. It's late and today was exhausting. We should eat and go to bed."

Harry considered the situation as a whole. If Roanoke hadn't seen the photos but other territories had, what were their chances of making it to Millington's border, and then the next territory's border, without being noticed?

If they stayed here until June felt livelier, he had a pretty woman and a fridge full of food at his disposal. Sounded like a damn good compromise to him.

"How long before you're recharged?" He studied June's face, her dark pink lips and sparkling blue eyes. Her snip of a nose. She still had a smudge of talc on it.

"A day or two." She pushed her hair out of her face. It was as soft and yellow as creamery butter. "I can't remember the last time I was this drained."

"Another thing." Harry couldn't believe how quickly his attention had flashed back to sex, but there it was. "Will there be kissing involved whenever you cast a disguise spell? If that's the case, I don't want any of your friends doing it. Just you."

Her gaze dropped to his neck as she blushed. "I…I had to get the talc into your system while we had witnesses."

"And the second time?"

"Douglas thought we were a couple. I apologize."

"There's nothing to be sorry about." Except for the fact the Roanokers had interrupted them. Oh, and her car was totaled, although he didn't see that as a misfortune so much as good riddance. "Is there?"

She eyed him, considering. "We're friends, Harry. We've been friends for eight years. Nothing has to change. We'll just be the guardians of one another's secrets."

He wasn't sure he believed her. His body didn't believe her. His love for Sandie was jumbled with how sexy he found June. Now that he knew, he wasn't about to block it out.

Things were going to change.

"When you came to me this afternoon," he said, piecing it together, "did you intend to tell me who you were?"

"I didn't think that far ahead." Their gazes locked. "I just wanted to help you."

His hands tightened on her hips. She smelled nervous. Desirous. "What would have happened between us if I'd continued to think you were Sandie's granddaughter?"

"I don't know." Her gaze slanted to the left, a sure sign she was hiding information. "I shouldn't tell you more. Please don't make me."

This was the second time she'd intimated he had control over her, but there was no way. Only pack alphas had much influence over humans. "Was there nothing else you hoped to achieve by pretending to be June?"

"I'm not pretending. I am June. The pretending was my grandmother's face."

"What if I'd fallen for you?" he asked softly. "What if I'd fallen head over heels in love with my...rescuer?"

She blinked several times before she answered. "You wouldn't have."

"You seem certain." He flicked her cheek with his finger, feeling the heat of her blood beneath the fine skin. "Did you see that in a crystal ball?"

She rolled her eyes. "I used common sense."

"How so?"

"You don't fall in love with your girlfriends, Harry. You're gun-shy." She tilted her head into his palm until he was cupping her cheek, his thumb at the corner of her lips. "It was a safe bet that aspect of your character wasn't going to change even if..."

"If what?"

"Nothing." The movement of her lips tickled his thumb.

He couldn't help that lots of women found him attractive. They came, they saw, he let them conquer.

Then he made sure they moved on to greener pastures because they were never enough like…

June. His best friend June.

Smart. Funny. Resourceful. A fabulous cook. But not that sweet, when it came right down to it—except for the way she looked. The way she tasted.

Oh, hell. He was starving, and she smelled like cake and fruit tea.

CHAPTER SEVEN

JUNE DIDN'T HAVE a chance to duck before Harry kissed her, one hand securing her head while the other tugged her hips against him.

Her brain told her to run.

Her arms snaked around his neck.

He slanted his mouth and plunged his tongue inside her, setting off a chain reaction of desire from her lips to her privates. He tasted wild. Vital. For a moment she wasn't conscious of anything but the need to be closer to him. She kissed him back, opening herself.

Harry murmured something she couldn't make out. Her head swam when he lifted her, almost roughly, and slid her onto the counter. The dish drainer clattered into the sink when he swept it aside.

He shoved her knees apart, his muscular body pressing the softness between her legs. His fingers dug into her hips, explored her back, gripped her hair in a fist that rendered her immobile. She held him tight, embracing him in a way she'd never been able to before.

He dropped his head to nuzzle her breasts through the thin fabric of her dress. When cool air hit the skin of her thighs, June realized he'd lifted her skirts. His questing fingers ripped a gigantic hole in her tattered pantyhose and she broke off the kiss.

"No, no, no, Harry. We can't do this."

"What about this?" His hot mouth laved her throat, licking the pulse. Then he returned to kiss her again.

And again, she kissed him back.

This was dangerous. Her defenses, literally, were down. Her skirt was up. Harry's tongue was doing things to her. This was leading straight to the situation all witches warned their children about, warned each other about, in grave and somber tones.

Never, never, never sleep with a shifter.

Male, female, straight, gay. Didn't matter. While there was no edict against befriending their furry companions in secrecy, those libido dampener spells came in handy. Independent wolves in particular tended to be drawn to covens. These things happened. Once a wolf decided to pursue you, the relationship could get volatile quickly.

And here she was, squirming in Harry's hands, wishing he had more of them. The better to touch her with.

This time cool air hit her chest. Her dress had pearl buttons marching down the front, and he'd freed them to expose her sensible white bra.

June tore her mouth away from his. "We really can't."

"Really?" He chuckled, his smile seductive and dark. "Which part can't we do?"

"All of it."

"Including this?" Harry palmed her breast, his thumb stroking her nipple, and she sank a little deeper under his sensual spell.

"Yes," she panted, but what she meant was—more.

He drew one bra strap down her shoulder. Her heart raced. She'd gambled Harry wouldn't be attracted to her true self. Even if he was, he didn't chase women. They chased him.

She'd assumed if she didn't flirt, this wouldn't be a problem. The kisses after the wreck had been necessity, not encouragement.

But there was a problem. A big problem. Harry was behaving out of character, getting in her space, getting in her...clothes. *Oh Goddess.* Her resolve was failing with every brush of his lips. The thrill of being close to him twisted her common sense into rumpled bed sheets.

When Harry's lips closed over her nipple, June arched her back, whimpering. He sucked harder. Sensation arrowed straight to her core. She wrapped her legs around his hips, her heels digging into his behind. When he ground against her privates, she thought she might climax right on her countertop.

He yanked down the other bra cup and raked his teeth across the rigid tip of her breast. The prickle of his whiskers, the liquid silk of his tongue, heightened her passion. When he went to pull off her ragged nylons, she raised her bottom to help him.

Harry smoothed his hands up her bare legs, drawing

them farther apart. When he reached her panties, he didn't stop. His thumbs swept her secret flesh, causing her hips to buck. He remained there, rubbing her through the cotton, which dampened with her need.

"I want you," he whispered against her neck. "I want to taste you."

She meant to say, "No," but it came out a helpless moan of desire.

"You smell so good." He kissed her cheek, licked her bottom lip. "I bet you taste better. My mouth is watering."

One thumb delved beneath her underwear, brushing her wet heat. June whimpered, and Harry muffled her with a long, sensual kiss. He smeared her juices up and down her slit, concentrating on the most sensitive area.

"You're drenched. This turns you on, doesn't it?"

It would be ridiculous to deny it, so she kissed him. Maybe he'd be quiet if she kept his mouth busy. His suggestive talk struck an answering chord inside her and made her want to be a bad, bad girl.

Because he was being a bad, bad boy. He broke off the kiss and continued his spiel, as if he knew how much it enhanced his touch.

"Do you want me to lick you?" He plucked and rubbed her slick flesh until her breath came in pants. "I can make it so good for you. I can lick you until you come, and then I can suck you until you come again. Unless you want something else."

"Harry," she said, twisting away from his face. "Don't."

"Don't talk to you? Don't kiss you? Don't lick you?" He kissed her cheek, her lips, between words. "Don't tell you how much I want to be inside you?"

"Don't... Oh!"

Harry sank a finger into her body. She clenched around him, far too close to her peak.

"But I want to." When he inserted another finger into her, pulling at the aching skin, the animal part of her stirred. Growled. Wanted.

Oh no. She moaned, fighting it. Yearning for it. If it clawed its way free, her life as a witch would be over. She'd lose the magic she'd struggled so hard to master. She'd lose her coven. She'd lose herself.

But it would feel so good to be with Harry. To take him inside her, his beautiful wildness pounding in and out until she disappeared in bliss.

He withdrew his fingers to fondle her breasts again, rubbing his moist, musky thumbs on the nipples. The ache between her legs was almost painful. He murmured against her neck. "The minute I saw you today, I wanted you. I don't care about the past eight years. I don't care about the pack or your friends. Things change, and it's okay. Change is okay. You're so sweet, I just want to eat you alive."

She dredged up every ounce of willpower she possessed. She had to stop this before it was too late. Harry's alpha side was enveloping her, his wolf calling her, and she was succumbing.

This was why witches went over the edge.

This was what she absolutely could not do.

But Harry lifted each breast so he could lick her juices from one nipple, then the other. He growled and sucked, drawing something out of her to meet him.

He would do that between her legs with his hot, hot mouth. Growl. Suck. Madness and lust whirled inside her like a tornado, a violent wind that flung aside her caution.

She wanted to devour him, wanted him to devour her, until they were inside one another. Forget the consequences. This was Harry, and she had to have him.

She slipped a hand beneath his T-shirt, his warm skin gliding beneath her palm. In response, he yanked off his shirt, practically ripping it. Lean muscles bunched in his arms, his abdomen, his skin golden-tan. The hair that grew on his chest was as silky as she'd always imagined.

When she followed the path downward and tried to free the button on his jeans, something inside her popped.

No, not inside her. Thank the Goddess, it was her sprained wrist. The pain restored a semblance of sanity.

She closed her eyes so she couldn't see his dark head bent over her breasts, her legs spread wantonly around him.

"Harry."

He pinched her nipples, his whiskers rubbing her raw. Delicious.

So she bent her hand backward until her wrist

flared with agony. June clenched her teeth against it. "Harry, stop."

His teeth scraped her tender skin, and she wondered if they'd sharpened. If his eyes were pale blue. If Harry continued to exert his alpha to persuade her into bed, what was she going to do?

She wasn't strong enough. A few witches claimed to have bedded a shifter and kept their magic, but June feared she'd be one of the others. One of the lost ones.

She shoved him. "I hurt my wrist, Harry, and my cut could get infected. We can't do this right now."

He rested his forehead against her, his breath sighing over her moist nipples. "You're right, honey, you're right. Give me a minute."

She did. When he raised his head, his expression was tight but not angry.

"I can't believe how much I want you," he told her. "Did you cast a spell on me?"

"Of course not." There were spells for that, but she'd never cast one. "In fact, I normally..." Her face heated.

Harry raised the straps of her bra and buttoned her dress with lazy hands, caressing each inch of skin before he concealed it. "Normally?"

"I run a...well, we call it a dampener. For the libido." She didn't want him to think she'd been drowning in lust the past eight years. "I dropped that spell along with my older face to conserve magic. I didn't think it would be a problem."

"Really." He didn't phrase it as a question.

"Yes, really." She sighed.

"Being horny isn't a problem, June. It's healthy." He finished her top button and winked. "Besides, what else are we going to do until your power comes back?"

He made it sound so casual, something to pass the time. She was no virgin, but she didn't hop in bed to relieve her boredom.

And she absolutely couldn't hop into bed with Harry.

"What can we do? All sorts of things." She slipped off the counter, bumping him with her elbows and knees. "We can eat. Sleep. Surf the internet. Bake a pie. Play poker."

"I was teasing." He stepped out of her way when she stomped to the sink to tidy the dish drainer. "If you're not in the mood, I get it."

"It's not that." She couldn't tell him what it was. "Sex would complicate matters."

"Matters are already complicated." He winced and adjusted his jeans, which bulged at the crotch.

She tore her gaze away. "Complicate things more." If she slept with Harry and lost her power, she couldn't imagine how she'd be able to help him tomorrow—or herself.

He bent to pick up a plate, his jeans hugging his heinie in a way she had always appreciated.

Just not with such erotic hunger.

His light brown eyes gleamed when he caught her watching, and he smiled—wolfishly. "I think I can handle it. Can you?"

No, she couldn't. "End of discussion. Put some food in that mouth and quit arguing with me."

"Now I definitely believe you're Sandie," he grumbled, but he opened the fridge, just the same.

June retreated to her stillroom at the back of the house as fast as her feet would carry her. She couldn't explain why sleeping with him was a horrible idea, and it both thrilled and disturbed her that he'd been so aggressive. From what she'd heard from his dates, who'd all adored Harry's sweet old lady friend, his habitual indolence had extended to his love life. He didn't hunt. He didn't pursue. If he'd been roused to seduce her today, he might be roused out of it again.

She had no idea why. The nerve-racking situation? Their friendship? Her resistance?

Didn't matter. As soon as her power returned, she was going to hit herself with a dampener spell the size of a tractor.

Right now she lacked the strength to soothe a sunburn. To tend her wounds, she'd have to dig out her stash.

The Millington coven didn't just specialize in cake. They were also one of the top producers of primed medicants, pre-spelled substances that could heal without more magic. Nothing fancy—no cures for cancer—but her coven's ability to combine psyches gave them an edge over other covens in this lucrative area. It took a lot of power to create medicants, power that solo witches rarely had.

Nearly all their product went to market. June didn't

have much on hand. Burn cream, a few orals, an all-purpose healer. She had more in her emergency pack, but she didn't think she'd need it. After donning clean clothes and washing her arms and hands with anti-bacterial soap, she smeared a dab of healing salve on the cut.

Then she gritted her teeth and counted to one hundred because it burned like fire as the wound closed.

For the wrist she popped ibuprofen and slapped on an elastic bandage. Time and patience could work their own magic.

AFTER JUNE RACED out of the room, Harry considered shoving ice down his pants instead of fried chicken down his gullet, but then he smelled the meatloaf.

His stomach growled like two badgers fighting over roadkill.

He piled meatloaf, baked beans, scalloped potatoes, cornbread and, what the heck, some chicken on a plate and nuked it. The odors of beef and carbs slowly overpowered the scent of woman. He squeezed the bridge of his nose, only to realize his hands smelled like June's body.

His erection sprang back to life as he remembered how he'd spread her out on the counter like a wishbone waiting for his wish. Christ, he hadn't been this horny since he was a teenager, the man and wolf inside him struggling to break free.

Teenaged shifters had it rough. Not only did they have raging hormones, pimples, growth spurts and bottomless pits for stomachs, but their wolf stirred around that time, as well. Their animal nature tormented them. Their senses sharpened too, which made things worse. Fucking, eating and their hair was pretty much all they thought about. When they weren't having an existential crisis, that is.

Not that different from human teenagers.

In a biological blessing to parents, no shifters turned four-legged until they controlled their animals, usually in their late teens. Mastering the wolf was a huge rite of passage. Wolves who displayed weakness afterward were considered feral. Defective. Pack risks. They were banished, and after a day or so in foreign territory, the defective wolf lost his powers, maybe his life.

Indies who lost control—well, their best bet was to never do it in the first place.

Harry had been in California at the time of his first change, with one of the packs that took in orphans. His mother had told him to go there before she died. The human social services system was no place for a shifter. He'd been considered a prodigy because he'd shifted before he got his driver's license.

Combine that with the alpha gene that revealed itself after the shift, and he'd had more chicks than he could handle. Werewolves dug alphas, even when the alpha wasn't pack. But women, he'd found, wanted you to date them. Stay with them. Join their packs.

And so Harry had quit handling them. Unless they brought food.

He was a sucker for a woman who could cook. If she wanted him to mow her yard, he showed up with the John Deere and an appetite. If she wanted him to help pick out a car, he found her an awesome deal. If she wanted him in her bed…

Well, he had limits. He didn't go for married women, miserable women, underage women or pack wolves.

Hell, a man who could cook could probably talk him into a lot of shit too, but men never showed up with pie. Sometimes a six-pack, which wasn't as persuasive.

That being said, if June's cooking skills had been equivalent to his, meaning nonexistent, he'd still have wanted her. Since now wasn't a good time to have her, when would be?

Next week, when this was all over?

Tomorrow morning, when she'd rested?

After supper, when she'd bandaged her arm?

To keep his mind off sex, Harry scrubbed her odor off his hands with dish soap and followed with a slice of onion to be safe. The pungent veggie brought tears to his eyes. He sniffed, rubbing his nose against his shoulder.

When his meal dinged, he fixed June a plate with chicken, potatoes and beans. Her favorites. As he waited, he cracked the window over the kitchen sink and listened for any signs of shifters outside the house.

Nothing but tree frogs and birds. He poured two glasses of milk and went to fetch June.

He'd been to her neat-as-a-pin house any number
of times. It was surreal to walk down the hall knowing everything was different. June wasn't the same,
obviously, since he got hard as steel when he thought
about kissing her. But the more he considered the day's
events, the more he realized her mannerisms, her way
of speaking, her inherent bossiness—her dislike for
profanity—were all Sandie.

While he hadn't had any complaints about Sandie
the past eight years, her new appearance roused him
in a way her previous one hadn't. His feelings for her
were being transformed by a major dose of lust.

If that made him a shallow bastard, nobody ever
said wolves were profound.

Her bloody dress was draped over the foot of her
bed. The bathroom door stood open, lights out. No
sign of her in the Florida extension, watering plants.
He finally found her in the back parlor she'd converted
to a craft room. The sink, fridge, counters and cabi-
nets were organized with the supplies she used for
potpourri and fussy stuff.

And, apparently, magic spells. His nose twitched
at the odor of grapevine and herbs.

She was immersed in whatever she was doing,
using a tiny ladle to sift green flakes onto an elec-
tronic scale. A book lay open on the counter. Muttering to herself, she bent forward to squint at the digital
readout. A pair of jersey pants hugged the curves of
her rear.

Harry swallowed.

"June."

When she didn't turn, he advanced on her. "June, I heated you a plate."

She lurched forward with an "eek," bumping her skull on the counter. Her ladle flew one way; she flew another.

Harry caught her before she hit the floor, and his hands lingered after she gained her footing. Her fitted T-shirt was as blue as her eyes. He'd never seen her so casually dressed.

"You startled me." She rubbed the top of her head where she'd hit the marble. "Don't sneak up on me like that, wolf man."

"Your arm looks great." He traced the nearly invisible scar that had recently been a claw slice. "You should patent that. You'd be rich."

"I agree, we should go public with the fact we can magically heal cuts." She pulled a face. Her other wrist was wrapped in a tan bandage. "Right after you wolf out on national TV, okay?"

"Touché." He pretended he was fascinated by her healed wound as an excuse to keep touching her. "Are you ready to eat?"

"I'm overhauling my kit." She inclined her head toward her giant purse on the next counter. "I need to be better prepared."

"Can it wait?" He smiled. "You know I don't like to eat alone."

Her eyelashes lowered as her gaze ventured down

his torso. He hadn't put his shirt back on after their encounter.

"Hmm." She wet her lips. "What are we having?"

If she kept looking at him like that, he'd be having her. She was clean now, her cut healed and her wrist taped. "Chicken, potatoes, beans."

"I should finish up." She plucked up the ladle and rubbed it with a cleaning wipe before hanging it on a swivel rack.

He caressed her arm. "This stuff isn't going anywhere. Come on. The food will get cold."

She followed him into the kitchen, and he seated her at the dinette table where he'd enjoyed many a meal. Conscious of her stare, he slipped into his T-shirt. A gentleman did not come to the table bare-chested or wearing a hat.

Unless his companion was bare-chested, but she wasn't. More's the pity.

"Thank you," she said as she rubbed her hands with an antibacterial wipe. He wasn't sure if it was for the food or putting on his clothes. "I checked my messages, by the way. My coven suspects I'm helping you, but they think we're long gone."

"Are you being censured?" He set his plate across from hers. It didn't seem right that her friends would punish her for kindness.

"Not as of right now."

"Good." For several minutes, they tucked away leftovers in silence. The sound of forks on plates provided quiet background noise, along with the fridge's hum.

"Want anything else?" He rinsed his plate in the sink and reached for hers. When they had meals together, she cooked, he cleaned. Annette and the other ladies wouldn't let him lift a finger, but his relationship with Sandie had always been egalitarian. He didn't even mind that she went behind him and redid everything.

She swirled her milk, watching the liquid. "There's cake and ice cream. None for me, though. It's too late for sweets."

It was never too late for her cake. He glanced around the kitchen until he spotted the tin. Harry cut himself a slice of the chocolate dessert and scooped vanilla ice cream on the plate beside it.

This time he sat beside June instead of across from her. In the other room the grandfather clock struck twelve. "Hey, it's your favorite time of day. The witching hour."

A smile curled her lips. "You know I go to bed at ten sharp. I'm hardly ever awake at midnight."

Yet here it was, and he hadn't seen her yawn for some time. "Can you turn people into pumpkins?"

"Myth."

"Frogs?"

"Myth." She rested her head on her hand and watched him enjoy the cake.

"Broom?"

"I use a vacuum."

"For riding?" It wasn't much smaller than the Smart car.

"For cleaning the floor," she said with a laugh. "It's bagless. Fancy, huh?"

He loaded the perfect-sized bite of cake, icing and vanilla on his fork. "Cake?"

"I'm full."

"You know you want it." And he knew it too. June had a sweet tooth to rival his own. "Just one bite. Open up."

After a second, she complied. Their gazes met. He withdrew the fork from her mouth and deliberately licked the tines.

She exhaled, her eyelids lowering halfway.

Oh, yeah. After supper was the perfect time to finish what they'd started.

Harry took another bite, allowing his knee to brush her leg under the table.

"You're bossy," she observed after she swallowed. "Why didn't I notice that before?"

He readied the fork with more cake. "What can I say? There are more things I want from you now."

"Harry," she began unsteadily, "we can't—"

He fed her more cake. She accepted it, desire warring with uncertainty in her expression.

What was she afraid of, sex with a shifter? No reason to be. His kind was devoid of STDs and unable to breed with humans. Shifters might get rowdy in the sack, but they didn't hurt their partners. They had more control than that; their painful teenage years saw to it.

If she was afraid of screwing up their friendship, that was plausible, but he didn't think it would hap-

pen. With few exceptions, his exes didn't become enemies. Some of his best customers were former dates
and their families.

June was single, he was single. They were attracted.
They liked each other. They trusted each other. They
spent half of their free time together. They'd survived
a near-death experience together. No reason they
couldn't hook up.

He alternated bites between them, teasing with hers
and making her work for them. By the time the cake
was gone, she was practically sitting in his lap. Either
she wasn't wearing a bra or it was a thin one, because
it did nothing to conceal her nipples.

She clearly wanted to sleep with him. He intended
to see she got what she wanted.

Harry circled the last bite around her. "Do we need
another piece?" He'd go for whipped cream this time.
And nothing else.

She licked a dab of icing off her lips. "You're a bad
influence."

He smudged ice cream on her cheek. "Oops."

"You rat."

When she raised a hand to wipe it off, he stopped
her. "Let me."

He leaned forward and licked the vanilla off her
skin.

"Ohhhh, boy," she said, "I already explained—"

He slid the last bite of cake in her mouth. After a
moment, he pressed his lips against hers.

It didn't surprise him when she opened for him,

the sweet flavors of cake and ice cream lingering on her tongue.

Harry took his time kissing her. Earlier, he'd been so excited, he'd had her on the counter before he'd given her a chance to adjust to the change in their relationship. Now he kissed and fondled, nothing heavy, learning her breathing, the sound of her heart. He rubbed her back, on top of the shirt. As long as he kept it light, she displayed no hesitation.

Encouraged, he drew her into his lap. He intended to place her legs to one side but she straddled him, her pussy close to his groin. His hands dropped to her hips, but he forced himself not to grind their lower bodies together. He began to caress her thighs through the thin jersey pants.

Her fingers threaded through his hair, and then one hand dipped beneath the neckline of his shirt in back. She rubbed his spine, her tongue winding around his. Her hips rolled against his cock as she reached farther down his back. Finally she tugged his shirt over his head.

He didn't return the favor. In fact he avoided the standard erogenous zones, concentrating on her legs, the back of her knees, her midriff and shoulders. He focused on kissing her, on seducing her instead of charging forward.

It wasn't easy. His cock was hard, throbbing like a bass drum. Something about June roused an aggressive streak in him that rarely emerged when he made love.

With shifters, sometimes—you had to be firm if they were alphas and you didn't want them taking control.

Which he did not. That was a good way to wind up chained to a bed with a cock ring shoved over your genitals and a Polaroid camera capturing the moment.

Harry cupped June's face in his hands and delved deep with a kiss. She sniffed, fidgeted and drew back for a moment.

"Why do I smell onions?"

He bit back a laugh. "I sliced one earlier."

She inspected his face, their eyes level. Her fingers twiddled the back of his neck. The elastic bandage on her wrist rasped against his skin. "This can't go any further."

"You mentioned that." He kissed her temple, blowing into her ear until she shivered. "Something about your cut getting infected."

"And complications."

"It's not complicated." He nuzzled his way down her throat. "It's very, very easy. You undress me, I undress you, we go to the bedroom, where I—"

She palmed his mouth. "None of that."

"Just sharing my thoughts," he said, muffled. He thrust his tongue between two of her fingers, and she gasped before removing her hand.

His jeans constricted his cock, so he spread his legs to make space. He needed to get out of these pants. "Is there someone else?"

"No." She continued to pet his shoulders, down his

arms. If she were unwilling, she wouldn't be stroking his muscles and smelling like sin.

"Are witches celibate?" He pulled her forward until her breasts rubbed him, his fingers wrapped around her ribcage.

"No," she said, her voice a little strained.

He drew his hands up her curves until his thumbs were almost touching her nipples. She was, indeed, without brassiere. "Then what's the problem, sweetheart? Do you think I only want one thing? Trust me, I like your cooking too."

"You're ridiculous." Her pale skin glowed with a blush.

He rubbed her nipples slowly, around and around. Her breasts were more than a handful, their bouncy softness the perfect receptacle for his head. Or his cock. "We've been friends a long time. I'm willing to see where this goes."

"It's not that."

"I'll still respect you in the morning."

"I never considered that you wouldn't."

"Then you've considered it." He leaned forward and latched on to the tip of her breast, moistening the fabric. He wanted her to take her shirt off herself. She'd be more willing to follow where he led if she thought she was picking the path.

"Ahhh." She arched her back, her hands digging into his hair. He responded by biting down, increasing the friction. Her hips rocked against him, so he dropped one hand to knead her cushy ass. This position had definite possibilities.

"Here's something else to consider," he told her as he fondled her other breast. "I want you bad. Bad enough that I'm willing to wait until you're ready." As long as she was ready in fifteen minutes. "I'll do whatever it takes to get you hot and wet."

"That's beside the point." She shoved his hand under her shirt, sighing when his fingers found her bare breast. He pushed the material until it was above her nipple, the dark pink gumdrop beckoning. "The thing is, I can't...ah!"

Can't. He didn't like that word. He sucked her nipple, licking and pulling. Impatiently she shrugged out of her shirt, returning his head to her breast.

Oh yeah, he was in. Once they started tossing off their clothes, they'd reached a decision whether they realized it or not.

Obligingly, he kissed and caressed her gorgeous tits until she was squirming and panting, rubbing herself against his crotch in a way that felt good to them both. Well, it would feel a hell of a lot better if he weren't bruising his dick against his zipper seam. He let his teeth sharpen and rake across her skin. She moaned.

He nibbled up her neck until he reached her ear. "Come on, June," he whispered, licking her earlobe. "Neither of us can think about anything else. This is going to keep happening until you give in."

She shook her head, her eyes squeezed shut. Her golden curls danced across her milk-pale shoulders.

He kissed the dimple beside her mouth, and her lips parted, anticipating his kiss.

He didn't kiss her, not right away. "I want you. I want to be inside you. I want to make you come while I'm buried inside your body."

And then he kissed her, his tongue slipping into her mouth. She met him eagerly, the kiss of a woman who wanted her lover to take her to bed.

He squashed their bodies together, letting his fingers sink into the supple flesh of her ass. She wriggled against him. He slipped beneath the fabric of her pants, delighted to find she wasn't wearing panties either. Her butt was like two silk pillows. He squeezed and released, reaching until the tips of his fingers brushed the hair that covered her mound. Moisture dampened her pants between the legs. The scent rose around him like steam from a shower.

"Tell me you don't want me," he dared her. "You ache for me, don't you?"

She leaned forward, her forehead on his shoulder. Her hot breath gusted across his skin. "You don't understand."

"Then tell me." He stroked her soft, private hair, not touching her labia.

"I can't."

Since that was the entirety of her sentence, he didn't have to cut her off with a kiss. She was close. He could smell it. Sense it. Her heart raced and she hadn't pulled away from him.

"If we can't make love, let me taste you."

"Cheese whiz." She fell against him, her face in his neck. Her fingers tightened on his shoulders, like she was ready to hold on for the ride.

He probed her lightly, flicking her clitoris. She flinched. Juices dampened his fingers. "I'll just use my mouth. My hands." He stroked faster as she panted. "I want to slide my fingers deep inside you, one at a time. Two at a time."

"I have to…"

Her feet hit the floor and she tried to stand, but he wouldn't let her. "How about three fingers? Imagine them pumping in and out of you and my mouth—"

"I'm not sure I like the way you're talking to me," she said breathlessly. "It's not nice."

She didn't smell unsure, and she didn't act it. In fact, she pulled his face to her breasts. He nipped the tender skin, licking her nipples until she trembled. When he drove two fingers roughly into her body, she gasped.

"I don't want you to feel bad." He sucked one of her nipples hard, letting his teeth dig into her. "Shifters can sense things. I smell it, June. I know how close you are."

"I am," she said, her voice barely audible.

"I want to make you come. Just a little lick, honey. You can decide if anything else happens." He started peeling her pants down her hips. Her soft, curved stomach was so perfect he had to force himself not to throw her on the floor.

Why was she so resistant? He'd never hurt her. He'd

never let anyone hurt her. Harry might be an alpha, but he was no asshole.

"I can't do this." She caught his hands, her pants barely covering her privates.

"You won't be doing anything." He flicked her nipple with his tongue. "I will."

This time when she tried to stand, he let her, but he held on to her pants. They slipped past her rounded hips, baring her damp curls. Because she was so aroused, he could see the hot pink skin there, glistening with dew.

Harry felt as if someone had put a perfectly grilled porterhouse on the table before him. He reached to cup her feminine heat, staring up into her face as he did so.

June's eyes were wide and brilliant blue, her cheeks flushed. Panic and lust ebbed off her in tandem. She wanted him. She was frantic for him. But she was frightened.

"What are you afraid of?" he asked. "If you say no, we can stop right now and I'll never touch you again." He'd touch himself, harshly, in a cold, cold shower. "But, honey, I am praying that won't be your answer."

He rubbed her pussy with his whole hand. Heat poured off her skin. Heat and indecision.

"If we're together I could...lose myself." She gripped his shoulders.

He didn't sense any dishonesty, just desire. "You're afraid to lose yourself."

It sounded like woman-talk for falling in love. Hell,

why was that a problem? He was halfway there already.

"Yes. And that's why—" she swallowed "—we should probably stop."

Probably, his ass. If she wanted him to stop, she'd had ample opportunity to tell him.

He knew this one. If he stopped, she'd be ticked. If he didn't stop, she'd be ticked. But at least she'd enjoy herself. Without another word, he hefted her onto the table, yanked off her pants and dropped to his knees.

June gasped with surprise, but she didn't kick him in the head—a good sign.

"I'll keep my pants on if that's what you want, but you should know. You're too late to stop me from tasting you."

"I don't think…ohhhh!"

Harry spread her apart and licked her from bottom to top, with particular emphasis on the middle. He didn't want any thoughts in that pretty head right now except, *Do me, Harry.*

She squirmed around so much he had to push her onto her back and hold her still to get a good taste. Her musky sweetness filled his senses and sent his cock into overdrive. His jeans pinched him like a lobster. He ignored his discomfort, lapping her cream and sucking her clit. God, she tasted good. He could do this for hours.

She pulled his hair, but only to urge him on. As promised, he inserted one of his fingers in and out of her, followed by two.

"More," she said. "I want more."

By the time he got to three, she was starting to keen. She was a tight fit, so he pushed harder.

She tensed, her hands in his hair. "Harry," she cried. "Oh stars, Harry, please!"

He raised his head. "Please what?"

"Do…do what you're doing. I'm close, I…" She couldn't get the sentences out, she was so agitated.

He pulled her clit into his mouth, laving with his tongue. He should set up a rhythm and finish her, but he loved a desperate woman. Loved how they begged him to take them, make them come. Loved when they gave themselves up to him. He wanted June to feel that desperate, that willing, so when she came she'd feel that much pleasure.

June whimpered, her hips surging. "It's so hard to fight it. I can't fight it."

"Then don't." He nudged his fingers deeper inside her. He flicked with his tongue, butterfly light, driving her wild. Her scent sharpened as she neared her climax, so primal she almost smelled like a shifter. God, she was magnificent. "Let go, June. Let go."

"I can't." A sob quivered at the edge of her voice. "I want to. I want to. I can't."

Harry felt a surge of sympathy but not enough to stop. That's not what she wanted. She wanted to come, and come hard. She was wound up so tight, she was going to go off like a rocket. Besides, she wasn't asking him to stop.

She was asking him to take over.

He started working his fingers in and out of her, simulating what his cock would do later. With a growl, he latched on to her clit and vibrated it.

June gasped. "It's close, it's here, I can't…"

He knew the moment she surrendered. She widened her legs and gripped his hair. Her pussy grew hotter and slicker. She thrust against him with the abandon he'd been seeking.

That was it. She'd let go. She was his now.

Harry relished this moment. If he wanted to mount her, fuck her pussy, her ass, she'd let him. She'd take his cock wherever he wanted to put it and beg for more. If he wanted to spank her until her butt was cherry-red, she'd hand him the whip. Anything he wanted would push her over the edge.

And what he wanted was to suck her pussy until she cried. Until she lost herself to him, the exact thing she feared.

As if signaled, her sheath convulsed around his fingers. She moaned her satisfaction, and he milked it until she drooped, licking and probing until she batted him away.

"Stop." Tears glistened on her cheeks, proof of the intensity of what he'd made her feel. "It's over. I lost."

Lost what, her composure?

"It's hardly over." He swept her into his arms, her body small against his chest, and carried her to the bedroom. He wasn't done with her by half. He kissed her, nuzzling the skin of her neck, until she chuckled weakly.

When he licked his lips, tasting her musk, something niggled at him, something he couldn't quite iden-
tify. A woman's flavor bloomed when she climaxed,
and there was something familiar about June's.

It was more than the fact he'd known her eight
years. Wolves were very good with scent. The memory went deeper, back to a time he hadn't known her.
Had he been living in New York? Before that? Had
he been a teenager?

He dropped her onto the bed with a whoomp and,
ignoring her protests, buried his face in her crotch,
trying to place the marker.

And then he did.

Harry shot to the head of the bed and pinned June
in place. She squeaked, but he cowed her with every
ounce of dominance in him. He knew his eyes had
blazed out white-blue. When she trembled, it only fu-
eled his anger.

Somehow, some way, she was a shifter. A young
one, but a shifter just the same.

"What the hell are you?" he demanded.

CHAPTER EIGHT

HE KNEW. NOT only had she slept with a shifter and lost her powers, but now he knew the big secret.

"I'm a witch." It wasn't a lie. Witches weren't precisely shifters, after all.

"You're a shifter." His grip on her arms tightened. "You're a natural alpha shifter."

"I'm alpha?" That was news. She'd never known any witches who would have been alphas if they'd gone through the change.

His jeans rasped her flesh as he shoved a knee between her thighs. "Don't play stupid anymore. First, though, tell me you're over twenty-one. Jesus! I did not just sleep with a kid."

"I'm quite a bit over twenty-one." Witches aged well. Very well. But so did shifters.

He blew out an irate breath. "Are you a shifter?"

Did it matter what she told him? Once her incipient conversion was complete, the coven would erase both of their memories. In the gentlest way possible, of course. They wouldn't even have a headache after the ceremony. They just wouldn't remember the truth about her life.

They'd think she'd always been a shifter. They'd have no idea witches existed.

"All right." June sighed. His fury ebbed when he realized he was getting his way. "I'm a shifter. Sort of. But it's like hiding the fact I'm a witch or you're a werewolf. We don't share this outside our community. It doesn't affect anyone but us."

"It affects the man you just screwed."

"I didn't. We didn't." She flushed, her innards twisting with guilt and shame. Or was it the arrival of her wolf? At least Harry could advise her when it happened. He'd been through it himself earlier in his life.

"Not that line," he said. "We did. Oral sex is still sex, and you popped like a firecracker."

That she had. "What I mean is it doesn't affect you."

"That's crap. When two alphas get together they tend to attract a pack. And I have zero interest in starting one. If this was some way to trick me into a bond, I'll—"

"It's not! The coven isn't a pack, and we don't want to be wolves." She had no idea whether she'd want to be pack or independent after she transformed into a werewolf. But she did know she was happy with her life the way it was.

"But you *are* a shifter." He whuffed her neck. "I can't believe I never noticed."

"You didn't notice I could do magic, either," June pointed out. Not that she could anymore.

"You smell like a juvenile whose wolf is trapped. It took me a while to place it. I haven't been around younglings in years." Harry frowned. "I've never heard of a juvie your age."

"It wasn't easy. You know when you finally get control of the wolf to release him? We take it a step further. We master the wolf and never shift. If we give in, we're no different from other shifters."

"Is that why you can do magic and I can't?"

"Yes." Good Goddess, he was quick.

"Let me see if I understand this." His gaze canted to the right, and his grip on her arms loosened. "When we're young we're filled with potential. If you don't shift, you can use it for something else." He returned his attention to her face, his glower gone. "How long would I have to stay two-legged before I can do magic?"

"You can't."

"You sure? Because it seems pretty handy."

"I'm sure." Experiments had been done. A single shift meant no magic, ever. She could discuss magical philosophy with him until winter solstice, but witches themselves didn't agree on the reasons.

"Damn, woman." Harry's brow wrinkled. "Why don't shifters know?"

"Because you curse too much."

"Come on."

She bit her lip. "Custom."

"That isn't the whole truth."

He might not like the whole truth. It didn't present shifters in a flattering light. But she wouldn't lie to him anymore.

"There are more of you than there are of us, and you've hidden yourselves for a long time." Their ability to keep humans from finding out was a testament to shifter resourcefulness. It helped that they had no interest in positions of power outside pack structure.

"So?"

"If shifters don't like the fact that we lock our wolves away and have powers they don't, it might not go well."

"That's jumping to a pretty big conclusion. They tolerate independents."

She noticed he sometimes referred to the wolves as "they" and not "we." "You believe that, with the situation you're currently in?"

He shrugged. "Millington's pack is prehistoric. So are most of the Southern packs. Indies just don't go south."

"A lot of packs are like that," she said. "The bond causes such fierce loyalty, packs can be less than philanthropic. They're blind to humanity in general."

He nodded slowly. "So you hide from the wolves."

"If they knew what we could do, what we are, they might try to bond us to the packs. We aren't sure what would happen if they tried." She shuddered. "Alphas can control us, the same as any indie. Less ethical people might abuse that."

Something flashed across Harry's handsome features. In a serious voice, he asked, "Have I abused you?"

"I…" She'd let this happen to herself, hadn't she?

She'd known all the variables going in. He hadn't. He'd demanded and dominated, but he'd assumed it wouldn't affect her.

"You even told me I was being bossy," he said.

And he had been, but Goddess, it had felt so right to give in. How could she possibly be alpha? Her body had been one giant pulse of joy as she released her self-control, trusting Harry to take care of the rest.

"I could have said no," she told him, not sure it was true.

He closed his eyes. "I'd never have pushed you into anything."

Her throat tightened. "I know that."

That's why Harry was independent, not pack. While he'd seemed to enjoy mastering her in bed, he had no desire to run anyone's life. First thing tomorrow, before her house protections faded, she'd beg the coven to protect Harry. It was her duty to let them know what had happened, and they'd figure it out anyway. Covens had a nebulous link to one another, and their coven had stronger connections than most.

"Of course, you did push back," he observed. "You're alpha too."

"Are you saying I abused you?" Alphas did have more ability to resist other alphas—if they wanted to.

Harry, shaking off his disquiet, gave her a slow grin. "My alpha's bigger than your alpha."

"If you say so." The smile was a good sign. His hostility had dissolved like sugar in hot tea.

He wound one of her curls around his finger. "I

hope you have condoms. I assume we could get pregnant?"

Where had that come from? They'd been discussing alpha dynamics, the dangers of discovery and the meaning of life. Not sex. She was about to sprout her first full-body fur coat. That would put a damper on things.

"Level with me." Harry stared down at her. As far as she could tell, he didn't have an erection, but that could change. She was nude, and he was thinking about condoms. "Why were you reluctant to sleep with me? You know you can trust me. Too stressed out? Too tired? Too soon?"

"It's—"

He cut her off, realization flashing in his eyes. "It's because I found out the truth. You're afraid we'll realize you're shifters."

"That tends to happen." The witch in question generally experienced his or her first change shortly after the sex whether the wolf put two and two together first or not.

"I promise you, June, I won't tell. We're already sharing secrets. What's one more?"

The problem was, this secret would tear her apart. As a teenager, the wolf had been a constant gnawing in the back of her soul. When she'd finally conquered it, when she'd cast her first spell, it had faded to nothingness.

But it was back. Or it had been. She'd sensed it rise to meet Harry and take over her awareness, her passion. The only question was when her body would shift to match it. A delayed change like hers was rumored to be a sudden, violent process, but she didn't think the coven librarian would appreciate a 1:00 a.m. phone call asking for details.

"One more secret is the straw that broke the camel's back."

Harry kissed her, eyes twinkling. "Have a little faith."

Lionel from the Millington pack was a former witch who'd been lured to the hairy side years ago. He didn't remember. The coven had ceremoniously poppied him—standard operating procedure. Many witches had remained friendly toward him, inasmuch as they could, but he was a shifter now. He wasn't the same.

That would be her. Poppied. Changed. She'd forget the pertinent details of the coven, her friends, her family, her magic, her life. The coven would alter whatever was needed to maintain the veneer, and all witches, including family, were complicit after a wipe. Too much was at stake. She'd think she was an indie shifter who worked in a tea room—but everything else would be different.

The enormity of what she'd traded to sleep with Harry crashed into her, and she closed her eyes.

"Look at the positive side," he continued. "When your magic comes back, you won't have to hide anything from me. There's no reason we can't continue to have sex."

"That's the other part of this." June took a deep

breath and tried to be strong, but tears escaped her anyway. She never cried. This was terrible. "My magic's not coming back."

"What do you mean?"

She couldn't look at him. June turned her head to the side, squeezed her eyes tight. "If we become intimate with a shifter, your wolf calls ours to the surface. That's why you sensed it. I'm like you now."

For a moment he didn't answer. Then he said, "Is that what they tell you?"

"It's true." The New York coven was in serious need of shoring up because they'd lost so many members. Apparently the wolves in that area were persuasive. And horny.

"You must be an exception."

She opened her eyes. "I felt the wolf inside me, Harry. I haven't felt her in years." And years, and years. "My magic is gone. I'm a werewolf now."

"I know you think you are. Your wolf isn't unbound."

"How do you know?" Her voice cracked. "Have you ruined the lives of a lot of witches?"

Harry rolled off her and presented his back, hunkered at the edge of the bed. "That was a low blow. I know because your scent marker tells me. You're nowhere close to shifting."

"I felt it." June curled in on herself. "I don't know why I haven't shifted already."

"Because you're not going to. Your wolf's so buried I only noticed because of the...degree of exposure."

"Really?" She sat up, hugging her knees.

"I've been told I have a capable nose." He shrugged, muscles rippling.

"It *is* supposed to happen fast." She tried not to acknowledge the hope surging inside her as wildly as the wolf had before. What if she were resistant? She racked her brain, sorting through her knowledge of shifter sex. The only thing that came to mind was *just say no.* "I thought you could help me through it."

He waved her off. "It's not going to happen."

"It happens ninety-nine percent of the time." She had no idea what the actual statistic was. When young witches faced the choosing, they had a lot of assistance. It's how they emerged on the other side with magic instead of fur.

"That's not a hundred." He bent his head, rubbing his face with his hands. "When you had sex with me, you thought it was going to change everything, didn't you? You thought you'd lose your magic."

"Yes," she said in a very small voice. A chill goosebumped her skin.

The muscles in his back tensed. "Why didn't you say something?"

"I tried." Her face burned, and she plucked the raised pattern on the chenille bedspread. "I'm sure being a shifter is great. You like it, don't you? I shouldn't have said that thing about ruining my life."

"This is my fault."

"It's not." June reached for his shoulder and stopped herself. "We aren't allowed to tell anyone, not even…

Sometimes the shifter never finds out. That makes it easier."

"I've already found out," he snapped. "Now what?"

She wished she could slip into something more comfortable—like a robe. Or a hairshirt. During a quarrel, her nudity seemed out of place. She pulled the bedspread until she could wrap it around herself. "Covens have ways of dealing with exposure risks the same as packs do. We consider transformed witches a risk. If they submit to a pack bond, they might spill the beans for the betterment of the pack. Then we're all in trouble."

"Are you saying they'll kill you?" Harry asked, horrified. "Honey, I'm flattered, but it wasn't worth dying for."

"That's not how it's handled." June wished he'd turn around, at least halfway, so she could read his expression. "We alter memories."

"What about me?"

"Er." Now she was glad he had his back turned. "You'll have to forget a few things too."

"Or not," he growled. "This is bull crap."

"It's for everyone's safety."

"It's for nothing." Harry whirled and grabbed her shoulders. "Nobody is laying a hand on you. You're coming with me when I leave tomorrow."

"We discussed this." His body weighted the bedspread, dragging it off her shoulders. She tugged. "The pack will catch us if the coven doesn't, and this Gavin guy? In my voice mails the coven didn't mention him."

"Hell." Harry glared at her. "Woman, you have the worst timing in the world."

"Must you have such a trucker mouth? This wouldn't have happened at any other time."

"So you say." He flicked her cheek with a finger. "I guess that means you haven't been champing at the bit to get me in bed for eight years."

"No," she said. The man was as changeable as... as a shifter.

"Too bad. That would be kind of hot." He released her and ran his hands through his hair, giving his scalp a scratch. "We can't change the past, but we can plan for the future. Are you still against setting out tonight?"

"We're safe here until morning. The coven thinks we're gone, and the wolves can't sense us from outside." She updated the house protections every morning like clockwork, before coffee. They hid irregularities for twenty-four hours minimum. "After that, I can't cast spells, so it's anyone's guess."

"With Bianca's lockdown, you're right. There are probably photographs on every shifter's computer between here and Indiana. Not all of them will be as clueless as Roanoke. So after, say, 10:00 a.m.—"

"Seven." She was an earlier riser than Harry.

"After eight-thirty, if we stay, we're toast. If we run tomorrow, we're toast—but at least we're on the move. This is assuming your magic doesn't come back."

"We're toast." Without the coven, there was no way to avoid it, and would they help or erase? She wrapped the bedspread more tightly around her. This was all her fault. She could have saved Harry, but she'd thrown it away to sleep with him.

It was as bad as a horror movie, where anyone foolish enough to have sex got slashed by the killer. She'd be sure not to wander outside in a skimpy nightgown to investigate strange noises.

"There's got to be something we're not considering." His fingers rat-a-tatted his side of the bedspread. "Is there any way you could convince your coven to hide us?"

She shook her head. "They're going to know I shifted, so even if they hide us from Bianca, they're going to wipe us. I hope they let us stay together. I… have a soft spot for you, Harry." The coven knew how much June cared for him and teased her frequently— when they weren't suggesting libido-dampener recipes.

He glanced up and smiled. "I have a soft spot for you too."

Nothing about their current situation should be giving her butterflies, but his statement did. Heavens, she was a silly person.

His gaze dropped to her knees, covered by the bedspread. In a thoughtful voice, he said, "If you don't shift, what happens then?"

"I don't know." As the minutes ticked by with no sign of her wolf, more and more optimism filtered through her gloom. Surely she'd have transformed by now. Instead, she felt normal—or as normal as anyone did who'd survived a car wreck, feuded with a pack, drained herself of magic and had sex with her best friend in the past several hours.

"If I'm a witch, we return to plan A," she said uncertainly.

"Which was?"

"Hide here until I'm strong enough to disguise you better." If she didn't shift, it could fix a lot. She'd have enough magic to protect Harry as long as her friends didn't interfere.

He stretched, his muscles bunching. "I'll agree to stay here because I think your magic's coming back and you need to rest. So 9:00 a.m., sharp, we'll drive the Caddy to Roanoke. If you can disguise me, great. If you can't, I'll drive twice as fast."

"Roanoke?" His hatred of Gavin had surprised her since she'd never known him to dislike much of anything. And now he wanted to drive straight into Gavin's territory? "That's where the Householders are from."

"Exactly." He finished his leisurely stretch, his spine cracking. "They're here, not at home. Their pack is a weak spot in the lockdown. Everyone knows indies aren't safe in Roanoke, so why would we go?"

"The police will pull us over if we speed."

He scooted closer. "That can be plan B. Get arrested. If the police take us down to the station, the shifters can't touch us."

June sighed. If only it were that easy. "The coven can."

"How so?"

"I can neither confirm nor deny that we have representatives in law enforcement."

"Don't be defeatist. All we need is magic and luck. Do you feel lucky?"

"Punk," she responded automatically.

Harry laughed, his teeth gleaming. He reclined on the bed, fluffing a pillow. "It's settled. Why don't you pack a bag in case we have to move fast? Most women don't like to travel without underpants and shampoo and stuff."

"Um." She knew shifters were comfortable with nudity, but parading in front of Harry, starkers, caused her to flash hot and cold simultaneously. So did the image of him settling onto her bed as if he intended to sleep there. "If I could have some privacy?"

"You're kidding, right?" He rolled to his side and gaped at her. "I'm the one who took your clothes off. I know what's under there."

"I can't help it." Heat flooded her cheeks. "There's an extra blanket in the hall closet you can use to sleep on the couch."

"Now I know you're kidding." He patted the pillow beside him. "Long day today. Long day tomorrow. Quit wasting time."

Her bed was queen-sized, but she didn't know how restful a companion he'd be. "I don't sleep nude."

"Then put something on. Christ, woman." Harry toed off his socks. She had no idea when he'd lost the boots.

Something else occurred to her. "What will happen to my clothes if I shift?"

"You're not going to shift." He unbuttoned his pants. "But hey, if you're worried, sleep naked."

Okay, she was no longer convinced she was going to shift. How…liberating. She'd research later. The more timely question was, if she were resistant to the call of the wild, would it be taboo to sleep with a shifter…again?

No. Be sensible. They needed rest. She, in particular, had magical energy to recoup. "You're not planning on sleeping naked, are you?"

Harry halted with his thumbs in his waistband. "I guess not."

June inched off the bed, dragging the spread. Harry shook his head and stripped his jeans down his legs. His boxers were plain blue cotton.

"Better set the alarm," he recommended. "I'm beat."

She should finish restocking her kit. Toss clothes in a suitcase. Sterilize her worktable. Run the dishwasher—she wouldn't want to leave the house with a dirty kitchen.

She should do anything besides slide between the sheets with him, the memory of what his hands and tongue could do to her far too fresh for comfort.

In the end she put on panties and pajamas, Harry smirking the whole time, and climbed in bed. He rolled over, kissed her and punched his pillow before settling down with a satisfied groan.

"Comfy mattress," he said. "Thanks for sharing. Your new couch is pretty, but it sucks."

"You're welcome." Her couch did kind of suck.

She waited to see if he'd say anything else, but he dropped off to sleep almost immediately, his weight and warmth an unfamiliar but reassuring companion.

CHAPTER NINE

HARRY JERKED AWAKE, listening intently in the darkness. It wasn't daylight. June's even breathing remained undisturbed. What had woken him?

Then he heard it, the scuff of paws in the grass outside. He wouldn't have noticed if he hadn't been a shifter.

Harry allowed his wolf to emerge enough to heighten his physical abilities. He padded to the window. The drapes were drawn. No lights on in the house. Carefully, he pushed aside the lace to study the yard.

Nothing. He couldn't see hide or hair of the animals he'd heard.

June still asleep, he slunk through the house, checking locks. He didn't know what June's magical protections muted. Sound? Smell? No reason to take chances. He paused in the kitchen where he'd cracked a window earlier and listened intently.

Scritch. Click. Whuff. There it was. Front of the house.

If the wolves had found him, there wasn't much he could do besides hope June had another spell up her sleeve.

Or he could dial 9-1-1 and pray the cops got here fast. He grabbed the portable phone and headed for the picture window in the living room. There he concealed himself behind a bookcase. Several large shapes paced around the Caddy under the awning. Tails wagged and noses sniffed. One wolf reared up and gazed into the driver's seat, claws ticking the metal door.

A man in dark clothing emerged from the side of the house. "Man up, you idiot."

The wolf whined and lowered its head to the ground. It blurred and emerged on the other side as a nude, dark-skinned man Harry recognized from earlier. One of the Roanokers.

"What did you smell, Maurice?" the first man asked. Harry couldn't make out the man's features. They had zero reason to be here. This location had already been checked by Bianca's people.

"He's been in the car, maybe a week ago." Maurice straightened, but his shoulders remained hunched. "No recent trace."

"Bianca said Smith hangs out with the old woman who lives here. He left a scent trail from his house to her restaurant a juvie could follow." The man stepped into the light of the moon.

Gavin.

Hate shivered across Harry's skin like a chill. No time to reexamine his old resentments. His goal was getting himself and June out of here. Why the hell was Gavin looking for him, to help Bianca out? That would mean she was still fixated on him and hadn't held the ceremony yet.

Maurice shook his head. "Dude, nobody's here and now I'm form stuck. How will I get back to the cabin?"

"Nike Express," Gavin suggested. The two other wolves bumped Gavin's legs. One glanced toward the house. Harry tensed. Four against one wasn't as bad as his odds yesterday, but it was bad enough. Luckily, the wolf didn't seem to sense him.

"This was a waste of time," Maurice said.

"Bianca thought it would be a waste of our time too." Gavin didn't seem concerned they might wake the occupants of the house; he and Maurice were speaking at regular volume. "But we know something Bianca doesn't."

"Maybe." Maurice glanced at the front porch. June's spells must be working overtime if the wolves thought nobody was here. Harry released a breath. This didn't have to become dangerous as long as Gavin stayed outside. "Are you sure your dad came here?"

"There are his tire tracks, idiot." Gavin jerked his thumb toward an area in the driveway that was more dirt than gravel. "You're supposed to be the best nose in the pack."

"There's been a lot of traffic," Maurice said defensively. "Bianca, shifters, humans, cars. I was trying to isolate Smith and the old man, not the truck."

Was Gavin here to find out about Harry or Douglas? Harry inched closer to the glass so he'd be able to make out facial expressions.

"If he didn't drop them off here, where did they go?" Gavin ripped the head off one of June's daffo-dils. "Old bastard never tells me anything."

While Harry wished Gavin wouldn't vandalize June's plants, that wasn't enough of a reason to call the cops. Millington had a conscientious police force who'd report quickly once Harry dialed, which could turn a neutral situation into a bad one.

"He could have taken a wrong turn. Lots of houses around here."

"If he recognized Smith and didn't tell us, he could be laying a false trail." Gavin destroyed another flower, crushing it. "I don't know how they fooled us. If they've got some agreement with Pop, I'll make them tell me. Should have known he wouldn't stick to the plan."

So Gavin had put two and two together—maybe he'd seen a photo—and realized they'd intercepted Harry Smith in No Business and not a stranded human. Who else knew? Obviously no one had told Bianca or she'd have shown up hours ago.

"That dude did look familiar." Maurice nudged the flower Gavin had destroyed into the flower bed, hid-ing it. "The chick had blood on her. She's all over the old man's truck, but there's no marker here."

"She was a tasty piece of ass." Gavin chuckled darkly. "When I find her, I'll enjoy convincing her to tell me everything she knows."

Maurice rubbed his close-cropped hair. "Maybe she doesn't know anything."

"Who gives a crap? She can shut up and take it. Once I'm alpha here, not even human bitches will tell me no." Gavin put his hands on his hips, gazing toward the house. "I'm missing something. I can feel it."

Harry shifted his weight to the balls of his feet. Gavin was interested in the Millington position. It didn't bode well for anyone if he got the job. Why, oh, why had Bianca refused to consider any candidates but Harry? If she'd gone through a normal selection process with interviews and such, this wouldn't be happening.

"You could ask Douglas," Maurice said. "He's here until tomorrow."

"He'd never tell me." Gavin stalked around the Caddy, testing the handles. "Bianca has no idea Pop came with us. She sent us here because she assumed we'd strike out. I bet she knows I wouldn't turn Smith in if I found him."

Harry rotated the phone in his hand, considering. Could he use the fact Gavin would try to trick Bianca to his advantage?

Maurice crouched between his wolf brothers. "If something happens to Smith, she'll be suspicious. You have to treat him like the others."

"He pissed me off," Gavin growled. "We're doing Bianca a favor. She didn't want candidates nosing around, and we made that happen. If some won't leave peacefully, that's not our fault."

From the sound of it, Gavin and his friends had been encouraging candidates to disappear. Thinning the herd. Were Douglas and the others part of the plot to set Gavin up here? Hopefully they wouldn't succeed. Harry didn't wish Gavin on anyone, not even Bianca.

"This is Bianca's home turf. If she finds out..." The wolves huddled closer to Maurice's nude body, keeping their form stuck compatriot warm in the cool night temperatures.

"If she finds out, it will be too late." Gavin's sharpened teeth flashed in the moonlight. "One way or another, I'll be a pack alpha before the next moon."

Harry frowned. It was a toss-up which of them would be a worse alpha in Millington—him or Gavin. If Gavin became alpha, Harry would have to relocate. No way would he live in a territory overseen by that feral piece of shit.

Uprooting himself—he hated the very thought. Would June come with him? It wouldn't be safe for her here anymore, maybe not even as Sandie.

Maurice put his arms around the wolves. "What if something goes wrong and we have to go back to Roanoke?"

"Then I guess I'll feed my parents cyanide and find some dumb recessive bitch to marry," Gavin snapped. "Where's the faith, man? We mapped this years ago, and finally there's a vacancy. This is our shot." He felt under the wheel wells of the Caddy, probably for a spare key.

"It's a joke," he continued, sounding like the teenager Harry had known and not a mature alpha ready for pack responsibility. "I don't know what Bianca's thinking. Everyone knows Harry Smith is a shit choice for a pack wolf. Even Pop said so."

Since Harry had expended some effort making sure everyone knew it, he was gratified to hear his reputation had spread. Too bad it hadn't gotten him off the hook when it mattered.

"Douglas wants this as much as you do," Maurice said. "You wouldn't have been able to get so much help with the candidates if he weren't here to anchor us."

"Yeah, Pop's a saint," Gavin said. "He agreed because Mother won't let him banish me. That's what he gets for letting a woman order him around."

Another strike against packs—they tended to be patriarchal. Women weren't without rights, but many packs treated females as lesser. Harry gripped the phone as if he could shoot Gavin with it. His mother had removed him from that poison at the expense of her life, and he was grateful to her every day.

"You're not worried about somebody else finding Smith?" Maurice asked.

"I don't care." Gavin spat on the ground. "No matter what, I will make sure his loser ass is never a contender for pack alpha again."

Even on two legs, Gavin's threat raised Harry's hackles. There were a few ways to ensure an alpha never became a pack alpha, but the easiest was to kill him. Gavin's vehemence solidified Harry's determination to avoid a confrontation at all costs—a confrontation he had little chance of escaping with his life.

Maurice cleared his throat. "I don't think he wants to be alpha. You don't have to—"

"If Bianca tries to instate him, I'll challenge before the pack bond ceremony. I'm already pack. He's not. He's a dead man."

If candidates wished to unseat a new alpha, they had to challenge before the next pack bond ceremony when the new alpha reached full strength. Although tonight there wouldn't be a gap, sometimes it was weeks between instating a new alpha and the next pack bond ceremony, which were two separate rituals. Challenges were primitive, brutal and an embarrassment to shifters everywhere. Kill or be killed, with your reward a lifetime of pack.

It was Harry's worst nightmare, multiplied.

Maurice crossed his arms. The wolves on either side of him hunkered onto their haunches. "You'll have to challenge Bianca too if she doesn't want you."

"Bitch'll get in line." Gavin swaggered toward the porch. "She's a woman. What the hell does she know?"

Probably a lot, Harry realized. She had the good sense not to want another Bert, though replacing him with his polar opposite—Harry—seemed extreme.

From the flagstone walkway, Gavin studied the house. "I don't like this. What was Pop doing here? There's no trace of Smith or the blonde."

Maurice huddled against his companions' bodies. "What does it matter, Gav? There's nobody here."

"Then there's nobody to stop us from going inside. Maurice, check those planters for a key." Gavin ascended the stairs. "Let's see if we can figure out what our esteemed leader was doing."

Shit, Harry and June couldn't be here when Gavin came in. He'd recognized Harry, and things would get ugly. Harry couldn't protect June if he couldn't even protect himself.

Time to do that running thing he was so good at.

He dialed 9-1-1 as he headed for the bedroom. In the quietest voice possible, he told the operator a version of the situation. But when he reached June's bedroom, she wasn't there.

Where did she go? He yanked on jeans and boots. No time for a shirt.

When he concentrated, he could make out the shifters on the front porch discussing how to get into the house without leaving evidence. Veteran burglars, they were not. He wasn't sticking around to find out what window they broke.

Something tinked in the back of the house. Ceramics on glass.

Harry shot down the narrow hallway to June's still-room. She was there, frantically stuffing packets and bottles into her big purse, her hair in wild ringlets.

"They're coming in. I dialed 9-1-1." He grabbed her arm above the tan bandage. "Out the back. Move." If Gavin had half a brain, he'd have lookouts on all sides. Harry was counting on Gavin being as brainless as he was ambitious.

"No." She shook out of his grasp. "We're not in any danger."

"Then why are you shoving your pantry into your handbag?"

"I should have done it earlier." She startled when a loud thump resounded from the front porch. "I hope they don't break anything."

According to the 9-1-1 operator, the cops were on their way, but June had an excess of confidence in the police if she thought that was the only protection they needed.

"Gavin's not here to play poker, June. Let's go." Harry would carry her if he had to. She wasn't wearing shoes.

"Seriously, it's okay." She shoved her hair out of her face. "They think we're human, and the talc spell components are still in our bodies."

Harry didn't want to scare her, but she had to realize the shifters wouldn't just let them go. "They know I'm Harry Smith. They must have seen a photo since Douglas dropped us off."

"Then we'll pretend to cooperate with them until the cops get here." She fastened her purse and secured it around her body like a bandolier. It contrasted with the pink flannel of her PJs. "We have to stay. I can't have the cops tear apart my house looking for me."

"This is about your place getting wrecked?" June hadn't overheard what he'd overheard. "They're going to do more than hurt us. Gavin wants to kill me and rape you."

She turned big blue eyes on him, uncertainty growing. "Are you sure?"

"If you thought Bert was bad, it's because you never met Gavin." Harry cupped her chin. "I can't let that happen to you too."

"What do you mean by *too?*" When he shook his head, she conceded. "All right."

"Let's go," he repeated, two seconds away from tossing her over his shoulder. June didn't keep a spare key anywhere Gavin would find it, so it wouldn't be long before the wolves kicked in a door or window.

"Better idea. Hide in the cellar. I'm sure the dispatcher told you to do that anyway." June bumped her arm on the counter and flinched. "My wrist hurts."

"I'm not getting trapped down there." Harry had helped another friend of theirs build shelves in the low, dank room carved into the hill behind June's house where she stored canned goods, bulk items and old clothes. As far as he knew, she didn't store weapons and guns. "We're running."

"We won't get trapped. There's a back door." She shook a small pill out of a nearly empty bottle and popped it in her mouth.

"You mean that vent? Too small."

"The root cellar is bigger than you think. The door is concealed." She slipped her feet into a pair of plastic clogs. "They won't even know we're there."

What was she talking about? The cellar door was beneath the hallway floor, covered by a fluffy rug. The rug disguised the edges, but any wolf who crossed over the door would notice the change in pitch.

"I'm not taking that chance." Harry was done arguing. He picked June up and carried her to the Florida room. Beyond it was a screened porch and the woods. The mountain rose sharply behind the house, but he knew a way up the cliff. "They're pack, June. That means they're strong enough to—"

The remainder of his statement was cut short by a crash from the living room, followed by laughter. The picture window. That answered the question of how the shifters were getting in.

"Jerks," she muttered. "Glass is expensive."

He hustled her out the rear door, alert for sounds of pursuit. Gavin was cussing the hell out of whomever had broken the window. Harry scanned the backyard, thankful he'd repaired the formerly squeaky screen door.

"Will they chase us?" June whispered.

"Who knows what those idiots will do?" Their breath steamed in the frosty air. "We'll climb the bluff, hit Horse Mountain Road and steal a car." A semi-flat area atop the mountain boasted a small community of houses.

"We most certainly will not steal a car." She wrapped her arms around herself. "It's cold after that rain."

"Shhhh." They crossed the yard as silently as possible. Shifters had astute senses in human form, but the housebreakers would be focused on searching a house they thought was empty, not listening for escapees.

Once past June's property line, the manicured landscape disintegrated into trees, scrub and rocky slope.

The mixed evergreen-and-deciduous forest blocked what light the stars and moon offered. Harry had navigated this on four legs, not two. Since June had no wolf, shifting wasn't an option.

Though she did have a shirt. Good thing they hadn't slept nude. Who'd have thought he'd be wrong about that?

Wet brambles thrashed Harry's chest as he endured the brunt of the trail blazing. The frigid air nipped his skin. If the wolves gave chase, they'd have no trouble locating this path. He had to hope they wouldn't realize there was anyone to follow.

Small bluffs began to dominate the landscape along with the trees and laurel. Slick ground cover created unstable footholds, and several times they knocked rocks loose.

When June tripped and fell the fourth time, Harry realized their mad dash up the incline wasn't working. The tree cover was dense, the lighting limited. Scratches crisscrossed his skin and hands. He could only imagine how she felt.

Pebbles clattered as he muscled her to her feet. Her warm breath tickled his chest, and her damp pajamas grazed his belly.

"You okay?" he whispered.

"I can't see a thing." An owl called overhead, and June trembled. "Isn't there a cliff around here? What if we accidentally walk into it?"

He smoothed her hair out of her face. "I can see okay. We'll be all right."

She rested against his chest, her heart thumping. "Instead of going up, what if we follow Route 56 to town? We can hide in the back of the tea room."

"Too obvious. Apparently everyone knows I go there." And here he'd thought his love for the tea room had been a secret from the pack. So much for his cleverness.

"Especially the coven," she agreed. "I wish it weren't so dark. I can't see where my feet should go or what's safe to grab."

If he weren't careful, she was going to get hurt. "I've got an idea. Hold on to my back pocket."

"Okay, but you'll have to slow down. I don't want to make both of us fall."

"Don't worry about that. Just hold on." She couldn't knock him over unless he let her. He'd wolfed out as much as possible without growing fur. It increased his stamina and steadiness. He just had to be careful not to bite his tongue.

Muttering under her breath, she clung to the back of his jeans with one hand. He paused frequently so she could use him to lever past obstacles. The strenuous exercise ought to keep her from getting chilled.

"Wait, my shoe fell off." She crouched, patting the ground. "Can you see it?"

The clog was wedged several yards downslope, a splash of neon against the dark leaves and rocks.

"Gotcha." He fetched the shoe and straightened to inspect their location.

They hadn't gotten far, but it was far enough that

he could no longer hear the intruders at June's house. They were several hundred feet above town elevation-wise, a mile distance-wise. The woods were pretty old growth, the night creatures loud enough to muffle other creatures—like wolves. Water dripped from the trees onto their heads in cold splats.

They should reach the big cliff soon. The rock face was too sheer to attempt without proper equipment. They'd have to work their way along the bottom to the cleft he used as a wolf.

On the plus side, the canopy thinned at the base of the cliff and June would be able to see. On the minus side, so would anyone looking for them.

Several boulders loomed up the slope. Harry searched for an easy way around. In the distance, he heard police sirens.

June grabbed his pocket and hauled herself beside him. He snuggled her against him, rubbing her arms. From the feel of it, her pajamas weren't doing much to protect her from the cold.

"Harry," she said between pants, "when the shifters run from the cops, are they going to head this way?"

Shit. She was right. He and June needed to take cover—fast. The shifters might go east, toward town, but they might tear straight up the mountain.

"Let's hide."

"We should have hidden in my cellar."

Beside the boulders was a sturdy pine with low branches. "Up there."

The closeness of his wolf heightened Harry's body

temperature, which June seemed to appreciate. Her arms tightened around him. "Where? It's so dark I might as well be in a cave."

"There's a tree beside two boulders. We'll climb it. They won't be looking up." In his experience, shifters on four legs were remarkably unobservant of overhead areas, and shifters on two legs would be too busy trying to keep up.

June gusted out a big breath. "Tree-climbing. Sheesh."

He half carried, half led her to the tree. With a boost on his part, she hoisted herself into the bottom branches. It wasn't as wet beneath the thick covering of needles. One of her shoes promptly fell on his head.

"Rats." June's voice floated down through the swish of pine.

He shoved it in his back pocket, the material squishy and malleable. "Take your other shoe off."

She rustled above him. Water rained down as she jostled the branches. "My clogs are great for gardening, but this is ridiculous."

"We're doing great." Harry wiped his face. The thin wail of the siren had become stationary at June's. He doubted the cops would glimpse the shifters, but they'd wonder about the broken window and why Miss Sandie wasn't in her house. They'd also wonder who'd placed the 9-1-1 call.

June's absence would raise more alarms than the ones on the roof of the squad car. She was well liked in the community and not known to associate with rough characters.

Bark crunched as she ascended. "I haven't climbed a tree in ages. How high should I go?"

"Higher." He pulled himself onto the bottom branch. The boughs quivered as they fought to squirm through them.

Pines were difficult to climb at best, with tight branches and sticky sap. Thousands of needles blocked the light from the trunk. Harry could only see down. Sap dotted his fingers, stinging the scrapes. Prongs and rough bark awaited every movement.

At twenty feet up, they should be able to hop to the boulder. It would be more comfortable.

Harry was reaching for the next sizeable branch when hands latched on to his ankle, yanking him straight down through the dark.

CHAPTER TEN

WITH A CURSE, Harry crashed into the ground, a stick jabbing his ribs. His head banged a rock and stars exploded in his vision.

"What happened?" June called. "Did you slip?"

"Stay where you are." He groped for the stick in his side. His hand came away wet, and the scent of blood flooded his nostrils. "Who's there?"

The hands grabbed him roughly, tugging him to his feet. "Dude, a better question is, who's climbing a tree?"

He'd heard that surfer guy accent twenty minutes ago. Maurice, Gavin's minion.

Maurice tried to yank Harry's arm behind his back. Ignoring the throb of his head and ribs, Harry broke the man's grasp so easily it surprised him, using a martial arts move he'd picked up at some point.

His wolf snarled closer to the surface in a rush of strength.

Maurice attempted to tackle him. They grappled, neither able to land a punch. Maurice's wiry body was nude and slippery, but Harry had the upslope advantage. He shoved the other man back.

Undaunted, Maurice regained his footing and lunged. Harry struck out, his fist encountering Maurice's face. Maurice reeled and came at him again.

This time Maurice reached him. As they stumbled back, the lower branches of the tree whacked their heads and shoulders like whips. They exited the limbs and thudded into the boulder.

Maurice's fingers wrapped around his neck. The other man's pack-enhanced strength would cut off Harry's breathing if he didn't do something quickly. He'd gathered from the earlier conversation that Maurice was a bloodhound, not a fighter. Definitely not a leader.

"Back off," Harry commanded, asserting his alpha.

Maurice paused, his fingers loosening. "What? Hey, I know you."

To hell with sportsmanship. Harry brought up his knee, slamming it into Maurice's crotch.

Maurice wheezed out a pained breath as he doubled over. Were the other shifters close? Harry prepared to stun the other man with an uppercut when Maurice dropped to his knees.

He couldn't kick a dog who was down, could he?

"Sorry, dude," Maurice groaned. "Uncle."

"Are you insane? A naked man attacks me for no reason, I've got a right to defend myself." He decided to play dumb. "Who are you and why did you jump me?"

"You're Harry Smith." Maurice hunched, practically groveling. He bobbed his head. "People are looking for you."

It wasn't just the knee to the balls. From his posture, Harry had quelled Maurice with alpha vibes. Amazing. He'd always been able to influence other shifters, but not this much. Either he'd gotten stronger or Maurice was spineless.

"Are you one of the people looking for me?" Harry asked.

"Depends." Maurice rubbed his jaw. Mud smeared in various places, he smelled as much of dirt as he did shifter. "What are you doing up here—camping? This is a shitty place to camp."

If he had to ask why Harry was here, Maurice didn't realize he'd been inside the house. That didn't mean he and June were in the clear.

"Hell no, I'm not camping. I was out for a run." He inspected the scrape on his side. Surface wound, but it stung. "Are you part of Bianca's group?"

"No." Maurice eyed him suspiciously. "How are you masking yourself? I can barely sense you and I'm standing in front of you."

The other three housebreakers were probably booking it on four legs way ahead of poor, form-stuck Maurice. But once he caught up to Gavin, he'd point the way to Harry. June's talc spell wouldn't cover a trail this obvious, and if Maurice could sense him, the disguise must be wearing off.

He could try to knock Maurice out and tie him up, but bribing him might be easier. It was certainly more Harry's style. "Why, do you need tips on staying hidden?"

Maurice's face twisted. "Maybe."

Harry approached him, and Maurice ducked his head. "Who do you need to hide from?"

"Nobody," Maurice lied.

"Tell you what." He put as much pressure on Maurice as he could without turning him into jelly. "I'll give you all the tips you want if you don't tell anyone you saw me."

"Yeah, about that." Maurice's hands protected his privates. "It's not safe here. You and your girlfriend should get out of the territory until…forever."

Interesting—he was willing to warn Harry instead of being blindly obedient. "Why forever? Once the ceremony's over, I should be in the clear."

"I dunno." Maurice's dark eyes darted from side to side as he tried to avoid answering. "The new alpha doesn't like you."

"The new alpha, huh." Gavin wasn't alpha yet, and if Bianca had any sense, she'd find anybody else. The Roanokers couldn't possibly clear *all* the candidates from the territory. "Who'd Bianca pick?"

"Uh, well, uh, nobody yet. She still wants you."

"Then there isn't a new alpha." Harry deliberately kept Maurice on the defensive. It wasn't hard. He was pissed, and Maurice was easily cowed. "Are you going to tell Bianca where I am to get in good with her?"

"I won't see her before the ceremony. Won't matter by then. Just get your girl out of here, okay?"

Harry nearly growled. "Why her? Not that I'd leave her, but she's got nothing to do with this."

"I shouldn't have said anything." Maurice shuffled backward several steps. "You got cut on your side. My bad. Sorry."

"I'll heal." In the distance, the wail of the police sirens shut off. If he immobilized Maurice, Gavin might realize his whipping boy had fallen way, way behind and come looking. It wasn't like Harry was going to kill the guy.

So he risked a half-truth. "I'll level with you, packer. We're headed out of town. All I want is to be left alone."

If Maurice had been in wolf form, his ears would have perked. "Where are you going?"

"Anywhere but here." Harry crossed his arms. Perhaps Gavin would give up the hunt if he thought Harry and June were gone. "When you see your friends, make sure they know I'm never coming back to this dump."

"Dude, I didn't say I was going to tell anybody," Maurice claimed, and Harry didn't smell dishonesty. Maybe he wasn't as subservient to Gavin as he appeared.

"I'll hold you to that." Harry dismissed the smaller man. Maurice picked his way across the slope to the east until Harry lost sight of him.

The pine tree vibrated as June descended. "Can you help me down?"

Harry fought his way back to the trunk of the pine tree. "Stay up there."

"The shifters are gone." *Rustle, rustle.* Water spattered him. "I need to go back to the house."

"We'd better not." He was torn. They couldn't stay here, but showing up at the house was also risky. Half the town had police scanners. Everyone around, pack and coven included, would know everything that had gone down at Sandie's by morning—including any mention of Harry Smith and a blonde woman.

June halted her descent. "Why can't we go home?"

"The cops will be all over that place."

"That's my point. I don't want them all over my place."

"You mentioned that. Is this because you didn't run the dishwasher?" He'd waited for her to tidy the kitchen or her stillroom before they could proceed with their plans many a time.

"I can't guarantee a certain person on the police force will be there to cover up any oddities." She started sliding off the branch, and Harry caught her. "They might come out of there thinking I'm a drug dealer or something. I have a lot of lab equipment. Herbs. Substances."

She'd always been obsessive about leaving her house just so. Was it cleanliness—or secrecy? "You got anything illegal?"

June's forehead scrunched. "Maybe."

"You're yanking my chain."

"Medicinal purposes only." Her lips quirked. "Imagine the scandal."

"I'd rather not." He peered down the mountain. All they needed, on top of everything else, was June to get tossed in jail for possession. "Is it out in the open?"

"It depends how thoroughly they search the house. If we get closer, you can hear what's going on." She started down the slope, but he stopped her.

"If we show up, they still won't know where Sandie is," he pointed out, his hand on her arm. "How are you going to account for that?"

She placed her palm over his hand, her fingers chilly. "I'm the granddaughter. I'll tell them she's on vacation."

"They might not believe you." He began chafing her cold hand. "None of us knew Sandie had a grand-daughter."

"You'd vouch for me." June offered her other hand for warming. "Why would they think we were covering anything up?"

"Because it's their job. We need to stay under everybody's radar. What if they bring in a K-9 unit?"

"I've got it!" Her face brightened even in the darkness before dawn. "I'll call the station and tell them I'm okay."

From his pocket, Harry withdrew his phone. "That won't work. One, there's no reception. Two, what if they want you to come to the station?"

"I do have the supplies to change myself into Sandie," she said, patting her purse, "but then I couldn't renew the protections on the house. I haven't slept long enough."

Harry slipped the phone into his pocket. "What's this about spellcasting? I thought your magic was gone since I ravished you."

"Ravished me. I swan." She lowered her gaze and shivered. "As you can see, I don't seem to be turning into a wolf."

"I hate to say I told you so." He drew her against him, sharing body heat.

"No, you don't." June snuggled, her breasts cushy and her hands icy. "Mmm, you're so warm."

"It's the wolf in me." Her body was increasing his temperature by the second. "Since you didn't convert to the dark and furry side, does that mean we're free to—"

She placed a finger on his lips. "Hush. I can't be sure. We didn't do...everything."

"Hmm." Harry's libido perked at the idea of what he and June hadn't done yet. "We should remedy that."

"Give it a rest, Romeo." She ducked her head to hide a grin and inspected the scrape from his confrontation with Maurice. "This looks painful."

"I'll shift it away."

She traced his collarbone. "Did you know shifters are physically fit because they alter their bodies during the shifting process?"

"That's ridiculous," he scoffed. It was common knowledge their fitness was enhanced by the caloric burn of wolf form. Shifters who rarely changed could grow as corpulent as a human, but once they shifted, their agility and strength returned.

Being a wolf was better than kickboxing and vitamins.

"Ridiculous, is it? So is the fact you can vanish and recreate your clothing if you're skilled enough," June said dryly. "We suspect there are other possibilities you haven't discovered."

Shifter philosophies about why they could do what they did varied. Some believed they'd evolved beyond humans while others believed they had alien DNA. A few believed their ability was a gift from a deity. Shifter scientists had confirmed many facts, like the lack of a lunar connection, but spent most of their time making sure fellow scientists didn't stumble across their species.

A minority of shifters believed what they could do was magic, and few believed in magic of other types. It would take away from their specialness.

Harry now knew differently.

"Are you saying I could alter my appearance?"

"It's a theory. We haven't been able to experiment."

"You looking for a guinea pig?" He liked new things—yet another reason he was no packer.

"No." But her gaze lost focus as she considered it, just like when she had an idea for pie.

"How about a compromise?" He started grooming her PJs, removing pine needles. "If you stay in the tree, I'll see what's going on at the house." He could sneak down there, listen in and sneak back before Maurice caught up to Gavin.

"No, sir. In horror movies when the actors separate, neither of them make it."

"I can outrun Michael Myers." He stroked her back and enjoyed the supple feel of her body. He doubted Gavin would return to the house, and Bianca obviously considered it a dead end. It wasn't a bad place to stay—as long as it had a hide-a-wolf spell and no cops.

He'd still rather be in Vegas.

"Better not," she said. "Shifting would probably negate whatever's left of your talc spell. Any wolves in the vicinity would sense you."

If restricted to two feet, Harry wasn't as confident of his ability to eavesdrop without getting caught. "All right, we stay together."

"Glad you agree." She laced her fingers behind his neck. "We need to get you inside that house and the police out of it before the talc wears off."

"I agree with that too." If anyone did come sniffing around the house again, they'd conclude it was empty. Maurice hadn't seemed aware Harry and June had been inside. Why would anyone break in to her empty house a second time?

She rested her forehead against his chest, and the rest of her words sent puffs of air across his skin. "I apologize to you in advance. With the cops there, we'll have to use the back entrance and hide in the cellar. Darn it, I knew I should have maintained it better."

"What are you talking about? Back entrance?"

June rubbed her eyes. "Remember when I said the root cellar was bigger than you realized? Coven members usually have secret passages in and out of their houses, and that's where mine is."

CHAPTER ELEVEN

HARRY WAITED AT the bottom of the rock pile, holding out his hand in case she needed assistance, but June managed on her own. Without losing a shoe. What she wouldn't give for a touch of shifter resiliency right now.

Her thighs trembled with exertion. Her hands stung with cuts, aggravated by smears of pine sap. One of her toes throbbed where she'd stubbed it. Good thing her sprained wrist had nearly healed since she'd swallowed one of her last all-purpose curatives right before they'd fled.

At least heading down the slope was easier than dragging themselves up it, even with the complication of covering their old trail and laying a false one. The increasing sunlight helped, as well. She could see what was a bush and what was a briar.

Finally she and Harry reached her property. This close to the house they could hear voices. Cars in the gravel drive. No dogs.

If Pete had been on duty this morning, he would make sure the cops didn't find her cellar. She didn't think she'd left anything irregular in the stillroom, but cops, in her experience, were skeptical individuals who might question why Sandie—mysteriously missing Sandie—needed professional-grade lab equipment to construct holiday crafts. Granted, some of her tools were specially manufactured by a coven in Georgia and wouldn't be that recognizable, but not all of them.

If, in searching for Sandie, the cops felt compelled to analyze her computer files, they'd really be in for a shock. Well, maybe this would spur her to install that data-washer program from the coven in San Francisco.

"What can you hear?" she whispered to Harry, clinging to his arm. "Are they still at the house?"

"Yes." The tiniest of shudders thrummed through him. She wouldn't have noticed if she hadn't been stuck to him like a vine. "They're looking for evidence of theft or violence. Someone is taping up your window. Someone else said he couldn't find your purse."

They sat for a moment while Harry listened. June tried to breathe quietly. "Has anyone mentioned the root cellar?"

"Not so far."

Since Harry already had ideas about who her fellow coven members were, she asked, "Do you hear Pete Bowman, Annette's husband?"

"He's the one who said you don't leave home without your purse."

Relief flooded through her. "Then we've got nothing to worry about. We—"

"Wait a minute." Harry shushed her. "Somebody mentioned Bert. Why would they connect his burglary with this? It's not like he's at large. I need to get closer."

"I need to get inside." Oh, she'd hoped to avoid this. The access tunnel had mushed in the center, and it had always been harder to crawl up than down. Scuffed knees and unmentionable sludge were in their immediate future.

That's what she got for installing her escape route too close to the field line. Civic engineer, she was not.

"Where's this back exit?" Harry asked.

"Technically it's a side exit." They picked their way to the west of the house, where the hill sloped into a scrubby area. She'd tried to cultivate grapes a couple years ago, and the remnants of her unsuccessful terraces remained.

Finally they dropped into a gulley where mountain laurel grew in front of the secret passage. The narrow highway wound past on the other side of a ridge. A drizzle began to fall, the beginning of a gray, nasty day.

"We're here," June whispered. She hoped the cops did a good job taping up her picture window or her new couch would be ruined. Surely Pete would take care of it. As one of their elders, he was a good friend and true asset to their coven.

He was as committed as she had been, prior to yesterday.

Harry put his hands on his hips. "Where is the back door?"

She pushed aside the wiry bush with a cedar limb,

not her bare skin, and started poking the wall. The door was camouflaged with sod and had been set into the hillside like a hobbit hole. It was also protected by the magic on her house.

As she plumbed the area, rocks detached themselves and plopped to the ground. Glints of metal shone through the dirt.

Harry's sharp eyes picked out the irregularities, despite the cloaking spell. "That's the door? It's barely three feet tall."

"Easier to hide." She manipulated the latch and the little door creaked open. A dark hole shored with concrete yawned into the hillside. A few creepy crawlies scuttled away from the inrush of light. "Don't worry, it's only a couple hundred feet long."

"I'm not a fan of tight spaces."

"I'm not a fan of you being made alpha of the Millington pack or Gavin Householder trying to kill you," June countered. "Get in there."

"Is it safe?"

"Far as I know." She'd tested it in the fall and survived.

"This is nuts."

"You go first." If he were in the tunnel, he'd be protected by her house's spell, however much longer it lasted. She had to be in the root cellar to renew it.

He squatted at the hole, squinting into the darkness, before muttering about Indiana Jones and snakes. Duck-walking the tunnel wasn't an option for a guy

Harry's size, but at least he wouldn't have to squirm on his belly.

Probably.

"It's okay, Harry. There shouldn't be many critters." If you were going to place an enchantment on your house, you might as well include pest control.

"It's not the critters that worry me. Something stinks." His denims scraped the floor as he crawled. When his boots disappeared, she purified the evidence of their passing with a tweak of magic through the cedar before pulling the door shut. Darkness blanketed them like a physical sensation.

So it hadn't been as dark as a cave in the forest earlier this morning. Hoo boy. If that middle section had gotten worse, they were in for it.

The tunnel dipped down and back up, ascending the hill to her cellar. When she exited from the house, she lay on an oversized skateboard and whizzed along like a bobsled. The dip slowed her before she reached the door.

Near the dip, the rustling of Harry's jeans against the concrete halted. "What the hell?"

Her head bumped into his bottom. "What is it?"

"Some kind of disgusting slime."

Uh-oh, it was the sludge, and sooner than expected.

"Gosh, there must be a leak," she said. "It's mud. Don't worry about it."

He squished through and June gritted her teeth, following as quickly as possible. She sank a couple inches into icy muck, soaking her pajama legs. The stench was part earth and part decay.

Emphasis on the decay.

The sludge lasted a couple yards before the tunnel rose. Against the left wall was a drainage channel where the goo had trickled down from a breach in the concrete. Her field line dispersed gray water into the environment, nothing hazardous, but food particles and detergents resulted in a pretty intense slime on this end.

She decided not to tell Harry it was about to get worse.

"How long has this been here?" His voice echoed through the tunnel. Their wet pants slapped the concrete like flippers. Her hands encountered a few bug carcasses that crunched like potato chips. *Ugh.*

"Since before you came to town." Lionel had been their master builder, such as he was. He'd agreed to dig the tunnel near her field line, after all. Since he'd been lost to them, upkeep of the secret passages had been a hassle. Pete and Annette's son—Lionel's apprentice—was in California, but they had doubts the kid would return to Millington. California's varied covens were quite the lure for a youngling beginning his first pass-through.

"Do you use the tunnels often?"

"Sometimes." In the history of Millington, no tunnel had been used for anything besides hijinks and Halloween. That wasn't the case with other covens, especially in the past. "Aren't you glad I have one?"

Something skittered and Harry cursed. "Not particularly. That was a stinging centipede. It's dead now."

June guesstimated they'd crawled fifty feet. Her bottoms clung to her like glue. In the summer, the tunnel radiated a chill that helped cool the cellar, but right now it was just cold.

Too bad it wasn't freezing. They could have skated over the sludge.

"Harry," she warned, "you may encounter an area with a little dirt up ahead."

"Does that mean we're there?"

"Halfway."

After another minute, he stopped again. "June?"

"Yes?" She crouched on her haunches, rubbing her mucky fingers on some dry leaves. She hated being unclean almost as much as she hated improvising spells.

"This is more than a little dirt."

It had been more than a little dirt in the fall too, but it had been navigable. The concrete ceiling had cracked. Goo and stuff had trickled through, and reinforcing the passageways was hard. She needed to hire a coven builder to fix it, but she wasn't made of money. "Is there still a roof?"

"We crawled up here with the chance we'd be roofless?"

She swatted his behind. "Just check, you big baby."

Harry scuffled and pried, rocks clattering in the darkness. "It doesn't block the whole passageway. There's space on top. I think I can move this big rock."

He grunted, something thunked, and a shaft of light entered the tunnel from above.

"There's a hole in the ceiling," June observed. Her tunnel had not fared well this winter. In the fall, it had been a crack. If light could filter down here, there must be one heck of a sinkhole in her grape terraces.

"The tunnel opens up on the other side of the mound of dirt." His voice floated back to her. "I'll go first and then you… Oh, good Christ!"

A moist splatter preceded his backward scuttle. He crashed into her, and she flattened herself against the wall.

"I've been slimed," he said with a groan. "This is really fucking gross."

"Language."

"Can't help it. Fucking gross is the most accurate description."

A vile reek filled the air with choking swiftness. Harry's arms and stomach appeared to be coated with a dark sludge that oozed in rivulets to the tunnel's floor.

June squinted, looking for alternatives, but it didn't help. The same vague hole in the ceiling, the same anonymous mound in the path, the same muddy were-wolf. "How bad is it?"

"Bad enough," he said through gritted teeth. "We can get past it if you don't mind visiting the fourth level of hell."

"And here we are without a handbasket." She wrinkled her nose. If she had to, she could leave him hidden in the tunnel, walk to the house and have Pete convince the cops to leave. Was there any way she could do that without confirming she was neck deep in Harry's business?

Probably not. The coven suspected her and she was a terrible liar. Lying was too much like adlibbing.

Harry elaborated. "Once you get past the top of the hump, it's coated with this cold, revolting sh—stuff. God, this odor is going to kill me."

"I can do something about the smell." June dragged her purse into her lap and searched through it until she found the last wet wipe. First she de-slimed her hands, and then she unscrewed her menthol rub, which she smeared under her nose. The medicinal odor cut through the reek.

She held a bedaubed finger to his face. "Want some?"

"Seriously?" He stifled a cough, accidentally smearing sludge on his lip. "Oh, fuck me, it's on my mouth." He gagged and spat.

Poor, foul-mouthed Harry. As Sandie, she'd threatened to wash his mouth out with soap more than once. Maybe this would teach him a lesson. "Parts of my shirt are clean. Try the shoulder."

He scooted around and scrubbed his mouth on her pajamas. In the near dark, she poked her finger toward his face, missing his nose and hitting his cheek. But once she coated his upper lip with menthol, he breathed a sigh of relief. "That helps."

"I vote we go through the puddle." She daubed more

menthol on her lips and, for good measure, her cheeks and chin. It would function as a moisture barrier if goo dripped in her face.

"You aren't going to like it," he warned. "We're going to have to wiggle through it."

"It'll wash off."

"Okay, but no fair getting mad at me when it makes you want to puke."

"It has to be done." Once they got past this area, the tunnel rose steeply. When they reached the top, she'd cast the protection spell and add an element of scram. Then everyone would leave, freeing her shower for immediate use.

"No time like the present," she continued. "I'll go first so I can open the door at the top. And we'll need to start being quiet."

"You're sure there won't be anybody in your root cellar?"

Relatively. Shifters could find it, but the other cops were human. Pete would check it for clues when he was alone.

"If there is someone there," she suggested, "we'll say we were hiding from the bad guys. I'll be the granddaughter house-sitting while Sandie's at…Virginia Beach on a vacation."

"Hiding in a secret tunnel none of them knew about before today."

"This is Millington. Do you really think anyone will find it strange that I'm eccentric?" June approached the mound and peered over, her head scraping the crumbling ceiling. Beyond the circle of weak light was sludge and darkness. *Hoo-boy.*

"Go fast," Harry advised. "Maybe less will soak into your pores."

She took a deep breath. There was enough space on top of the dirt mound to belly over it. Water and goo had started to dribble from above at a faster pace. The weight of the dirt above the damaged concrete might cause another cave-in.

"Here goes nothing." She held her purse as high as she could and dove like a penguin into slick, disgusting slime.

Sludge spattered her face and enveloped her body. June floundered on one arm in the muck, supporting her handbag. The bag was waterproof, heatproof, cold-proof and probably gooproof, but it was extremely expensive, as were many components inside it.

Her teeth chattered. She clamped her lips shut. The menthol quickly failed her as the frigid sludge stole her warmth and breath. Boy howdy, this was the most repulsive situation she'd ever been in, and she'd gone to great lengths to harvest certain herbs and fungi. June pushed forward, the sludge filling half the tunnel. Was it packed with worms, bugs and creepy crawlies?

And bacteria. *Ack, ack, ack!*

It was hard to gain purchase on the slippery concrete. She pressed against a wall, wedging her fingers in a groove to pull herself forward. She inched upward until the sludge level sank to her elbows.

"Okay," she called to Harry, her voice weak as she

tried not to throw up. There were worse things than the mud created by her nice, soapy, sort of harmless gray water. Like adding vomit to the mix.

Harry splashed through it, cursing. He quickly caught up, bumping her rear.

"Think of this as a spa treatment," he said, his teeth clenched. "Our skin is going to glow when we get out of here."

"Don't make me laugh." The essence of the sludge entered her mouth and sinuses no matter how she tried to fight it. Suddenly June couldn't resist any longer and retched.

"I was afraid of that. You okay?"

"Suuuuuuuuure," she moaned. She forced herself forward, inch at a time. They lost what little light they'd had, but soon the sludge was behind them.

Not that it felt like it. Muck had invaded every part of her. Her shirt, her hair, her ears. She had no idea how her stupid clogs had remained on her feet, but they were full, as well. Her toes squelched. She kept crawling up the slanted tunnel until they reached the door.

"Do you hear anybody?" she whispered to Harry. The only sound June could detect was the droplets of sludge falling off them. No light bled around the door's edges.

"No," he said. "Not sure about the house, though."

She fumbled the latch. The door creaked, another sign of her neglect. They clambered into the lightless safe room, shivering. Harry latched the door while she inched around the wall to the switch.

When she flicked it, a welcome sight greeted her—her utility sink in the front corner, complete with towels, antibacterial wipes, hand sanitizer and dish detergent. Her stash of emergency water underneath was down to two gallons after the power outage this winter. She couldn't crank the faucets because it would echo through the pipes, but she could scrub her hands clean enough to renew the protections on the house.

"What is this room?" Harry whispered.

"My safe room. The cellar is through there." She indicated a steel door between an industrial cabinet and a deep freeze. The skateboards for quick escape lay atop a cabinet. The low hum of the freezer added a mundane element to the scene. "Can you hear anyone?"

Harry paused by the door. She held her breath.

"A couple men upstairs. Somebody's running a vacuum cleaner. This room seems fairly soundproof," he answered.

"They can't hear us if they aren't shifters. I bet one is Pete. He wouldn't let them search the house without him."

Harry glanced toward the ceiling. "Can Pete hear us?"

"Our senses aren't as sharp as yours." June kicked off her clogs, which spattered muck all over the concrete floor, and plonked her purse on the sink counter. She grabbed enough wipes to clean the muck off the leather exterior. Otherwise when she opened it, the contents could become contaminated. "What time do you think it is?"

Harry reached into his back pocket gingerly and dragged out his cell phone. "Wow, it's still working. 7:00 a.m."

Perfect, she had thirty minutes to spare before standard renewal time. The root cellar stood at the central point of the spell's boundaries. Her body acclimated to the temperature of the room as the sludge dried on her skin.

And then she began to itch.

Harry gestured with his phone. "Want me to preserve the memory? We look amazing."

She rubbed her nose and instantly regretted it. "We smell even better."

Blackish green sludge coated Harry's jeans and torso. Two featureless blobs masquerading as his boots tracked goo on the floor. Except for one smear near his mouth, he'd kept his face and hair relatively clean. With a smirk, he held his phone at arm's length and snapped an image of himself.

June couldn't imagine how much worse she looked. She could feel muck spattered over her face, pasting her hair to her neck. Her favorite pajamas were ruined. But they'd made it into the house, increasing their chances of surviving this fiasco tenfold.

Harry aimed his phone at her and clicked.

"You big goomer. Delete that," she ordered.

"Blackmail." He set the phone on the counter and rubbed his arms. "What now?"

After spot-cleaning her purse, June turned her attention to herself and her crawling skin. "We get out of these disgusting clothes."

Harry quirked an eyebrow. "I took pictures too soon."

"I'm going to barf again if I can't get this off me." No time for modesty. Or photographs. "If you touch that phone, I will hex you."

"Can you do that?"

"Totally." She peeled the flannel pants off her legs with a gross, sucking noise. Sludge had worked inside the pants at the waist and up to her knees, but her thighs were startlingly white. Then she tried unbuttoning her top. Her fingers were too chilled.

"Let me." Harry's toasty body closed in, and he released the buttons. Shifters did run hot. Their temperature hovered two degrees higher than a human's, but witches, like young shifters, had more human-like vitals.

"Thanks." She shrugged her filthy shirt onto the floor and studied her torso. Not much of her had escaped the muck. Goddess, this was disgusting.

To his credit, Harry didn't get fresh though she had on nothing but panties. The muck probably had as much to do with it as anything.

June turned back to the sink and uncapped a gallon of water, her back to him. She shivered and then had a good scratch. "There are spare clothes in the cellar. Would you get me something warm?"

"Just a sec." Harry removed his boots and jeans. The denim had protected his legs more than her pajamas had protected hers. His boxers were clean. He twisted the knob on the door and peered into the root cellar. "I can't believe I never noticed this door."

"It's not as soundproof out there," she whispered. "Don't let the door latch behind you, and don't turn on the light."

"Gotcha."

While he rummaged in the root cellar, June sloshed muck off her arms and hands. The water was room temperature. Gradually she began to thaw. She scrubbed her hands with an old towel, wishing she had hot water, lots of soap, five gallons of antibacterial gel, a nail file, a pumice stone and an hour to spare. She couldn't allow any trace of sludge to pollute her spell. That would foul things up mightily.

Harry reappeared with a bundle of clothes.

"You got more water?" He reached for one of her towels.

"You can have my last gallon. The room drains in the corner." It would trickle back into the field line they'd just crawled through.

"On second thought, I could just pop into wolf form. Dirt won't stick."

"Better not. I don't know if the spell is strong enough for that with Pete in the house."

As quickly as possible, they dirtied her rag towels and emptied the water. The more sludge she wiped, the more she realized she was practically naked in the same room as Harry. June kept her back to him and focused on the grungy rags. Her ministrations worsened the briar scratches on her hands, but the slow ooze of blood would cleanse them. She used most of her water on her hands and face. The rest of her would have to wait.

At last she was satisfied her hands wouldn't sully the spell. After slipping into her clothes, she turned to Harry, who looked particularly fetching in yellow sweatpants. For her, he'd unearthed red shorts and a wool sweater that had always had an odd lanolin smell. She welcomed the warmth, if not the odor.

As she shoved her crusty hair out of her face, June said, "Can you guard the trapdoor while I cast the protection spell?"

"Sure." Harry held the door for her, his voice muted. "Are you going to dance around and light fires and stuff?"

"Hardly." Magic began as a neutral energy within the self. It gained purpose depending on how it was used. Or, more specifically, what organic ingredients it funneled through. The occasional mineral like talc functioned as an inert base. During a spell, a substance's natural properties were multiplied and transformed by the magic.

Protection spells involved forcing magic through preselected components and into boundary markers. Her markers were boxes of soapstone filled with herbs, scattered around her property in a precise circumference, with an internal set in the safe room walls. When cast properly, the magic shot into the components and out the other side infused with intent. The spell happened. A werewolf was calmed; a cut healed; her home space sheltered.

Magic, in fact, was about as showy as making pot-pourri.

When the door to the safe room closed, June allowed herself a deep, restorative breath. The low light in the cellar shouldn't give them away to anyone above. She and Harry were going to get through this without her losing her magic, without him becoming a packer. Hopefully without the coven insisting he needed a memory adjustment.

Because, did she want him to forget? Perhaps it was time to retire Sandie and begin her second pass-through as Sandie's granddaughter, June. Like hope, the familiar scents of old clothes, pickles, herbs and dusty potatoes overpowered the odor of the sludge.

Could this possibly work between her and Harry? Could they be together after this?

"Harry," she began, but he shushed her.

He pointed at the trapdoor, the ladder to the upstairs folded against the ceiling.

A few thunks sounded above them. People in her stillroom? She'd left it in a mess.

Well, criminy. She hoped the police investigation didn't cost her too much money replacing components. Or hiring a lawyer.

June blocked the vision of the police dumping her costly Spanish saffron, trying to figure out if it was an illegal substance. She settled into the room's center and dug through her purse until she located her travel mortar and pestle. Cayenne from yesterday powdered the surface. Careful not to touch the specks, she cleaned the tools with a wet wipe. No telling how cayenne and poppy would alter her protection spell.

Satisfied it was sterile, she wiped her hands. To the mortar she added premeasured packets of chicory, salvia, bay, thistle and caraway, then sprinkled in black tea leaves so the police would experience a sudden desire to be elsewhere. All this she pulverized before meditating on her power reserves. Pieces of hair tickled her neck and face, courtesy of the sludge. Her nose itched. Twitched. The briar pricks on her hands stung.

Through it all, Harry watched her, his whiskey-brown eyes trained on her every move.

This wasn't working. Thoughts of what she and Harry might do once they were alone—and clean—kept intruding. She could shelve the image of the cops costing her hundreds of dollars in saffron, but not the one of Harry kneeling between her legs.

"Stop watching me," she whispered. "I can't concentrate."

He raised a finger to his lips.

She shut her eyes and imagined Harry. Naked. Looming over her and...

A much louder *thunk* rattled the trapdoor.

A muffled voice said, "Does Miss Sandie have a cellar? I think it's hollow under here."

The stomps of the policeman thundered through the cellar. "Definitely hollow. Where do you reckon the door is?"

Her heart racing, June poured the spell components into her hand. Powder escaped her fingers; she caught it in her other hand. Leaning so close to her doubled fists that her sludge-stiffened hair tumbled over them, she tightened her inner self…

And released.

It was like taking a deep breath to blow out a candle on the other side of the room. Magic rushed out of her. She reeled. Wow, either she was more drained than she'd realized or adding the black tea was going to make the policemen really quick-step out of here.

Footsteps trotted away from the trapdoor and faded, exiting the house. Another set followed. Another.

June straightened, dizzy, and shook her head to clear it. Dried sludge speckled her hands, falling from her hair like the world's most disgusting dandruff. Her reserves seemed to be empty again—three depletions in less than twenty-four hours.

"They're gone." Harry watched her with intense speculation. "You did that?"

"Yeah." The first time she said it, it came out raspy. She cleared her throat. "Yes, I did."

"Cool." He scratched his arms. "Can I shift?"

"Now? You'll be stuck in the cellar." She'd never seen Harry up close as a wolf, only flashes in passing. He wasn't gigantic—more fleet and rangy, with long legs, lots of creamy white on his underside.

"I can shift back and forth." He indicated his side, where sludge fouled the reddened wound. "This hurts, and I've got a wicked headache."

The injury marred his muscular torso. She'd seen more of Harry's body in the past several hours than she had in eight years as Sandie. A definite perk. "Wait until we're sure they aren't coming back."

They lingered five minutes, ten. Harry held his head cocked to the side, as if it helped him hear better. Her knees and behind began to ache on the hard concrete. It seemed the spell had worked.

"Anyone up there?" she asked.

"We're clear."

She rose, depositing the inert components in the wastebasket before dusting her hands. "Then I guess we can…"

Before she finished her sentence, Harry had lowered the ladder and disappeared upstairs in a flash of buttercup fleece.

CHAPTER TWELVE

HARRY SHIFTED AS soon as he got upstairs. The pain relief was instantaneous. Not only did it negate his wounds but his wolf form improved his energy and mood, like yoga or meditation. Cleansed and whole, he rolled blissfully on June's rug in the den before prowling through the house.

With his wolf side engaged, he could trace the paths of humans and shifters here. He detected traces of Gavin and Maurice, the policemen. Pete's marker was strongest in the stillroom and near the trapdoor, as if he'd been guarding June's secrets. Good man.

Gavin had intruded into her bathroom, stillroom, kitchen. He'd been in her bedroom. Her underwear drawer was open.

Harry growled. Bad man.

His claws clicked on the kitchen tile as he stared out a window. The shifters had exited through this door. The police had too, at some point. Would the protection spell allow him to leave the house to inspect the property?

"Harry?" June's voice drifted through the house. "Where are you?"

He padded down the hall until he found her, his snout wrinkling at the sludge still clinging to her. She was inspecting the garbage bags taped over her broken window, her purse slung over one shoulder. As far as he could see, nearly all the glass had been swept up. Her couch had a few glistening slivers and a tear on the headrest. A stone garden gnome with an evil expression lay on the coffee table, possibly the item that had broken the glass.

He gruffed out a small bark to let June know he was there.

She turned. When her gaze dropped to him, her face lit up. "There you are."

He bumped his nose against her thigh, where her skin was cleaner. In wolf form, he retained memories and thoughts, as well as personality, though he was less able to resist primitive urges. Or communicate with two-legs. Or twist doorknobs.

Cautiously at first, June stroked his head and ears. His eyes closed halfway as he enjoyed her caress.

"Did you smell anything weird?" she asked, scratching his ruff.

Her stillroom and her house were filled with a myriad of scents. Even so, the weirdest thing he could smell was her. What was that crap in the escape tunnel, radioactive waste?

Harry bumped her toward the door of the living room with his head. He might be able to cleanse himself when he transformed, but nothing beat a good, hot shower—except for a good, hot shower with a woman in it.

When she didn't budge, he brushed against her, wagging his tail. He hoped he wasn't out of line assuming June would share suds with him. They were inside the house, safe and sound, and she hadn't exactly been giving him the cold shoulder.

"What is it, boy?" she asked. "Did little Timmy fall down a well?"

Harry bonked her with his head again. Shifters were the size of regular wolves, though some were larger. He outweighed June by twenty pounds.

She fondled his ears. "As much as I appreciate you letting me see your better half, this would be a lot easier if you'd shift back."

It might drain his abilities, but she had a point. He trotted into the hallway for a little privacy, rested on his haunches and allowed the tingle to fill his body.

Natural process—or magic?

Just like cowardice, it didn't matter as long as it worked.

The tingling continued longer than usual as his lowered energy levels responded sluggishly. When he came out the other side, he was disturbed to realize he was nude.

Not because June was admiring him as if someone had given her a present. That part was good. He hadn't lost his clothing between forms in years.

"Weren't you dressed when you went upstairs?"

"Yeah." Before he'd learned to relocate his possessions, he'd undressed first or squirmed out of his clothing post-shift. *Good Lord.* What had happened to the sweats?

"Does this mean I'm never getting my fat pants back?" June quipped, her eyes trained on his face. "Good thing I already lost my winter weight."

"I don't know." He assessed his physical state. Were her trousers embedded somewhere in his DNA? "That was unexpected."

"You're tired." She ducked into her bedroom and returned without her bag. "It's okay."

He'd worry about it later. Harry grabbed her hand and pulled her toward the bathroom. "I'm not that tired. Let's take a shower."

June followed him until they neared the bathroom door, where she balked. She inspected the rest of his body, lingering where he'd been wounded. He might have disappeared her fat pants, but at least he'd been able to heal himself.

"You're already clean," she said.

"You're not."

She chuckled. "This is true."

"We're housebound until you can cloak us or the Caddy, right? The pack can't sense us, and anyone looking for us will think the house is empty."

"The coven won't be fooled as easily as the shifters. They'll know about the 9-1-1 call."

"Pete searched the house." Harry snagged two towels out of the linen closet in the hallway. "He won't come back that quickly. We have time for a shower."

She crossed her arms, and her gaze cut to the half-open bathroom door, clearly tempted. "How can you be sure?"

She must be longing to bathe, as finicky about hygiene as she was. Why wasn't she already scouring herself? He could help her scrub those hard-to-reach spots. "Because the police went to search the tea room. Won't he stay with them?"

"It's not open yet," she said. "Well, no matter. He will be with them if they're going there."

"If anybody else shows up, we have the option of leaving the way we came in." The door to June's safe room was completely concealed by the wooden panels on the walls. He'd constructed the shelves down there and hadn't even noticed.

"Ugh."

"Don't you want to wash the mud off?" he coaxed, careful not to exert his alpha now that he knew it affected her. His native charm and good looks would have to suffice. "I bet it's flaking off on your carpet."

"That's horrible." She eyed the floor around her feet. "But—"

"We're here. We're alone. We might as well get clean."

And do a few other things. Even in a manky sweater and baggy shorts, surrounded by a miasma of muck, June turned him on. When his cock hardened, there was no hiding how he felt about the idea of getting naked with her.

Harry lowered the towels over his hard-on anyway. It seemed like the polite thing to do. Her cheeks pinkened, proving she wasn't as unaffected as she was pretending to be.

"We can't get too distracted." She blushed more. They both knew what she meant by *distracted*.

"You're wasting time arguing." He couldn't tell if her reluctance stemmed from shyness, the tense situation or fear she might wolf out.

She followed him into the yellow-and-white bathroom. Her tub and fixtures were new, but water usage caused a terrible banging in the pipes.

"It will conserve water if we shower together," he said. June didn't have the biggest hot water heater on the block.

"You go ahead, I—"

He grabbed her before she could exit. The towels dropped to the floor. A cold shower was not on their agenda. Not physically, not figuratively. But if she insisted... "Is something wrong? Are you not interested?"

"I'm interested." She focused on his chin. "We just need to stay alert."

"There's nothing like a shower first thing in the morning to wake you up." Harry shut the door behind her. "How hot do you like it?"

Her eyelashes fluttered down before she averted her face. "How hot?"

"The water." He had a good idea how hot she liked the sex. God, he couldn't wait to slide between those creamy thighs. His cock ached and she hadn't so much as touched him. "Why don't you adjust the temperature to your liking?"

June sidled past him, careful not to brush his body. She leaned over to twist the faucets, her shorts riding up her thighs. The muck coating her pale legs like grunge knee socks should have been a turnoff, but Harry's hard-on seemed here to stay.

For the time being. He planned to rectify the situation after he sanitized his lady in a hot shower.

Water gushed. The pipes clonked. June cranked the shower and drew the curtain. Without asking permission, he slid her sweater over her head. The air puckered the tips of her breasts before she crossed her arms. But she stepped obediently out of her shorts and panties when he drew them down her hips, allowing him to appreciate her rounded curves along the way.

Once they were under the steaming shower, she loosened up. She was right about one thing—he was clean already, so he could concentrate on washing her. He sudsed her hair and scrubbed her back with one of those fluffy mesh things chicks always had in their bathrooms. He kneeled in front of her and worked on her legs, ankles and toes. When he rose, their wet bodies slid together. The glide of his cock across her stomach was excruciating.

When she held out her hand, he gave her the soap. To his disappointment she used it on her face instead of him. He took it back and started washing her front, rubbing away traces of the muck, telling her how dirty she was. It had gotten on her neck, so he washed her neck. Her stomach, so he washed her stomach.

It hadn't gotten on her breasts, but he washed them anyway, rubbing around and around until she was leaning against the wall, her hands clutching his shoulders. Water sprinkled her face like diamonds. When she closed her eyes and sighed, he pinched both nipples at the same time. Her grip on his shoulders tightened, and Harry decided the foreplay was over.

He dipped his head and captured her lips. Their tongues touched. Curled. He pressed her against the wall and kissed her deeply, still plucking her breasts.

With soapy hands she caressed his shoulders, down his arms, around his hips. He loved how much smaller she was, how soft, how she yielded to him. Her hair clung to her head and neck in dark ringlets. When she kissed, she tasted him as much as he did her, nibbling and licking. Her teeth against his throat, her tongue on his neck, her hands pulling his body into hers.

Rather unexpectedly, June rubbed the bar of soap down his ass. It slid between his cheeks, grazing him from behind. His cock surged against her. She soaped up and down, fondling and exploring, until he could feel every inch of flesh as if it were raw.

His balls tightened as he thrust against the hot gloss of her skin. When her fingers closed on his cock and pumped, he nearly climaxed before he had a chance to appreciate the sensation.

He latched on to her wrist. "Too much."

"Really?" She squinted through the spray. Her free hand swiped him again before squeezing the head.

He grabbed her other wrist. A few more touches like that and he'd come before they could properly consummate their relationship. He wasn't a one-blow Joe, but it would take time to regroup. Instant erections were the only thing he missed about being seventeen.

She licked her lips, angling her face out of the spray. He slowly stretched her wrists above her head, watching her for her reaction. Some women liked to be overpowered. Some got pissed off. Yesterday she'd had qualms about sex with him she shouldn't have now, so her responses would be more genuine.

Instead of moaning or struggling, she twisted her lower body against his cock. It didn't have the same effect as her hot little hand, but it would eventually.

"So that's how you want to play?" He bent his knees and slid between her thighs, prodding her folds. If she was going to tease, he was going to return the favor. She clamped around him tightly.

When he thrust, the friction felt pretty close to the real thing.

The water gushed over them as Harry moved. His cock bumped her clit. The moisture between her legs became silkier, and he caught the scent of arousal. When she tilted her hips, the head of his cock nearly entered her body. Her feminine heat seared him. He froze there, neither pushing nor withdrawing. He ached so much every miniscule shift of her softness against him was torturous delight.

He could take her here. Now. He was one thrust away from paradise. His grip tightened on her wrists.

June licked water from her lips. "How close are you?"

He inched forward, pressuring her with his cock. "Why do you ask?"

"I want you inside me but…"

He didn't wait for the rest of the sentence. He pushed into her molten smoothness. They both groaned. At this angle, the penetration wasn't deep, but it was so, so tight. He bent his knees a little more and she slid onto him like a glove.

June's eyes flew open. Their gazes locked as they connected physically, emotionally. Her lips moved, forming a word.

Alas, it wasn't *yes.*

"Condom."

She was right. But God, this was hot. Water poured down their bodies. Steam surrounded them. She was pinned to the wall, panting. Soaked. Her sheath tightened. He sank into her another half an inch.

"Do you have any?" He didn't mind them, but they weren't in reach, and her body was.

He spread her arms farther apart, sliding along the wet wall, and she swallowed. "They're put away. You're the skirt chaser. Don't you have something?"

"I didn't think I'd need any for movie night," he gritted out. He slipped almost out of her body.

But not quite. June whimpered and her inner walls squeezed him. Her hard nipples rubbed his chest.

If he dropped her wrists he was going to lift her up and shove her all the way onto his cock. But restraining her was its own kind of turn-on. The knowledge she was alpha only made him want to take her more.

"Kiss me," she said. "Don't move your hips."

Harry complied. The kissing grew quickly out of hand, their tongues doing what their bodies couldn't risk. Water cooled as the heater drained. He concentrated on the way her warmth clasped the tip of his cock like a hot mouth, the way she moaned, the way her slender wrists felt in his fists.

June tugged her arms. His cock swelled as she struggled to free herself. Harry growled. His urge to dominate broke through the surface.

To his surprise, hers did too. He could feel it all over.

She squirmed, and he held tight. Pushed her body against the wall. The result of her resistance wasn't her freedom. It was more kisses. Frantic kisses. Her breathing became ragged, as did his. Her hips jerked as she fought him and kissed him at the same time.

His peak approached, and he willed himself to withdraw, to be safe, but June took control. She twisted a leg around his hips, pushing him deep.

Ah, God.

"Harry, it feels so good," she whispered.

It was about to feel better. Harry dropped one of her wrists, reached between their bodies and pressed his fingers on her clit.

Rubbing. Rubbing. Holding still and rubbing. Her scent sharpened. Her breathing caught.

With a choked cry, June convulsed. Her muscles clenched him. Loosened. Tightened. She sighed and gasped. Called his name. Her reaction almost undid him.

Baseball. Bass fishing. Blue balls.

Her eyelids opened. "More."

"No." He held himself even stiffer than his cock. "I'm not going to be that guy." His knees started to tremble. She was shorter than he was, and their pelvises did not line up.

She blew out a breath. "What guy?"

Their shower went from lukewarm to cold. "The one who talks you out of a condom when you ask him to use one."

"We don't have one handy." She smoothed her palm across his chest, her fingertip rounding his nipple. "I'm not fertile this week, and STDs aren't an issue. Can't you just—"

"No." Harry pulled out. His cock popped free, bobbing against her stomach.

"I'm sorry." She rested her cheek against him, breathing deeply. "This can't be satisfying for you. Again."

"Oh, it will be. Let's go to bed." Lack of a condom didn't mean they had to cancel the festivities. It just meant they had to get creative. "The water's cold."

"You can handle it." June pushed him into the spray

and ran her hands down his chest. She followed the hair until her hands rested on either side of his cock.

"June?" If he weren't mistaken, her alpha had just come back out to play. He could sense her strong will pushing him along with her hands.

She smiled. "I'll take the edge off."

He plucked a tendril of wet hair out of her face. "What do you mean?"

"Guess." She grasped his heft in one palm, stroking. Her other hand cupped his testicles. Before Harry could answer, she dropped to her knees and took him into her mouth.

Shock flooded him, and he nearly bent over double. The chilly water splashed past him into her face. She spluttered, releasing his cock. Goose bumps broke out across her flesh.

"Sorry, sorry." He reached behind him and twisted the faucets off. June shoved him against the cold wall and raked her fingers down his thighs.

"Bad werewolf. Now I'll have to punish you." This time she lapped the head of his penis, her tongue twirling around the opening and sensitive underside. Harry clenched his fists—not in her hair—and willed himself not to unload until he got to enjoy this for at least ninety seconds. Maybe two minutes. His last affair had been months ago, with a schoolteacher from Wheeling now engaged to the auto-parts salesman he'd introduced her to.

June toyed with him, tasting every inch. She placed soft kisses along his length and flicked her tongue across the head. While he'd rather be face to face, pounding in and out of her body, getting head ranked high on his list of Fun Things To Do With Women.

With pursed lips, she enveloped his cock. She took the tip, part of the shaft. Her eyelids closed as she relaxed her throat. Her head moved back and forth, a moist suction that drove him to the verge. Waves of tension built as his climax neared.

She grabbed the base of his cock with one wet hand. Her teeth grazed the underside, and his hips jolted. Her breath feathered the wet skin.

When she patted his rump, he thought she would head for the bed. But she didn't. Instead she practically swallowed his cock and began to suck him at such a fierce tempo, Harry's orgasm came out of nowhere in a blinding flash of pleasure.

June sucked until he had to pull her away, too sensitive to handle the treatment. She released him and stood, her lips swollen and red. Her nipples were hard as pebbles. She was obviously aroused.

He ripped open the shower curtain and dragged her into her bedroom. The sheets were still rumpled. Gavin's scent hadn't marked her room so much it was a distraction. Harry threw her onto the bed and covered her with his body.

This was going to be good. Every inch of their naked flesh pressed together. He poised over her, trying to decide where to start. The water droplets on her skin? Her rosy lips? Her breasts?

Her knees rose to cradle his hips, bringing her in

contact with his half-hard cock. He watched her, not speaking, allowing the anticipation to build. Extending his senses, he detected a car on the highway, birds in the trees, the fridge humming in the kitchen.

Nothing between them. Nothing around them. Nothing to stop them from making love for the next twenty-four hours.

Okay, a few hours. June would need to sleep so she could cloak their getaway car.

Before Harry could make up his mind what part of her most needed his attention, the telephone rang, shrill and insistent beside the bed.

CHAPTER THIRTEEN

JUNE CLOSED HER eyes, but it did nothing to silence the telephone.

Closing her eyes didn't ease her arousal, either. Harry's weight pressed her into the mattress. His penis nestled between her legs. Her animal simmered inside her, but she no longer feared it would break free.

It had surged through her veins at her climax, but it only intensified her pleasure. She was wholly in control.

The phone rang again.

"Are you going to get that?" he asked. "It might be your coven."

"I'd rather not talk to them. They'll ask too many questions." She and Harry watched the phone as if it were going to jump off the hook and into June's hand. Neither could reach it without crawling across the bed.

He squinted. "It shows up as a local number on caller ID. Timothy Manns. Isn't he the chief of police?" The phone rang again. Her answering service would kick in after five rings.

"That's his home number, not work." She pushed

at Harry's shoulders. Why would the cops be at the Mannses' house instead of the station?

He rolled off her until he could reach the unit. "Want me to unplug it?"

"I know what I can tell him." When he handed it to her, June clicked the on button. "Hello?"

Static crackled across the line.

"Who's there?" she said, irritation bleeding into her tone. She had better things she could be doing, like having sex for the first time in two years. When your disguise was a senior citizen, your choices of partner were coven members and other senior citizens. Unfortunately, her tastes at this stage of her life ran to younger men, and no local witches interested her. One of the downsides of a witch's cyclic age discrepancies.

"Miss Sandie?" said a female voice she didn't recognize.

"Speaking." June altered her pitch to resemble an elderly human. Harry watched with his eyebrows raised.

"It's Donna Manns, your neighbor."

"Donna. Hi, honey," June said with a quaver. She'd seen Donna yesterday at the tea room. The Mannses lived on the same street she did, a mile down the road.

"Are you all right?" Donna sounded different on the phone, more measured. "I heard the sirens. I was worried."

"I'm fine."

"So what's going on?" Donna knew everything that happened to everyone. If Tim hadn't clued her in about the break-in, she'd be frantic to find out before lunchtime.

"Nothing important." Vague answers were safer, not that she could explain the truth to Donna anyway. In fact, she was surprised Donna had called. She and Donna had more of a baker-customer relationship than a gossip-sharing relationship.

"It didn't sound like nothing."

"I'm almost embarrassed to say," June protested. *Come on, Donna—take a hint. Don't badger the nice old lady.*

"No need to be embarrassed," the woman said. "You can trust me."

June couldn't, but to balk now would raise flags. Well, the tittle-tattle—and Sandie's alibi—could start here.

"I heard men outside the house this morning." Whatever she told Donna needed to mesh with the information the chief would share with his wife later. "I called 9-1-1 and hid down the road a piece. The police were gone before I got back."

"Do they know who did it? What they were looking for?"

"There's nothing missing. Tim got here in time. I need to bake him a cake."

"I don't know who'd break into your house, not with Bert Macabee out of the territory." Donna's statement perked at the end, as if Bert's absence pleased her.

Territory was an odd word for her to use. Perhaps it was a cop's wife thing.

"Your husband sure does a good job," June complimented her.

"If he has the right clues," Donna agreed. "Do you have any secret enemies?"

June tried to mimic her Sandie laugh. "My pie beat yours at the county fair last year. Maybe it was you, looking for the recipe."

Donna forced a laugh too. "Ha, ha, ha. Are you there alone?"

"No." Why did she want to know that?

"Is Harry over there?"

"Harry who?" June and Harry hadn't concealed their friendship from anybody, but it seemed an odd question for Donna to ask.

"Harry Smith. From the tea room."

"That Harry." June widened her eyes and shrugged at Harry, who rolled closer until their bodies touched. "He's not here."

"Then who is there? You shouldn't be alone after that scare."

"A repairman." Harry did repairs for her sometimes.

"Have you seen Harry since yesterday?"

"No," June lied. Harry began to draw circles around her breasts with his finger. "Is there a problem?"

"You were my last hope." Donna sighed, disappointment evident. "I need to track him down. A business thing, you know. It's that church bus again. If I can't find him, I'll have to hire a second-rate mechanic. Too bad it won't be Harry Smith. He was perfect."

She sounded more disappointed than a woman in need of a mechanic ought to be. The phone rasped as if a solid object had rubbed across the mouthpiece. Donna spoke to somebody on the other end, muffled. Then she returned. "Do you know if he was going out of town?"

"Let me think." What would she have told Donna two days ago, before Bianca decided to ruin Harry's life? "He travels to Wheeling a lot."

Harry leaned down and sucked her nipple into his mouth. June squeaked.

"What did you say?"

"I sneezed. Bless me." June knew her voice was an octave too high. She smacked Harry away but he only switched to the other side.

Warmth began to curl through her insides as he licked. And Donna kept talking.

"It's important I find him soon."

"I bet."

"There are other mechanics."

June couldn't respond, unable to form words as Harry's lips closed around her nipple.

"I know it's a long shot, but if you see him, could you give me a call on my cell?" She rattled off a number. "I'll be out the rest of the day."

"Of course."

"Don't you want to write it down?"

"I did. Bye now." June disconnected and clonked Harry in the head with the phone. "You devil!"

He leaned on his arm. "Did you know I went out with her when she was Donna Partin?"

June could name most of the women he'd dated in the past eight years, and she had no wish to discuss his past conquests when she was naked in bed with him. "Why?"

"Because I don't work on her church's bus."

"Are you sure?" June frowned at the caller ID. Donna had never called her at home before. Donna had seen Harry in the tea room yesterday, being pursued by Bianca, wife of the recently arrested Bert Macabee. Donna had asked several strange, pointed questions.

Donna used to date Harry.

"I'm sure," he answered. "I don't work on buses, period."

June clicked through the recent calls in the memory. Manns, unknown name and number, coven, coven, coven, unknown name and number, coven, coven, her mom in California, coven. No new voice mails since last night.

The thought of Harry and Donna, of Harry and any woman, made June want to bite somebody. Green-apple jealousy was an unexpected component to their changed relationship. Before, she'd had libido damp-eners and a general acceptance it could never be.

Now she had…Harry.

"Are you suggesting she wants something else from you?" she asked sharply.

"I don't know. I don't care." He reached over and unplugged the phone base. "No more phone calls."

No more women, she almost retorted but instead stared at his hairy chest. "What if there's an emergency? You don't have to unplug it."

He captured her hand and twined their fingers together. "We've had enough emergencies for the day."

"I agree." But not enough of…other things. His forearm brushed her nipples. "I can't wait until this is over and things get back to normal."

Harry drew their clasped hands down until he reached their hips. He began rubbing his knuckles, and hers, on her skin, brushing her stomach, the crinkly hair at the apex of her thighs. "There's no normal for us, June. If Bianca instates Gavin, I'll have to relocate. My guess is she has to pick someone as soon as tonight or her pack bond will dissolve."

"I know." She didn't know—didn't want to know. Her stomach knotted like their hands.

"Your whole coven may want to relocate." Harry gave a soft laugh. "Do you think they'd want a wolf for a mascot?"

"Harry." She cupped his face with her free hand. "I don't want to talk about tomorrow."

"Me neither," he said. "Right, then. Where are your condoms?"

Despite the fact they were naked, their hands clasped, their lips inches apart, she had trouble comprehending his abrupt change of topic. "What?"

He nipped her shoulder. "I'm not finished with you."

Her breathing quickened. "You don't have to finish

me." Although, if he really wanted to, the bed was a lot more comfortable than the kitchen table.

"How about I finish us both?" He took a nipple in his mouth, licking gently. He switched to the other side. Then back. His tongue sampled her skin as if testing wine, swilling it in his mouth, waiting for the full flavor to hit.

June rubbed her feet against the sheets. She wished he'd be a little rougher. The sweet lick of his tongue was delicious. Hypnotic. But she wanted more. She arched her back, encouraging him.

Harry blew across her moist nipples. He barely touched one with the tip of his tongue. She threaded her fingers through his hair and pulled. So he sucked harder, and harder, until she reached a nearly unbearable pleasure/pain threshold and wrenched his head away.

He released her with a sly smile, his penis hard against her thigh. "Where are they?"

"I'll get them." Her condoms were in the closet, packed away with other things she rarely used. Like her bikini. And her gym membership card. She kicked a plastic tub into place to use as a stepstool and yanked down a purple hatbox.

Sheets and pillowcases cascaded around her. She fumbled with the lid; the box slipped to the floor and spilled. Bathing suit, cards, sunglasses, gloves, Mardi Gras beads and condoms tumbled across the carpet.

"In a hurry?" Harry lounged on the bed and watched her.

"Hush." She spotted the condoms under her dust ruffle. "I hope these aren't too old." She tossed him the small, silver packages. "You read the date. I can't bear to look."

He shook out a packet and peered at it. "We've got two more months."

She hopped onto the bed and lay down. "Aren't you going to put it on?"

"It's not time yet." Harry traced a finger down to her mons. "I have plans for this body."

"I have plans too." Her fingers curled into the sheets like claws. And when he loomed over her and lifted her chin for his kiss, the fierceness inside her, her wolf, said *Not this time.*

With a strength she hadn't even known she possessed, June surged up, flipping Harry over. He tumbled onto his back with a look of shock on his handsome face.

It turned quickly to anticipation.

June's wolf sizzled through her, and she knew it for what it was. She climbed onto him. Pressed his shoulders to the bed. "You're awfully bossy."

"So are you." He reached between her legs, finding her heat. "And you're wet."

She considered the man spread on the bed beneath her. His hair dampened the sheet, and his brown eyes regarded her with curiosity and passion. What would he do if she wanted to take control, really take control, in the bedroom? Visions of bound arms and hot wax danced in her head. Her mouth on him. Her body over him.

Taunting him. Teasing him. Ruling him.

What would it feel like to be begged for release… instead of begging for it?

"What are you thinking?" he asked. "Are you thinking how I'm going to lick your—"

She shushed him. "No talking. Put your fingers inside me," she ordered. "Two of them."

Harry wasn't pack, but he was alpha. She'd always known that—and always known it wasn't his defining characteristic. She felt him balk before a slow, easy smile crossed his face. "Yes, ma'am."

He slipped his fingers deep into her until their base pressed her privates. She tightened herself, testing her power. When he adjusted his hand, it jolted her with gratifying pleasure.

"That the right spot?" he asked.

"I said no talking. Take them almost all the way out."

He did, drawing her cream across her until she was slick. One fingertip remained inside. She clutched his shoulders, their gazes locked.

"Now put them…"

He thrust his fingers into her, bumping against her swollen nub. She spread her legs wider, sinking, until she could feel the brush of his penis between the cheeks of her bottom. Without permission he grasped her hip with his other hand.

June bent and kissed his neck and chest, avoiding

his mouth. She licked his nipple, circling her tongue around the point. He tasted slightly of soap, slightly of male. Rising, she tried to ignore the fact he'd started wiggling his fingers.

But she couldn't. It made her hot.

"I want…" She paused, thinking. "Hold your hand still."

"Are you sure?"

"Don't question me," she ordered. But then their gazes met again and she could tell he was trying not to smile, which made *her* almost smile.

So she bent her head and concentrated on his body. She raised her hips, and as she'd asked—commanded—his hand remained stationary. His fingers slipped out, and she sank onto them, squeezing tight. Small sounds and a salty-sweet smell accompanied her movements. She rode his hand, and his penis bobbed against her.

This was good. Dominant. He would do as she wished. Releasing his shoulders, she straightened, and his gaze lit on her breasts.

She cupped them, watching him. Rubbed her own nipples. It wasn't as seductive as his touch, but she liked his reaction. His penis twitched against her backside.

Harry licked his lips. She rubbed his muscular chest. "Now I want…" But she couldn't decide.

He smirked and began to move his hand, her juices oiling her flesh. His palm worked her, his fingers inside. Delicious sensations began to tweak her center. She reached behind her and captured his penis.

Slowly she rose, and his penis slid until the head was nestled near her entrance. She pressed it against her. He continued to massage her and something inside her pulsed. Needed.

"Take your hand out of me and touch yourself."

He did, and his dripping fingers stroked himself all the way to the end. He *hmm'd* deep in his chest. She supposed that didn't count as talking. He maneuvered the tip through her folds and began to ply her with it even though she hadn't told him to. His other hand parted her rear, squeezing and releasing. Jiggling the flesh. He worked his fingers into…

She needed. Needed more.

The silver condom packet lay by his head. She ripped it open and smoothed it over him, her hands trembling. She poised above him, her insides aching to be joined.

She meant to be slow about it and savor every second, but as soon as the tip slid inside her, he yanked her down. Her inner flesh stretched and burned.

"Harry," she chided, yet secretly thrilled. "I didn't tell you to."

He caressed her legs as she seated herself. "I slipped. Won't happen again."

She wriggled, adjusting. She'd liked being on top. Harry as the man beneath her only made it better. His organ was sizeable but not painful; his body hairy but not coarse. His long fingers stroked her skin.

Her hands on the mattress, she began to slide up and down, rolling her pelvis. He glided in and out. Up and down. His fingers dug into her, snaking around to her bottom. His eyelids half-closed as his gaze shifted from her face to their intimate joining.

She changed position slightly so she could touch herself. Harry's eyebrows arched. So much moisture drenched her folds that her fingers grew slippery. She plucked herself and watched his face.

His organ swelled. He smoothed his hands to her breasts, pinching the tips.

She allowed it for a moment before she grabbed his wrists. "I didn't tell you to." She let her newly discovered alpha side flare. "Put your hands behind your head."

This time when Harry balked she didn't think he was going to do it.

She pushed. He caved. He locked his fingers behind his head and smiled up at her, daring her to try anything else. Promising that this was as far as he'd let her go.

She wasn't sure if she'd swayed him or if he'd just decided to cooperate, but either way, triumph spiraled through her like a small climax.

She shoved herself down on him, rubbed her clit fast, and it *was* a small climax. She trembled, tight and eager, and couldn't hide a sigh. He inhaled deeply, his eyes narrowing.

"Having fun?"

"No talking." She placed the finger she'd used to

give herself the orgasm over his lips. "You're not in charge here."

He sucked her finger into his mouth. Without permission. Exactly as she'd hoped he would. Her insides clenched with desire, and she knew he felt it.

"You're forgetting something." His eyes gleamed. "My alpha's bigger than your alpha."

"This again?" June dragged herself off him and tugged her arm, but his grip was like a velvet band. Delicious excitement flickered through her. "Is that a threat?"

"It's a statement of fact. Like this one." Harry stretched lazily, even though she could sense the wolf in him poised to strike. "In the next twenty minutes, I'm going to make you scream."

She yanked at her wrist, her heartbeat accelerating. "I'm not a screamer."

Without warning, he flipped her onto her stomach and himself onto her. His shaft prodded her rear. "You will be."

CHAPTER FOURTEEN

THE SHIFTERS WHO broke down the back door were much more stealthy than the first ones. Harry didn't notice them until it was almost too late.

A shadow darkened the round window over the sink three seconds before the back door rattled in its frame. Harry grabbed June, who was eating scones at the kitchen table, and raced her bodily to the trapdoor.

In the other room he heard the door smash open and Gavin's voice barking orders.

"Down." Harry and June had propped open the floorboard earlier and stored their overnight bags on a shelf. June swung herself into the cellar, missed the second rung and fell the rest of the way. She cried out as she landed.

No time to worry about that. Why was Gavin here? Were the shifters with him Millington wolves or Roanokers who'd do whatever Gavin wanted?

Probably the latter. Roanoke's press gang had a lot of practice digging out wolves who didn't want to be found.

Harry's gaze locked with Gavin's right before he leaped into the cellar, flipping the door as he jumped.

A loud boom echoed through the basement, either from the trapdoor crashing or Gavin trying to catch it. Harry fumbled the latch in place. Wouldn't hold long, but seconds counted.

June limped into the safe room, seizing an orange box off the closest shelf. He grabbed the overnight bags and followed. The thick door had two deadbolts, which he slid home, as well.

"Can they get in?" No way would Gavin miss the safe room when he knew his prey was in the cellar. He'd tear down the shelves, the walls, everything to find what he sought.

Which had to be Harry. No shifter was crazy enough to display this much firepower over a woman. He'd bet anything Gavin was hoping to eliminate him to get his hands on Bianca's pack.

"We'll be okay," June said. "The concealment spell is reinforced in the safe room. A protection spell inside a protection spell. He'll think we got away."

She hobbled to the center of the room. The fetid odor of muck emanated from the dirty rags in the corner.

"Even if he finds the door?"

She kicked aside a dirty rag and kneeled, grimacing when she twisted her ankle. Her blue sleep shirt hiked up her thighs. "Maybe he'll assume we made it out of the house and split his forces."

It wouldn't help. Half of the intruders would be more than enough to take them. In the cellar, wood splintered as the shifters burst through the trapdoor.

"Down the chute?" Harry asked. Their talc spells were gone, so he would be easy to find. Maybe June too. She hadn't thought they needed them inside the house, and she'd wanted to save her power for something stronger. Once outside the house, they'd be sitting ducks.

If Gavin didn't catch them, Bianca would. Right now he'd pick Bianca. He concentrated on the voices in the cellar.

"I know that mongrel's in here somewhere. I can sense him," Gavin said, followed by crashes and rips.

"I don't understand." June rifled through her carton of herbs and roots. "The spell worked. I felt the magic leave me. How can he detect you in here?"

"No idea." Harry had been wrong to put his trust in hoodoo. He'd heard Gavin's threats, the violence in his words. He and June should have made a run for it, and now they were screwed.

June babbled as she dumped the hatbox on the concrete. "We should have been safe. We covered our tracks. Why are they back? This could draw attention to all of us. How stupid is that guy?"

"Very stupid. The packs won't like covering this up either." Maybe they'd finally see Gavin for the loose cannon he was. Harry inspected the door to the cellar. Metal—but the walls seemed less sturdy. The wolf inside him paced, longing to be free—so he could run, run, run. He was one fast motherfucker in his wolf form.

"Do you think Bianca sent him?"

"If Bianca thought I was here, she'd have come herself. She's got to realize Gavin's been chasing off candidates by now."

"You told that boy we were leaving town. Gavin has no reason to be here." Crashes sounded from the cellar. Ripping. Tearing. Harry wasn't sure how much June could hear, but there was mass destruction in the next room.

"It doesn't matter why. It just matters that we get away." He opened the door to the tunnel, his nose curling. The caved-in area meant the skateboard things were useless.

Gavin's voice rose above the chaos.

"Can you hear me, Smith? I don't know why we didn't recognize you last night, but we do now." Wood splintered, and dust puffed around the safe room door. "You've been broadcasting signals this morning even a loser like you could pick up. Been banging your girl-friend? Way to get distracted, moron."

He had been having sex—crazy, powerful, alpha sex—but according to June they should have been protected.

"That can't be right." She threw twigs and roots in every direction. "The spell worked. It worked! There's no way they should be able to read you then or now."

But they could read him. June's spell had been a dud.

"I know you haven't run yet, Smith. In fact, I think you're right—" one last giant crash and the door between the safe room and the cellar jiggled "—here. By

God, there's a door. Looks like the old bat from the tea room has some secrets."

"He has no idea." June's hands trembled as she chucked herbs into a white bowl. She pounded a gray rock on the floor, creating a powder, and added it. "I must have screwed up the spell. Sludge was all over me."

"But you have some secrets too, don't you, Smith?" Gavin shouted between thumps. "Or should I call you John Lapin?"

Harry's blood ran cold. June paused to stare up at him. "What's he talking about?"

"Not now," he growled, his teeth so sharp he nearly cut his lip. Gavin had Harry's true scent…and the memories he had never wanted to revisit.

"I can't wait to tell Mom and Pop." Gavin whaled on the wall between sentences. "Little John Lapin is notorious pack hater Harry Smith. Good trick, you useless bastard. I don't suppose your mother's still around? I'd love to fuck her again, once I finally kill her mongrel brat. She should never have tried to run, little Johnny. Now you're going to pay."

June watched him with wide, frightened eyes. "Harry?"

He had a sudden, blinding understanding of why wolves went feral.

"Nah, I bet she's dead," Gavin continued, as if the conversation were sociable. "She'd never have survived severance. Which means the only thing I don't know is how sweet, tasty June can still be a juvie. She smells good to me, Lapin. Real good."

Harry growled.

Outside the door, Gavin paused to laugh. "You don't like that, do ya? She must be a moron like you, too stupid to shift. Too stupid to run."

"Hurry up, Gav," another voice urged. The door rattled again. "Bianca's going to sense him too and send somebody over here."

"She can go screw herself. I'll be alpha soon." More voices, Gavin's rising above them. "Love and war, baby."

"This can't be happening. Dial the cops. Pete will get us help." June fumbled a glass vial on the concrete and it shattered, exploding red powder all over the floor. "Criminy."

Harry indicated his clothing—underwear and nothing else. "My phone is on your bedside table."

"Well, hell. What else is going to go wrong?"

It was the first time he'd ever heard her curse. She didn't even realize how wrong things had gone. "Do you really want me to answer that?"

"No." She began scraping up red powder, cutting her hands on the glass, and sprinkled the powder into the bowl.

Harry couldn't stand it any longer. Her magic had failed once already. Gavin knew who he was and had double the reason to kill him now, because Harry knew how he'd gotten that scar—and why. Gavin wouldn't take any chances Harry might enlighten the Roanoke pack about what had happened to Christine Lapin. "June, we can't stay here."

She plucked out a few pieces of glass, her hands unsteady. "It's a strong door. We have a few minutes."

"Not strong enough. We need to run."

She glanced at him, anguish twisting her pretty features. Blisters began to form on her fingers. "We don't. You do."

Harry glared at her. "We're both going to run."

"I'll survive what he wants to do to me. You won't. You'll die, Harry, and I won't allow it." Her voice cracked. "After I disguise you and your wolf, you're going alone."

"No. Disguise us both."

"I can't."

"Then we run."

She ignored him, pounding a pestle into the bowl, the *tink-tink* a counterpoint to the werewolves trying to get into the safe room. Blood streaked the handle of the pestle, the sides of the bowl. "If I never improvise a spell again, it will be too soon."

She inhaled a deep breath, throwing back her head so her yellow curls tumbled down her back. She dumped the powdery mess into one hand, closed her eyes, made a double fist, and…nothing.

Until a pressure began to build in the air, a pressure Harry now recognized as magic. It popped almost audibly and she fell forward, catching herself on the concrete with one blistered hand. The other clutched her powder.

"What did you do?" He dragged her to her feet. She swayed, eyelids fluttering in semi-unconsciousness.

"Some spells take a lot out of me," she whispered. Then she wrapped an arm around his neck and kissed him.

Harry kissed her for a second and pulled away. The coppery scent of her blood hit him at the same time. "I'm not leaving you."

"You are." She smeared powder across his neck. Glass cut his skin but it was nothing compared to the slow, mounting burn that followed.

He clapped his hand over the area. "Cast a spell on yourself too."

"Not enough power. Shift so I can mask the wolf."

"No."

She stared him straight in the eyes. "I love you, Harry." Then she slapped him full across the mouth. "Now do it."

Her alpha flared up as if she were as pack as Bianca. He stepped back, his shoulders instinctively drooping, before growling at her.

"No." His own alpha responded in kind. "I stay. You go."

"Good grief, Harry, why do you make things so hard? I have a plan." She snatched a purplish twig from the floor and grabbed his arm.

Pressure. Pop. Calm washed over him along with the scent of lavender. Pandemonium around him, but his path was clear.

Protect his woman with every fiber of his being.

She lurched forward, clutching her stomach, her skin pasty. Her eyes burned a hole through him, their blue shade the most intense color in the chill room. Her pupils shrank to barely visible dots.

"Shift," she ordered again, her voice low and dangerous.

Harry felt the command's strength. Found it reasonable. The change fluttered over him, tingling through his extremities. The surface pain at his neck melted as his animal took control. He could do more damage in this form. He could hold the pack off while June got away.

The thunderous attack on the door halted. "What's going on in there? What do I smell?" Gavin asked. "Is June an alpha? My lucky day. I need a new alpha bitch in my pack."

Harry nuzzled June's crotch. She smelled of his body, of hers, layered with a pure thread of alpha. She fell onto her hands and knees.

Was she changing? Now?

She shook her head like a wet dog. He whined anxiously, unable to express his concerns any other way.

"Come here," she croaked. She extended her arm around his neck, rubbed down his spine. A few flecks of cayenne twitched like fire against his skin.

Pressure. Pop. June groaned and crumpled to the floor.

Harry nuzzled her and considered shifting back, but two quick transformations before a fight would weaken him way too much.

The door rattled. Dust fell from the jamb as the metal fixtures began to loosen.

"Get help," she whispered. Her last words to him, before she passed out, were, "You big dummy."

The door thundered. A crack appeared in the jamb.

Harry could stay. Fight. Lose.

Die.

Or he could go. Run. Get help.

If Gavin laid one hand on June, if the pack did anything to hurt her, Harry would find a way. He might be a man who'd never wanted much beyond good food, a pretty woman and the freedom to roam. He might be a man who'd comforted himself with the knowledge that the best revenge was a life well lived. But the past twenty-four hours had seared off his soft edges. Forged him anew.

He would find a way to make them all pay.

LIQUID SPLASHED HER face. June shivered awake, gasping.

"Get up." A tall figure loomed over her, an empty cup in his hand. "I've got questions for you."

Her vision blurred as beer stung her eyes. She tried to wipe her face but found her wrists secured behind her back. She blinked rapidly. The hazy shape took form—Gavin.

He stood with his legs spread, glowering at her. "Where did he go?"

"Who?" She was sprawled in the back of a pickup. Trees above, voices nearby, mostly male. The tailgate was down. A breeze puffed across her legs, exposed by the sleep shirt.

Gavin leaned over and captured her chin. "Where did John Lapin go? He was there and then he wasn't."

Snippets of memory filtered back to her. The door to the cellar bursting in, rough hands, her body given the potato-sack treatment. Harry must have gotten away.

Thank the Goddess he hadn't stayed in some futile effort to fight Gavin. Thank the Goddess twice her adlibbed masking spell had worked. Her head ached and her mouth tasted like a dirty sock.

How dumb should she play? She couldn't pretend to be human, but she could pretend to be uninformed. For example, she'd had no idea Harry had an alias until today.

She widened her eyes in feigned confusion. "I don't know a John Lapin."

Harry might have gone to the cops or he might have gone to the coven. It wouldn't be easy to convince either group to take on the pack. The cops would want proof and a search warrant while the coven... Well, she had no idea what the coven would do. They'd never been faced with a crisis like this.

Gavin patted her cheek sharply. "Harry Smith is a fake name. His real name is John Lapin. I know you're stupid, but think back. How did he get away?"

"He said his name was Warren." She examined what she could see of the terrain. Deciduous trees, pines, a thick canopy. Birds calling, squirrels chittering. She couldn't see any mountains, but there were no signs of civilization. A diesel motor coughed to life nearby.

"I don't care if he said he was Elvis. Answer my question." Gavin dragged her into a sitting position and propped her against the back of the truck. Wriggling her bound hands and her bottom, she inched her nightshirt over her hips.

"Which question? You asked two." Her arms were duct-taped from wrist to forearm. It wouldn't contain a pack wolf, but it would contain her, with maximum discomfort.

He crouched and mustered enough alpha that June felt pressured to obey. The flat skin of his scar darkened, and it pulled his mouth into a sneer. "I'm losing my patience, bitch. Where did he go?"

Witches followed certain protocol if detected by shifters: claim you were indie and hope they believed it. It was easier when the witch looked young enough to be a juvie. June shouldn't set off any immediate alarms with regards to her genetics.

"I assume he took off," she said. "I blacked out."

"Why, did he hit you?"

Gavin increased his alpha, and June struggled not to yield. Outside of Harry, she hadn't had much experience fending off alpha vibes. Bianca and Bert hadn't frequented the tea room.

"He shoved me," she managed to lie, hoping Gavin was on the weak side. "He said I'd slow him down."

Gavin's nostrils flared. "Bullshit. What did you do to help him?"

Rats, he could smell dishonesty. She'd have to choose her words more carefully. He didn't seem like the kind of guy who'd deal with frustration constructively, and all of Harry's dire warnings about Gavin ticked through her mind like the timer on a bomb.

"I was giving him a ride out of town," she said. "I had a car, and he's cute." All true.

Gavin rubbed the scarred corner of his mouth. "Is he going to play hero and come after you?"

She wanted to search for clues to her location, maybe spell ingredients, but it might anger Gavin if she didn't give him her full attention. She held his black, intense gaze with her own. "We met yesterday. What do you think?"

"I think he ran like the coward he is. Damn. I was hoping I'd get a chance to rip out his throat," Gavin said so casually it chilled her. "You're sure you don't know where he went?"

"I'm sure."

"How did you hide the fact you were shifters last night after your wreck?"

She couldn't think of a lie a human would believe, much less a shifter, so she deflected. "Look, Gavin, I feel dumb enough getting mixed up in pack politics. Whatever you think I did to you, I'm sorry. If you let me go, I won't tell the police. I just want to forget the past couple of days ever happened."

The sun painted the sky to the west in shades of yellow and red. Late afternoon. She'd been unconscious for hours. They could have driven a hundred miles from her house, and they could have driven ten. When she tested her center, a little magic had been restored. So she wasn't completely tapped.

"You're right about that, baby. You won't be telling the police anything at all."

"I told you I wouldn't." Another chill engulfed her. Shifters weren't murderous. Generally. When they were, they were more likely to eliminate rival shifters than humans, and there hadn't been a full-out pack war in decades.

Did Gavin see her as a rival or, worse, a danger to the pack?

He watched her with a malicious smirk. "Don't look like that. I won't hurt you if you treat me right. In fact, after tonight, you'll be part of my pack. I'm stepping up as Millington's alpha. It's no problem to include you in the bonding ceremony."

Her stomach lurched. "You can't do that. I'm a juvenile. I've never shifted." She wasn't even sure she could. If they tried to bond her, the pack would realize she wasn't a standard shifter. The coven could wipe her memories, but they couldn't transform her into a werewolf.

"You think because you're a juvie we can't bond you?" Gavin laughed. "We have ways."

She wriggled her fingers. Her hands and arms began to go numb. "How?"

"You'll find out soon enough. Why are you still a

juvie, anyway?" He fondled her breast. "This isn't a teenager's body."

She kicked at him, nearly falling over.

"Hands off," she ordered before she could stop herself.

He laughed again. "You know, I actually felt that. That's so cute, you trying to tell me what to do. Like a yappy poodle. You've got to be close to changing. Bonding you won't be a problem. Indies always end up thanking us after the fact."

"No thank you."

"Like you have a choice." He stared at her chest, covered by her thin sleep shirt. "Bianca's a dyke, did you know that?"

"No." Bianca must have turned him down.

"If she gives me much more shit, how about we get rid of her and you be my bitch?"

"I don't want to join a pack." June didn't want to anger him, but she couldn't pretend to be thrilled, either. He'd never buy that.

"Well, I'm liking this plan more and more. How old are you?"

"What does it matter?" Some shifters were twenty-one or so at first change. Not many, but it happened.

"You've got to be the oldest juvie I've ever met. Did you know a good screw can bring on the change? I guess Harry wasn't good enough."

"That's none of your business." She hadn't known that, but it confirmed what witches knew about sex with shifters—what she personally knew. It roused the beast.

Gavin grabbed her breast, bruising and cruel. "I bet you're screwing every shifter you meet so you can wake up your wolf."

"Leave me alone." She tried to kick him again, and he caught her ankles, his grip like iron.

"It's not a bad strategy." He pulled her legs, hard, and her torso whipped backward. She struggled frantically as he planted his hips between her legs. "Okay, okay, you convinced me. I'll do you."

"No!" Bile rose in her throat. The coven could wipe memories of trauma too, but that didn't mean she wanted to suffer through it.

"What are you gonna do?" He ground his erection against her, pinching her tender flesh. When he thrust, the top of her head thunked the wheel well.

"Cut it out!" Their position wrenched her shoulders, her bound arms trapped beneath her. She heaved. "Get off me."

In response, he laughed and banged her head against the truck again. His breath smelled of beer and meat. June's stomach roiled. "You don't like this? Is that because you'd rather suck me?"

She'd rather curse him with impotency. She could do it too, with the right herbs and a snoot full of magic.

Neither of which she had at the moment. But she did have witnesses.

June released an ear-splitting wail. "Help!"

Gavin struck her hard enough in the face that tears

sprang into her eyes. Fury and frustration swelled in her so quickly, she had no time to be afraid.

She screamed again. Her animal raged. Wrath curdled her voice.

Gavin flinched, half rising off her body. His shoulders hunched.

As soon as she stopped to draw another breath, he seized the front of her panties. "Shut the hell up."

Before he could rip her underwear, somebody jumped into the truck. Maurice, the kid from this morning. "Jesus, Gav, what are you doing to her?"

"Fan-damn-tastic, it's the moral majority." Gavin released her and rocked on his heels but didn't bother standing up. "What have I told you about interrupting me with a woman?"

June struggled into a sitting position to observe the byplay between the two men. Though both were dressed in T-shirts and jeans, Gavin's stocky heft outweighed the wiry, dark-skinned Maurice by fifty pounds.

"You're not with her, dude. You said you were going to question her." Maurice's gaze skidded across June as if reluctant to acknowledge her. "Did you find anything out?"

"I found out she's a whore." Gavin slapped her calf. "Right, baby?"

"Wrong." June focused on Maurice's young face. In the woods, he'd warned Harry to get out of town. He'd interrupted when June screamed. He didn't seem comfortable with Gavin's methodology. Maurice was likely her best bet for sympathy.

"I'm never wrong about women." Gavin groped her thigh. "If I am wrong, it's when they're dumber than I thought."

"I told him everything he asked and he hit me," she said to Maurice. "He threatened to hurt me. Would you let him do this to your mother?"

"Maurice's mommy was an indie whore like you," Gavin said. "He left her and joined a pack as soon as he was old enough."

Maurice glowered at Gavin, his expression darkening. "You can't keep doing this, Gav. The old man said next time it happened, you were done. You're just supposed to bring them in."

"What the hell do I care about Pop's rules now?" Gavin stood, finally, and adjusted his privates with a display of bravado. "Bianca's got to choose somebody tonight. If Smith got away from *us,* there's no way she'll catch him. As for the rest of the candidates, they're long gone. I'm Bianca's only option—just like we planned."

"What about the girl?" Maurice asked.

"Late bloomer. She's running around screwing everything with four legs to call her wolf." Gavin gestured rudely. "If you quit whining like a punk ass, you can stick it to her when I'm done. Only try not to knock her up, bro. That didn't work out so well last time."

Maurice cringed. "I don't think—"

"Did I ask you to think?" Gavin visibly dominated

the smaller man. As he ranted, his scar reddened. "Whores like her are fair game. No pack, no protection, no penalty. You know it, I know it, she knows it. She deserves it. Pack is the only thing that matters, and any wolf who refuses the true path is scum."

Another man, large and bearded, approached the truck. He had a plastic cup in his hand. "Is the puppy whining again? Ignore him, Gav. The ceremony starts at midnight. Our new pack awaits."

"That doesn't leave us much time." Gavin prodded June with his foot. "How about this? You suck me off on the way, and I promise to bone you later."

She glared at him. He'd be a fool to get his organ anywhere near her teeth.

The other man guffawed. "Save it for the after-party. You want me to chain her in the cabin?"

"I was thinking about making her pack. What do you think, Roy?"

"A juvie?" asked the big guy. "Harsh. Think she'll survive it?"

"Maybe." Gavin appraised her. "Worth a try."

June's head spun. She wanted to ask why juvies didn't survive pack bonds, but a typical shifter might know. It didn't sound good.

Maurice, his gaze pinned on the truck bed, said, "If you adopt her, she can register a complaint with the alphas about mistreatment."

"Hello, dumb ass." Gavin punched Maurice in the arm, hard. "I'll *be* the alpha, and alphas get their pick of pack whores. She'll be my first."

"Hardly your first," Roy corrected. Gavin didn't bristle when the larger man contradicted him. "Your first pack whore was the Lapin bitch."

"Like I could forget her." Gavin fingered his scar.

If something had happened between Harry's mother and Gavin, that would explain why Harry knew so much about Roanoke. Shifters rarely died from disease—just accidents, old age and severance. Did Harry's experience have anything to do with how his mother had died and why he had an alias now?

Maurice rubbed his shoulder. "Harry Smith knows we have her."

"*John Lapin* would piss his pants before he took me on. Sorta like you." Gavin fake-lunged at Maurice, who jerked away. "What can one indie do against a pack? Write us mean emails?"

Maurice stared at the ground. "If Smith can go incognito around you and Douglas, who knows what else he can do?"

Gavin's chest puffed out. "Maybe I did recognize him and wanted to wait until Pop wasn't around to handle it my way."

"I call B.S. You didn't know him," Roy said. Gavin's lips tightened but he didn't defend himself. "Did she tell you how they managed that?"

"Not yet." Gavin turned back to June. "I'll get it out of her one way or the other."

Maurice glanced at her, guilt written on his features as plainly as a book. "If we let her go, Smith won't have any reason to get on our butts."

"Would you stop whining? He's a loser. Hell, I thought he was dead. He never did anything about what happened forty years ago, and he's not going to do anything now. Look how his wimp ass turned tail. She's probably a pain in the butt. Most alpha females are, even juvies."

"She's a natural?" Roy leaned on the truck and studied June with an avaricious gaze. "I've never had an alpha bitch before. I think I'd like that."

"Trust me, you won't," she assured him. "I haven't done anything to any of you. I'd like to go home now."

"We should let her go," Maurice agreed, his brow furrowed. "This isn't right."

"I've had enough of you." Gavin shoved him off the truck bed. "You wanna stay in Dad's pack?"

"No," Maurice said. June couldn't see the younger man, but she could hear his pain. "I can't stay there after what happened."

"Then shut up and do as you're told."

"Yeah, shut up, puppy," echoed Roy.

Gavin and Roy laughed, and Gavin vaulted over the side. The truck bounced. "Roy, do you want to guard the slut? If she makes trouble, you can give her a good hiding."

"Maybe later." Roy took a long swig from his cup and wiped foam off his moustache. "I hate riding in the back of a truck. That's one thing I'm never doing once we're out of Roanoke."

"I'll ride with her," Maurice offered.

"Why, so you can let her go like the indie we caught in Virginia Beach?"

"I won't." Maurice dusted the back of his jeans.

"Yeah, right. Get me a chain and another beer. She's not going anywhere."

Maurice glanced at June one last time before obeying. Gavin and Roy spoke in low voices. She thought about maneuvering herself out of the bed and making a run for it, but Gavin periodically glanced her way. She wouldn't get ten feet before he'd be on her. On her and angry.

Better to rest and think. Build up her strength. Give Harry a chance. If the bonding ritual was at midnight, based on the sun they had about six hours. Eventually they'd relocate to Millington's commune for the ceremony, and it sounded as if she were going with them whether she wanted to or not.

Before she lost the light, she began to inspect the foliage for anything she could use in a spell. Trees, bushes, leaves. Cedar. Purification, to hide her tracks? There, on the ground was a clump of ferns—mild confusion sometimes, mental clarity at others. Not reliable. Oooh, mountain laurel. Any shifter she hit with that would vomit for several minutes. But she'd have to affect them individually, and as with any spell that harmed another, it would hit her, as well.

Whatever it took. She had to get away before they bonded her. To her knowledge, no witch had been bonded as a juvenile. She had no idea what it might do to her or how it might endanger the coven. Whether it might endanger witches everywhere.

Goddess, what could she do? She wasn't a super-hero. She was just a woman.

A really pissed-off woman.

A really pissed-off woman who could do magic.

She couldn't count on the coven, she couldn't count on Harry, she couldn't count on anyone but herself. Something would come to her. Until then, she needed to meditate if she could, to refill her well, but remain alert enough to react to anything and everything.

No problem. After all, she'd just had sex with a shifter and kept her own skin. Maybe she was a su-perhero.

CHAPTER FIFTEEN

FURY PROPELLED HARRY through the forest so fast he doubted even a pack wolf could have caught him. Fury at June, for forcing him to leave her. At himself, for succumbing to that damn lavender. At the situation, at his stupidity for not jetting out of town like a rocket and taking June with him.

Most of all, fury at Gavin Householder. If anger could lend one strength, he had no fear he'd best the other shifter in battle.

In fact, he longed for it.

Harry reached the tea room in record time. He could have gone back to June's house, but his efforts would be useless against Gavin's gang of shifters. That infuriated him too. So he did what she had asked and started sniffing around, tracing who'd been here, who was here, who might have the place staked out.

He had to slink through several backyards to reach his goal. The dogs and cats in those yards were used to him, although the chickens were never happy when he trotted by. He scanned likely routes into the woods— driveways, side roads. He ended in the gravel alley behind the strip of historic buildings that housed the tea room. Ruts in the center pooled with water from last night's rain.

Harry detected lots of foot and paw traffic. Several out-of-place humans, cops or witches doing their part to locate Sandie. Himself, yesterday. Pack wolves coming and going, unfamiliar scent markers that must be Roanokers. He no longer cared who was involved in the hunt for him because he wasn't leaving without June.

Gavin would never let either one of them be after realizing who Harry was. Because of that, June had value to Gavin beyond that of victim. Harry prayed to her Goddess that would be enough to keep her alive.

He would do anything he had to—anything—to make sure she was safe.

Harry paused near the Dumpster, the odor reminding him of the sludge. Sustaining wolf form in the middle of town made him twitchy, but he needed his enhanced senses.

One of the busboys popped out the back of the tea room for a smoke, a kid named Vern. Coven? He'd been working there about a year. As far as Harry knew he lived with his parents. Better not risk it.

Harry prepared to shift and remembered what clothes he'd had on before everything went down—his boxers. He wasn't shy, but he was about to beg a gang of little old ladies to bend their rules, rules as sacred as those held by shifters, and help him save June.

Partial nudity might not be his best approach, not to mention they'd never let him hear the end of it.

Hmm. Was there any truth to June's notions about shifter powers? He could erase wounds and transfer fabric, even cell phones, from form to form. Could he create them?

Harry concentrated, envisioning himself in clothing. Jeans, T-shirt, work boots, cell phone, wallet and keys. It seemed like weeks since he'd been dressed, but it had only been yesterday.

The prickle of the shift danced over his skin, and when he emerged he was wearing...

His boxers.

Damn.

Same ones too.

Though Pete was the only coven member confirmed by June, Harry couldn't imagine approaching the police station like this. He could go to the cops, sure, but the coven would be more effective against the pack— no search warrant required.

Annette, as Pete's wife, was suspect number one for being a witch. Vern, slumped against the brick wall puffing his hand-rolled tobacco, was not a candidate.

Harry stuck his head out from behind the Dumpster.

"Hey, Vern," he called to the busboy. "Is Annette here?"

The young man froze, cigarette halfway to his lips. He didn't look old enough to smoke. "Who's there?"

"Harry Smith, Smith's Auto Repair. I'm a frequent customer." When Harry nodded at him, Vern tensed, as most people would when confronted by a large, naked man in an alley.

"Yeah, so?"

Harry kept his alpha to himself. "I'm looking for Annette Bowman or her husband Pete. Can you tell her I'm back here?"

"Why are you hiding behind the Dumpster, Smith?" Vern demanded.

Harry thought it was rude for the kid to call him by his last name, but if Vern were coven, he could be any age. Hell, for all Harry knew, he could be an eighty-year-old woman.

"I was attacked," he said. "Had to make a run for it. I was hoping Annette could help me out. I'm a friend of the family."

"Uh-huh." Vern mashed his cigarette against the brick wall and pocketed the stub. The odor that drifted to Harry's nose was sweeter than standard tobacco. "Call the cops."

Jeez, he'd been surprised enough when June hinted that her supplies weren't one hundred percent legal. Was everyone who worked at the tea room a pothead?

Harry inched away from the Dumpster so Vern could see he had no weapons. Or pants. "I'm not sure I want to get the cops involved. It was a…personal matter."

"What'd you do?"

If the kid were coven, he'd have a good idea what Harry had been doing the past twenty-four hours. "Look, Vern, this concerns Sandie. Can you get Annette?"

Vern stalked across the potholed alley, halting several feet from the Dumpster. A foot shorter than Harry, he bristled with adolescent rage. "Where is she? What do you know about Sandie?"

"What do you know about me?" Harry countered, not missing the fact Vern neglected to address Sandie with the honorific "Miss." Either the kid was a disrespectful punk or he was older than he appeared. Harry tested the kid's scent, but all he could smell was herb.

Vern shoved his hand into his jacket and withdrew the butt, which he twiddled around his fingers. "I know I'm going to call the popo if you don't start telling me everything you know about Sandie in the next ten seconds."

"Please do." Harry crossed his arms. The police weren't his first choice of cavalry, but they'd listen after he presented them with Sandie's busted cellar doors. The obstacle would be their bureaucracy and their humanity, if the investigation turned up anything lupine. "I would have called them myself if I had a phone, which I obviously do not." He resisted the urge to call Vern "kid" or "little man" since he had no idea if it applied. "I'd rather talk to Annette or Pete about Sandie…and her granddaughter June."

The kid's eyes widened. "You know Junie?"

"I met June yesterday."

"You did, huh?" Vern glanced around the alley, as if looking for something that was about as tall as, say, a wolf. "Did you two get busy? And did—"

"None of your business," Harry interrupted, in a way he knew would confirm the question.

"Maybe it is my business." Vern stared at him. "Is there something you want to tell me besides the fact Junie's a traitor?"

A traitor? Why, because she loved Harry and he was pretty damn sure he loved her back? Did this kid think June belonged to him or something?

Harry felt his alpha rise, along with his frustration and fear. "I don't want to tell you shit. There's no time for dominance games, Vern. We both know who's the alpha wolf here."

"Don't you mean alpha dog?" Vern's nostrils flared as their confrontation heated. "That's what people say."

"I said wolf, and I mean wolf. If you aren't going to get Annette, I'm going to walk into the kitchen and start tearing the place up until I find her."

"You think I'll let you do that?" The cigarette butt broke apart in Vern's twitchy hand, seemingly by accident. Harry might not have noticed if June hadn't revealed her magic to him, including the fact it involved herbs and bodily contact.

"Do not throw that crap at me." For good measure he added, "Little man."

Vern lashed out anyway, flinging herbs. Harry dodged easily. They watched the dried leaves flutter to the gravel. He was coven, all right.

The kid shuffled back a step. "You'd better leave."

Harry gave up. Vern was infuriating, and Harry was already furious. His alpha side could influence other shifters so he pressed his advantage. He heaped it all on the unsuspecting kid—man, woman, whatever. "Get. Annette. Now."

Vern ran, calling for Annette.

"And get me some clothes!"

Within fifteen seconds Annette burst out of the tea room, followed by Vern and several employees. "Harry Smith, as I live and breathe. What in the world are you doing here?"

Harry knew shifters. Coven secrecy would be their biggest concern, and they'd sacrifice June to keep it.

He wouldn't let that happen. This situation endangered them all.

"Saving your ass."

Annette patted the knot of hair atop her head. "Is that so?"

The employees distributed themselves behind her in a half circle. Most carried twigs or leaves, and all wore resolute expressions. Vern sidled through the line, clutching an overcoat and a pair of large garden clogs. He tossed these at Harry from several yards away.

"I have reason to believe Gavin Householder from Roanoke kidnapped June," Harry said. Gasps and whispers swept the group. "I can find her if we move fast."

"You don't know for certain?" Annette asked, her face pale.

He shook the overcoat violently until a shower of herbs sprinkled to the ground. The employees exchanged glances, right before they crept forward, spreading out. Hemming him in.

"I'm ninety-nine percent certain." He ignored the people he was ninety-nine percent certain were witches about to wipe his memory. He recognized them all, and they were not all grannies. After turning the coat inside out, he slipped into it and knocked out the shoes.

Annette pulled a face and spoke quietly to Vern, so quietly he couldn't make out the words. Vern trotted into the tea room, and she turned her attention back to Harry. "Why are you coming to us instead of the police? What does this have to do with saving my behind, kiddo?"

Vern had called June a traitor. Annette suggested he call the cops. Were they prepared to desert June because they assumed she'd wolfed out? To hell with the coven's secrecy. How could they ignore the threat Gavin posed to June's life?

"Gavin is bad news," he stressed. "Bad, bad news. She did not go willingly."

"I have only your word for this. I don't know this Gavin person." Annette's lips were tight, her eyes moist. According to Harry's nose, she was lying. Several members of the group broke open paper twists of herbs and cupped them in their palms. "We can't do anything."

"Are you saying you don't care what happens to her?" Snarling, he advanced on Annette. He let his alpha emerge, his teeth sharpen, his eyes pale. He let

so much wildness bleed through his facade, he was
surprised his voice wasn't a lupine howl of frustration.

The coven, as one, stepped back. Most dropped
their gazes, staring anywhere but at him.

Good. They needed to stay out of herb-tossing distance. He had no desire to lose his memories before
he was able to save June.

Annette spoke first. "We do care but she…she made
her bed." One nervous snigger broke the silence. "I'm
sorry, Harry. I don't know what she told you, what you
think you know, but—"

"What I know is June's an amazing woman. I
shouldn't have to explain that to any of you." As he
spoke he became aware of a pressure in the air, like a
plane taking off. The times he'd felt that before, magic
had come of it. Annette and the others crept closer
to him.

Harry held up a hand. "Let me finish."

"Make it quick." She drew what looked like a grass
meatball from her apron pocket.

If he had to shift and run, he'd be form stuck as a
wolf for hours. That would help him track Gavin but
it wouldn't help him convince the coven to mount a
rescue.

Harry crossed his arms, prepared to stand his
ground until the oregano started flying. "June is intelligent, loyal, proactive and…extremely resistant to
change. Except I don't think she's equipped to resist
torture. Or a pack bond. I understand both of those
can really loosen a shifter's lips."

"Resistant?" Annette asked sharply.

"Not to my charms, I'm happy to say," he confessed, "but to other things, yes. Our girl's as two-legged as you are, Annette. Are you ready to talk now?"

She lowered the herb grenade. "That changes everything. You'd better come inside."

AFTER ANNETTE CONVINCED him there were no spells that would crucify Gavin from afar, Harry spent the next thirty minutes telling her everything that had transpired. He would have paced, but when he tried, he got in the way of the tea room employees.

No matter the crisis, the food must go on.

A slice of pie à la mode, large, helped him sit still long enough to spill his tale. Annette asked lots of questions, none about his sex life beyond confirming June hadn't lost her magic. The rest of the coven members fielded the lunchtime rush, while Harry and Annette ate pie at a table near the back door.

When Vern returned with Pete, the men wanted Harry to repeat the story from the beginning. Harry growled in frustration, evoking a variety of reactions from his companions—alarm, annoyance, amusement.

"When do we get to the rescue?" He banged his fist on the table. "Gavin could be—"

"We know." Annette grabbed his hand, her thin bones sharp. "But we think he won't kill her. If she heeds her training, she won't give him a reason to. She'll bide her time and wait for an opening."

Though Pete nodded his agreement, hovering behind his wife while he inhaled blueberry cobbler, Annette didn't look a hundred percent certain. Not even ninety-nine percent certain. She squeezed Harry's fingers.

"You'd better not put lavender on me." He sniffed but didn't sense any herbal interference. "I'm not going to bite anybody."

Her eyebrows raised. "How do you know about lavender?"

"Because I'm not blind." Every time June waved that stuff around, he'd felt peace and cooperativeness roll over him like ocean surf. She'd used it to convince him to leave her at Gavin's mercy. His self-esteem smarted like that cayenne crap. He didn't want to be mollified, and he didn't appreciate having his mood changed for him.

His mood right now was pure, gnarly alpha.

"You won't be so clever when we erase your memories, jackass," Vern grumbled.

Harry growled, low and threatening. These people should be doing what he wanted. Doing what was right.

Vern twitched before he flicked a piece of pie crust in Harry's direction.

"Did you feel that?" Annette asked her husband, who nodded. "It's almost like…"

"It is," Vern agreed. "How in tarnation did that happen?"

"I don't know." Annette stroked Harry's arm, trying

to soothe him without herbs, he guessed. There'd better be no herbs. "He's never ordered us around before."

"Good Goddess, don't tell him," Vern exclaimed.

"Don't tell me what?" Harry half rose, but Annette wouldn't let go. The lady was stronger than she looked. "Gavin could be hurting her. Why are we pissing around here?"

"Junie will survive the hurt, but it would endanger all of us if we charge in unprepared. It's not easy to control large groups of shifters. What you saw June do yesterday—well, the rest of us don't have that kind of power. But we can heal almost anything June suffers and help her forget anything she wants to forget. She knows that. It will help her get through this."

"That doesn't make it right." He should have gone to the police. What was wrong with these people?

Vern shoved his plate away. "Look, Romeo, we know where the compound is, but we don't know if that's where he took her. There are other variables too. Magic's not…magic."

"We have to get her out before the ceremony. I told you, I can—"

"Yeah, yeah, yadda yadda, you can find her. We can't keep up with you on the hunt, and you can't rescue her alone." Vern leaned back in his chair, fingers laced over his belly.

Flinging off Annette's hand, Harry banged the table again. Everyone jumped. A stupid testosterone maneuver, but it helped to see them rattled. "I could try."

"And you could fail." Vern snorted. "Then what?

It sucks to be June right now. It would suck worse if we outed ourselves to the shifters."

"I'll find her and call you. Give me a cell and I'll go right now." Energy brimmed inside him like a shaken soda, fizzing over the sides.

"Shifters are so hotheaded." Vern leaned on the table. "The pack and Gavin would be on you like white on rice as soon as you got within a couple miles. Are you stupid or have you just spent too long on four legs? Someone tell me why we haven't wiped his memory already?"

"Because you need me to find her." Harry leaned forward as well, matching Vern's posture like two lumberjacks about to arm wrestle. "June put a disguise spell on me before they took her. If they don't see me or hear me, the other shifters won't know I'm there. Every minute you sit here waffling is another minute I could be tracking her."

"She adlibbed?" Annette asked. She touched Harry's hand again, her eyes closing, and finally nodded. "It's wearing off, but it's impressive. This experience has been good for her."

"Give me a break. None of this is good for June. If you three don't come up with a plan in the next five, I'm out of here." He'd have to hurry if his disguise spell was fading.

"We're trying, but somebody's being an impatient asshole." Vern rubbed his temples. "Tell me and Pete everything. We're the tacticians. We need all the details."

Harry cursed, but he complied. He rushed through the story, an edge to his voice. Vern stopped him when he got to the part where June did not change into a werewolf. He didn't kiss and tell, but her resistance was a significant factor in the upcoming mission. If Gavin tried a pack bond on June, there was no telling what would happen.

"So…she's resistant, for real? I figured you just stunk in bed." Vern threw up his hands. "All this time and Junie's resistant."

As Annette laughed, Vern proceeded to curse a bluer streak than Harry had ever heard in life—and he'd heard a lot.

Finally he ended, out of breath. The vulgarities were at odds with his cherubic countenance and chubby body.

"He's a poor sport and a potty mouth," Annette said with a shrug. "That's what you get for playing the odds, old man."

"Oh, like it's obvious who's going to resist and who's going to eat Alpo," Vern snarked. "There was no reason on this green earth to believe Junie would be resistant just because she's crushed on Harry for eight years."

"No reason except that it's true. And you lose the bet. You owe the kitty two hundred hours." Annette spun her empty pie plate in a circle. "Might I suggest you spend your two hundred hours priming heal-all and cayenne?"

Vern flipped her off with both hands. "Might I suggest you eat a fast-food hamburger?"

Annette quit laughing. "Good Lord, no."

If there was one thing Harry knew about the grannies, it was that they did most of their own cooking. Not that he could call them grannies anymore. Who knew what lurked behind each facade?

"Honey," Pete said, in his quiet voice, "arguing with your brother isn't productive. If the pack tries to bond a resistant like June, we could have a real situation on our hands." It was the first time Pete had spoken beyond a hello when he arrived.

"Vern's your brother?" Harry asked, amazed.

"I'm younger. By a century." Annette grinned.

"I'm glad to hear Junie didn't tell you everything," Vern said sourly. "Did she tell you how old she really is?"

"Uh." Harry sank into his chair. "No."

"Shut up, Vern," Annette said, "or I'll put a cucumber under your pillow."

"If you two are finished," Pete interrupted, "I have an idea, but I have questions for Harry before we proceed."

Both Annette and Vern simmered down, giving Pete a chance to quiz Harry. He drew a notebook from the back pocket of his slacks. Harry was thankful to have Pete's investigative skills on the case but wished the slow-moving man would pour on some speed. His worries for June clawed at his insides like a hungry cat at a bag of kibble.

Annette handed her husband the pen tucked behind her ear, and he clicked the nib several times. He remained standing, his body blocking their conversation from the chaos of the kitchen.

"Gavin Householder has blipped the police radar a few times, so I can only imagine what he's really like." He paused when a girl bustled over to refill their fruit teas. "What can you tell us about him?"

Too much.

"He's feral," Harry said bluntly. "He should be put down."

"And we believe you why?" Vern asked.

Harry's whole body tightened. He had to force the words through his lips, words he'd never shared with anyone. "I was born in the Roanoke pack. My dad died when I was three, and Mom didn't remarry. It left her unprotected. After Gavin came of age, he picked her. She was nobody, a border monitor without a protector, and I was just a kid. Gavin got rough with her. Repeatedly."

"Oh, Harry," Annette said quietly. Even Vern appeared solemn. "The two of you couldn't go to the alphas?"

"He's the alphas' son. What the hell do you think?" Bitterness welled inside him like pus in a boil that had needed lancing for forty years. "One night I guess I thought I'd be the man of the house and tried to stop him. He hurt me, and she fought back. That's when he went feral. Tried to kill us. We had to run. I was ten. She didn't survive the severance."

"I am so sorry about your mama," Annette said. "Is this still going on in Roanoke?"

"I don't know what he's done since I left." He'd avoided finding out, the better to repress his memories. Harry's hands closed into fists. "They have a high attrition rate. Lots of runners. That's why they conscript indies. No indie with half a brain sets foot in Roanoke."

"The Wytheville coven has mentioned increased violence in the pack," Pete said. "Disappearances and skirmishes, stuff like that. They credited it to modern life's effect on such a traditional group. It wasn't a huge concern because the police have only picked up misdemeanors."

"The shifters cover it up. You have ways, they have ways." Harry stared at each of them. "Right now, I want to hear yours. This isn't helping us get June away from Gavin and the ceremony."

Pete frowned. "The ceremony is part of our problem. Bianca's got to instate someone or the pack will disband, and we don't want that kind of chaos here. Problem is, something happened to the candidates. Between yesterday and today, they've all disappeared."

"Roanoke," Harry said grimly. "Half the pack came, pretending to help Bianca with the lockdown, and chased the candidates off. Douglas came too so they'd have an anchor to postpone severance if needed. Now only Gavin's left."

"I never thought I'd say this, but Bianca was better off with Bert." Annette stirred her tea. "So were we."

"Old Bert wasn't all that bad," Pete mused. "If nothing else, he was predictable, up until he got caught breaking and entering. That didn't seem like him. Too sloppy."

"If you say so." Bert's arrest had been unanticipated, but no surprise. Millington, like Roanoke, typified the conservative side of the shifter spectrum. Only Millington hadn't run a press gang or tolerated ferals.

That would change along with everything else once Gavin was alpha.

"As for there being no other contenders in the area, I wouldn't say that's the case." Pete eyed Harry speculatively. "You're a good man, Harry. That's why I know you're going to hear me out, even though you aren't going to like what I have to say."

CHAPTER SIXTEEN

AFTER A BUMPY trip down poorly maintained roads, Gavin and his followers, with June chained to a tire in the back of the truck, arrived at the Millington compound a few hours before midnight. Her body ached, and her shoulders and arms had grown numb. However, her sprained ankle and throbbing head more than made up for any numbness. She hadn't been able to catnap, but she'd zoned out as much as possible.

June had driven past the compound a number of times on the river road. She'd been on a recon mission inside once, under the pretense of gathering signatures for a petition. Humans had little cause to trek this far downriver.

The compound itself was on the opposite side of the Hartsell, connected by a steel-cabled swinging bridge. The pack lined their vehicles on the public side, next to a narrow concrete garage for motorcycles. There was always at least one shifter near the vehicles at any given time, protecting one of the packs' most valuable assets as well as the bridge. Needless to say, the pack posted numerous no-trespassing signs, and shifters patrolled the woods to make sure no one came upon their utopia unannounced.

To the naked eye, the compound resembled a shantytown, with an open central area surprisingly free of debris and clutter. Because of the mountain on one side and the river on the other, the livable area was long instead of wide. The hodgepodge of dwellings clustered haphazardly, with ATVs, sheds, animal pens and the occasional swing set scattered among them.

June had been secured in a white plastic chair on the edge of the courtyard. She smelled like dried beer and anxiety. Sounds and scents rose in a tangle around her—the hum of generators, the babble of voices, the smell of grilling meat and baked beans, and somebody running a chain saw. Her ankles had been taped to the chair legs, and her arms remained behind her back. A cheap outdoor table beside her held the condiments for the meal after the ceremony.

Too bad it was nothing she could cast spells with. Ketchup, relish, mustard and hot sauce were too far beyond their native form to be of use for anything but hotdogs and burgers.

After some raised eyebrows at her bound status, the wolves had ignored her, even the young ones. No one was set to guard her, although Gavin warned her about getting funny ideas.

None of her ideas were funny, unless death and dismemberment amused you to no end.

June got as comfortable as she could and watched the preparations with an eye toward escape. Whenever she thought nobody would notice, she chafed her hands against the chair slats, using the poorly molded resin to shred the tape.

Pack wolves from Millington and a few from Roanoke milled around. A bonfire was in the center. Teenagers laid evergreen branches in a circumference around the area while two adults worked at a utility table near the beer kegs, doing something with roots, herbs and Crock-Pots. She assumed they were preparing the infusions each adult pack member would imbibe. June wasn't close enough to see what they were using, but traditionally it included passionflower, red clover, skullcap, peppermint and goldenseal. Others raked the ceremonial area over and over, sifting out unwanted items.

What the pack members didn't know was that they were preparing for a spell. Big magic. Not that it mattered. It was the only magic they could channel beyond changing their bodies from two to four legs.

With a lot of discreet wiggling, June scooted her chair farther from the circle until she was near a prefab shed. A few more feet and she'd be within reach of a laurel bush. She was beginning to hope she'd been forgotten when she noticed Bianca and Gavin, a pale wolf trotting behind them, headed her way.

The alpha's impatient stalk and jerky movements indicated all was not right with her world. Not surprising, since Gavin was about to become a permanent part of it.

June couldn't blame the other woman for wanting Harry as her partner, but Bianca had caught herself in her own snare—the clock ticking on the ceremony and nobody but Gavin left to choose from.

The shifters halted in front of June. The wolf, which looked familiar, sat beside the condiments table and regarded her unblinkingly. Bianca grabbed June's chin and tilted her face one way, then the other, peering closely at her features.

Would she note the resemblance between June and Sandie? Bianca released her and regarded Gavin with one thin, black eyebrow arched.

"This is the one you want to pack bond?" she asked dubiously. "That doesn't always work."

"We'd be doing her a favor." Gavin placed a heavy hand on June's shoulder like a warning. "Have you ever seen a juvie this old?"

Bianca bent until she was inches from June's face. Her nostrils flared and her fruity breath washed over June as she inhaled. "Why is she tied up? Didn't she agree to this?"

"I definitely did not agree to this," June said.

Gavin grabbed her hair, yanking her head back. "Shut up, bitch. Nobody's talking to you."

In a blur of movement, Bianca had Gavin up against the shed. The giant boom of his body against corrugated metal resounded through the clearing, halting the activity as everyone stared. The wolf beside the table rose to its feet, ruff bristling like a cat's.

June couldn't see Bianca's face, but the alpha's hands encircled Gavin's throat in a way June wished she could do herself. As it would be in poor taste to yell, "You go, girl," she kept her mouth shut.

"You aren't alpha yet," Bianca snarled, lifting him off the ground. "You will not treat the women in this pack with disrespect or you won't be alpha long."

June had to wonder how Bianca intended to make good on a threat like that. Ridding a pack of unwanted alphas was trickier than it used to be. The go-to method had always been murder. In this day and age, cops tended to investigate missing persons, dead bodies and killing sprees, even when the people involved were cultish.

Gavin didn't struggle. Wrath burned from his eyes. "Is that what happened to Bert?"

Bianca lifted him an inch higher. "None of your damn business," she said with a shake.

Gavin began to choke, so she flung him to the ground. The conversations around them restarted, unnaturally loud—people pretending this was business as usual, to allow the incoming alpha to save face.

Or because the encounter *was* business as usual.

June had no way of knowing how the pack operated. She had always assumed Bert and Bianca were a terrible twosome, and Bianca's aggression toward Gavin didn't disprove it.

Except for the fact her behavior had been spurred by his abuse of a weaker being.

He stood, rubbing his throat. "You know they won't find Smith in time. Or anybody. I'm your man, Bianca baby. Nobody's coming because I'm already here."

Bianca's fingers flexed into fists. Her guttural snarl was wordless and more than eloquent.

Gavin answered with words. "So we'll be including the girl in the bond tonight."

"I'd rather not drag any unwilling members into the pack," she said. "We're going to have enough trouble."

He laughed. "Harry Smith didn't want to join your pack, and you didn't give a rat's ass about that."

"I don't want to talk about Harry." In another display of alpha strength, Bianca hefted June's chair and replaced it beside the condiments table. *Oops.* The pale wolf sniffed June's leg.

"He's not even who he says he is," Gavin said. "Harry Smith is an alias."

June had heard this before, and apparently Bianca had too. The alpha didn't blink. "Lots of indies have fake IDs. I don't want to complicate the ceremony, and I don't want any bodies to dispose of. We have a lot of new members this month as well as…you."

"All right, all right. You win." Gavin's sharp teeth flashed in the glow of kerosene lanterns. "I'll keep her in a cage until she shifts. Me and my boys will help her find the wolf. We've done it before."

"You've got to be kidding me," Bianca snapped. "That's inhumane."

"I might care about that if we were human. But we're not, and we shouldn't pretend to be."

She gritted her teeth. "I won't allow it."

"In case you hadn't noticed, after tonight you won't

be in charge anymore. I will." He strutted away without a backward glance at the two women.

"What a piece of work," June commented, knowing Gavin could hear her if he wanted. "How can you stand him?"

It was in her best interests to exacerbate the strife here, maybe enough that Bianca would risk the pack's unit bond rather than instate Gavin. She could try to push it another night, give herself time to find someone else—and give Harry and the coven and the police and the Marines and the cavalry and the Easter Bunny time to find June.

"I can't stand him," Bianca admitted. The wolf that accompanied her nuzzled her hand, whining. "He's worse than Bert."

Interesting sentiment coming from Bert's legally wedded wife. With Gavin elsewhere, she sounded almost civil. She hadn't let him hurt June and seemed troubled by her presence. How else was Bianca different from the person June had always assumed she was?

And how could June use it to her advantage?

"Why him? Why can't you wait until you find somebody better?"

"You ever been in a pack, girl?" Bianca asked. "Maybe born in one before you took off?"

June shook her head. "Neither of my parents were pack." It was true.

"Then you wouldn't know." Bianca aligned the bottles and jars on the condiments table in order of tallest to shortest. "The lead-up to a ceremony begins weeks in advance. Once it's underway, if you drop the thread, it dissolves our bonds. All of them. We pushed it as far as we could. Tonight's our last night."

"Weeks?" Bert had only been sent to prison a couple days ago. Foreboding washed over her as the implications sank in. The Millington pack's annual ceremony usually took place in another thirty days. Either the Macabees had planned the bonding ceremony early or Bianca had planned it behind Bert's back... a month before Harry took his customary vacation.

Bianca nodded. "Then there's the ceremonial drink. The ingredients are expensive, and they have a use-by date you wouldn't believe."

"I would believe it." Certain herbs were the same way. They weren't effective if the item in question wasn't hours, even minutes from the ground fresh— problematic if you couldn't grow a local supply. "You won't really let him lock me in a cage, will you?"

Bianca placed the last salt shaker in the regimented line. "We'll try the ceremony. If you go into it with a willing heart, you'll probably make it through."

"Probably?" June exclaimed. "I don't know as much about pack bonds as you, but this is my life we're talking about. Mrs. Macabee, please."

Bianca frowned. "I'm getting a divorce. Call me Bianca."

"Bianca, I—"

"Actually, don't call me anything. If you aren't going to tell me how I can find Harry in the next hour and save us from that dog shit Gavin, I don't have anything else to say to you." The wrinkles in Bianca's forehead smoothed out and her exotic features became expressionless. "Other than welcome to the pack, sister."

FOR THE TWENTY-SEVENTH time, the Caddy's overworked engine failed to catch, so Harry motioned for Vern to turn off the ignition. The old car had coughed to a stop a mile from the compound. It was close to midnight, and part of Harry's job was to create enough of a diversion for the coven to infiltrate the compound.

The other part, he didn't even want to think about.

He cursed and slammed the hood. "I can't do anything without my tools. It's dead."

"Congratulations. You killed both of June's cars," Vern said. "Some mechanic you are."

"Shut up."

"No, you shut up," Vern replied with what had to be deliberate immaturity. Harry had never even met a preteen as annoying as Vern, and he'd been told adolescence was the most difficult age for kids.

June's original disguise spell had worn off. Vern had been sent with Harry to cast a spell the coven swore would protect him long enough for tonight's undertaking. The kid—man, whatever—was the strongest witch in the coven next to June, who'd be in no position to help anybody, they assumed.

Harry detested all the assumptions they were basing their plan on—like the assumption Gavin wouldn't hurt June, or that it didn't matter if he did, because they'd help her forget.

It mattered. It mattered to Harry.

He leaned through the back window to grab one of June's ubiquitous containers of wet wipes. That was when he heard it. The call.

A high, mournful ululation poured over him. He felt the urge to respond more strongly than he'd experienced since his childhood. Shifters who lived where there were no true wolves had to be cautious about the howl, so it wasn't something he'd heard in many places he'd lived. Like all indies he kept himself far away from bonding ceremonies to avoid this exact situation.

The call made him want to shift. To sing. To run. To join.

Moonlight broke into shards as his eyes changed. His fingers curled. His breathing quickened.

"Is that what I think it is?" Vern yelled through the window of the Caddy.

His voice shook Harry out of his trance. So did the answering howls scattered around them.

"Damn." He stalked around the vehicle and opened the door. "They're getting ready to start."

Vern popped out of the car. "Then let's go."

"Help me push the car onto the shoulder. It's blocking the road."

He wasn't sure how the coven intended to rescue June. They'd been crafty when pressed. June's scent marker led straight down this road. There was nothing out here but the compound and a lot of wilderness.

She was alive, or had been a couple hours ago.

Despite Vern's protests, they managed to inch the Caddy onto the shoulder. The grannies would be behind them soon. This section of the road was hundreds of feet above the river, and the next mile was all downhill.

The two men began trotting down the incline. Harry drew ahead of Vern, impatient to reach the compound. Would anyone be guarding the bridge? Would Gavin's men try to waylay him? How did the coven think they were going to manage this?

Vern huffed and puffed, a heavy pack on his back. "Slow down."

"No."

Vern broke into a resentful lope. "You're pretty strong for an indie."

"Pretty pissed too. I don't have time to wait for you. I should shift and go in alone. I can make it there in a few. I'm supposed to be Mr. Diversion—" he checked his watch "—as of ten minutes ago. Now the pack has been called home."

"You go in without my spell, you're dead." Vern stumbled on a rock. Harry caught him.

"Cast your hoodoo. What is it, a disguise?"

"Look." Vern panted between phrases. "I know you're not an inbred throwback, but we're not going to tell you anything we don't have to. It'll be that much less to erase from your memory."

"Good God, this again? I won't tell anybody." They'd been arguing all day. Why should his brain be wiped clean of June, for Chrissake? They couldn't let him keep that one thing when he was about to sacrifice his ass to save *them?*

"If you run ahead, I can't help you if anything goes wrong."

"Nothing's going to go wrong," Harry said, without conviction. "Why do you think they'll let you into the compound?"

Vern wheezed out, "I'm not going to tell you that, either. Just believe it when it happens."

"And when you screw up?"

"I don't—" pant, pant "—screw up."

"Then do whatever you need to do to keep Gavin from murdering me because I can't wait on your slow ass. They'll instate the new alpha first so he'll be in place to channel the group bonds. Once Gavin gets that far, we're screwed."

"Unless somebody shoots him," Vern said.

Harry gestured rudely. "Who's going to do that, you?"

"Nope." Vern pointed at him. "You are, killer."

"I'm not a murderer." Though he was tempted to ignore his principles in this instance. "Guns are a coward's weapon in most packs, and they're forbidden in challenges."

"Hey, if the shoe fits."

Harry bristled. "I'm not a—"

"Kidding. You'd have tried to take them all on this morning if Junie hadn't sent you to us." Vern rummaged in his knapsack. He pulled out a black pistol, checking the chambers. "If it works, who the hell cares what they think?"

Vern echoed one of Harry's favorite sentiments. However, while Harry had no problem being considered cowardly by packers, Vern had overlooked an obvious flaw in the plan. Shifters eschewed guns… to resolve pack conflicts. They were familiar enough with them otherwise and would never let Harry into the ceremony if he were armed.

"If I have a gun," he said, "they'll take it away from me. And they won't be happy about it."

"Not if they can't find it." Vern tossed him the pistol, which Harry snatched out of the air. Why was the idiot throwing a loaded gun around? "Can you shift this back and forth like you do your phone?"

"It doesn't matter. You think nobody's ever tried that?" Harry dangled the small, heavy weapon from his fingers. Outsiders weren't allowed into a compound on four legs, and the ceremony itself had a strict two-legs requirement until the end.

Vern chuckled. "Nobody's tried it with one of my spells on him."

"This is the big plan," Harry repeated incredulously. "I'm supposed to shoot Gavin."

"Since you won't wait for me…yeah. You need to shoot Gavin. Here's my advice." Vern laid a clean white cloth on the road and dumped a baggie of herbs on it. He followed with a beige powder and squirted the whole mess with oil from a squeezable ketchup bottle. "Shift to your wolf and stay there. The adults will be in the ceremony so the guards will be juvies. They'll let you pass because of the spell. Get really close, shift back and Glock that bastard in the head. It'll kill him instantly."

Harry would have to be close. He couldn't shoot the broad side of a minivan much less Gavin's head. If this was truly the coven's plan, he was disappointed. Who'd have thought the grannies were bloodthirsty? Had their fears of exposure pushed them beyond the pale?

"I would rather banish him than kill him." Harry might not be a murderer, but that didn't mean he had no vengeful spirit. Banishment meant Gavin's suffering would last longer.

"Well, your buddy Gavin wants to kill somebody, so you'd better buck up and make this happen. We'll take care of the rest." Without further ado, Vern wadded up the ingredients and scrunched his face. Harry's ears popped immediately.

Vern held out his clasped fists to Harry. Yellowish oil oozed between his fingers. "Eat some of this and shove some in the barrel of the gun. Rub the rest on your skin."

Harry accepted the gloopy mess dubiously, poking a few blobs into the gun. "Will this clog up the gun's inner workings?"

Vern rubbed the back of his hands on his forehead. "It's a gun, not a computer."

Harry checked the pistol to make sure the safety was on before shoving it in his jeans. His cell phone was in a back pocket and a bottle of pills the coven

had told him would heal almost anything was in another. He wondered if they'd heal a bullet to the head.

"What's in this stuff?" he asked before raising the
gloop to his lips.

"Little of this, little of that. If you feel like you're
going to barf, shift. Should take care of the nausea."

"Great." The mixture had a mineral flavor overlaid
with olive oil. Harry swallowed some and removed his
shirt so he could rub the rest on his chest and arms.
He tossed the shirt at Vern. "One less thing for me to
shift back and forth. Wish me luck."

Harry shimmered, his body morphing, while Vern
repacked his knapsack. Before he could dash off, Vern
yelled, "Hold on, I'm not finished." He grabbed Harry
by the tail.

Harry snapped at him, anxious to get on with it. The
wolves who'd answered Bianca's call wouldn't take
long to return home. He could smell Vern's marker
intensely in this form as well as the other man's anger.

He whuffed again. *Interesting.* The kid might be an
alpha too. Without the degree of exposure Harry'd had
to June, he couldn't be sure. Fine by him. He wasn't
about to get that exposed to Vern.

Vern wiped his hands on Harry's coat and did some
more ear-popping magic that made him want to howl.
So he did.

To his surprise, a number of wolves answered. One
or two close by, most near the compound. What was
that all about? Shifters responded to pack mates and
their alpha, not indies.

Vern flinched from the long, warbling sound. "Are you trying to deafen me? All right, I'm done. See you on the far side."

Harry didn't waste another second with the two-leg. He was off like a shot from the gun he carried, which was concealed with what June called magic.

It was a stupid plan, going in armed with a pistol and bravado, but the coven had refused his other plans and he couldn't do this alone. He had to trust them, because they were trusting him with a lot too.

CHAPTER SEVENTEEN

WHEN SEVERAL OF the four-legs erupted into eerie wails again, June nearly leaped out of her plastic seat, tape or no tape.

Gavin, dressed in nothing but a tacky loincloth, hurled a log at a yodeling wolf. "Shut the hell up!"

The wood struck its ribs, and the wolf's call morphed into a yelp. It was the pale four-leg June had noticed before. The wolf scampered to the side of the clearing, tail tucked between its legs.

Bianca emerged from behind the smoky bonfire, her inky hair loose around her shoulders and a predatory, somewhat malicious expression on her face. She wore little more than Gavin, but her sports bra and shorts weren't as absurd as Gavin's faux-fur breech-clout. She looked like a kick-boxing instructor—fierce, energetic and poised.

She did not look like an alpha disgusted by the turn of events in her territory.

"Way to win over the pack, big man," Bianca said to Gavin. A sack from a local discount store dangled from her hand. "Throwing shit at them really shows leadership."

Gavin indicated the wolves in the clearing. Most of the pack had disappeared to check on their children, meditate or do whatever they did before a bonding ceremony. "Why are they calling a second time?"

Bianca raised an eyebrow. "You didn't hear?"

Hear what? June wanted to ask. The commune had gone silent after Bianca had summoned the pack. For all she knew Bianca meant the ceremonial progress report and nobody had updated Gavin because they detested him.

"I heard you summon them fifteen minutes ago. Funny, they're still not ready." He paced in front of the roaring fire, scratching his heinie where the breechclout's string dangled. "You can't manage them?"

A gusty wind drove smoke in June's direction. It was so thick, she could practically cast a spell with it. Her eyes stinging, she coughed and missed most of Bianca's response.

"...our way of doing things."

The wind shifted, thinning the smoke. Through watery vision, June made out Gavin, hands on hips, rotating his trunk as if about to exercise. "How much longer?"

"It's not midnight yet." Bianca tossed a couple baggies of herbs onto the fire. Neon colors flared in the blaze.

"It's midnight somewhere." He pressed an arm over his chest, followed by the other. His shifter-enhanced musculature gleamed in the firelight. "Nobody's going to show up to challenge me. You might as well confirm me so we can get the party started."

She crossed her arms, the bag swinging in the crook of her elbow. "What if it doesn't work?"

He paused, his arm at an odd angle, and regarded her incredulously. "The confirmation? Why wouldn't it?"

Bianca shrugged. The fire snapped, and the scent of sage filled the clearing. That must have been what was in the plastic bags. "The girl's inclusion might disrupt things."

Gavin stuck his hands on his hips. "When has a pack bond ever failed to work on somebody that old?"

June would like to know the answer to that herself. Bianca's "probably" from earlier wasn't reassuring, and she doubted she could maintain a willing heart. Would the ceremony affect her? Would the fact she was a witch improve or worsen her chances of survival?

"I wouldn't know." Bianca's lips tightened. "I've never included a juvenile in a ceremony."

Gavin chuckled nastily. "Well, Roanoke has. Tell you what, baby. Since you don't seem to have a cage around here, after my confirmation I'll personally jumpstart her wolf. Then you don't have to worry about her being a juvie. I bet it would make for a great floor show."

"Absolutely not." The expression on Bianca's face chilled June even as it reassured her. June had escaped Gavin's sadism earlier today, but if rape were incipient…

No, she wouldn't let herself be distracted. She'd made progress removing the tape around her hands. She wasn't sitting around to wait for impending doom—or rescue. For all she knew the coven had trapped Harry, erased his memories and thrown June to the…wolves. And it wasn't as if the coven had ninjas at their disposal.

What they planned to do about her being resistant, she had no idea.

"What do you do with hags like her?" Gavin jerked his thumb at June, who quit twisting her wrists and ankles.

"We all find our wolf eventually." Bianca blinked at the fire, her profile limned by the blaze. "Except for challenges, this pack does not include violence in its ceremonies."

Gavin laughed. "Then you're in for a treat. This is my pack, baby, and a lot of things around here are going to change."

Bianca exchanged a look with the wolf lurking near the grills, or at least that's what it seemed she was doing. The four-leg let out a gruff and sank to the ground, nose on paws. Its eyes gleamed red in the firelight.

"Nothing to say to that, B? That's what I thought," he gloated. "A pack won't hold without a man in charge. This is how it's supposed to be. You'll thank me someday."

June doubted Bianca would thank Gavin for anything. Ever. Considering what Bianca had revealed earlier, June wouldn't be surprised if she were hatching
an evil plan to rid herself of Gavin, just as she might
have done with Bert.

Or was it evil, when it achieved a beneficial goal?
Did it mean the pack would be after Harry again soon?

Next time, June would be better prepared. If there
was a next time. She might be singing an entirely different song after tonight.

And she might be dead.

Gavin began stretching his calves. Did the ceremony involve running? If it did, Bianca required no
warm-up. She just stood there, glancing between the
flames and the bridge.

Watching. Waiting. Expecting.

Expecting what? Had someone tried to interrupt tonight's ceremony? Another challenger. The police. She
had to assume Harry hadn't been captured or they'd
have dragged him here to duke it out with Gavin.

Nothing like a little blood sport to make a commitment ceremony binding.

Or, apparently, a rape.

June's stomach roiled, its emptiness no guard
against nausea. She sawed at the tape on her hands,
knowing her movements were obvious but risking it
anyway. If she couldn't get her hands free, she had
zero chances for surviving this unscathed.

Her efforts were rewarded when a section of tape
parted, the rip loud enough that surely Bianca or Gavin

would hear. If not them, the shifters preparing the ceremonial beverages. Or the wolf near the grills, glaring at Gavin with lupine eyes. But nobody noticed.

Encouraged, she sawed more. Pushed harder. Wriggled her fingers and ankles. Started bumping her chair out of the circle again, easier now that she could grasp the slats and lift.

Every inch was closer to freedom. To escaping the circle of pine around the clearing. To that laurel bush growing beside the shed. It would have to do.

Gavin had obviously grown impatient. Bianca was obviously stalling. The sequence of events would be Gavin's confirmation followed by the pack bond portion of the night. Whether the two halves would be punctuated by her rape, June didn't want to find out. She, Harry, the coven, Bianca and her pack—all of them were adlibbing now.

How she hated adlibbing!

At least she had a secret weapon. Something inside her nobody would be expecting.

A few more inches of tape, a few more feet in the chair. June pulled her hands as hard as she could, and the tape yanked the hair on her forearms. She grabbed the rungs, lifted the chair and toed herself backward.

The legs of her chair brushed the pine. If she could scoot out of the circle and somehow, miraculously, be forgotten, the bonding magic wouldn't affect her.

A naked man June didn't recognize jogged to the log pile, added an armful of wood and began rounding the ring, shutting down kerosene lanterns. All remaining wolves disappeared from the circle or shifted up. Soon the only light was that of the bonfire.

In the darkness, June wrestled with the tape. Soon the only bit left was around her wrists. She rubbed her arms up and down, trying to squeeze out of the binding.

Bianca glanced at her watch and frowned. She clapped her hands.

"Let us gather." She motioned to her herbalists. One of them struck an iron triangle hanging near the table.

The clang shattered the silence. Wolves barked. People shouted. Excited voices converged on the courtyard. The herbalists ladled the Crock-Pots' contents into the paper cups they'd set out across the table surface.

June bumped her chair, pushing pine aside. Another foot. She was almost there.

Gavin bounced up and down. "I can't believe it. This is it."

His men entered the clearing, stepping over the pine ring. Maurice hung back like a censorious shadow. He focused on June a moment before taking a spot inside the branches.

Although it was obvious she was struggling to free herself, he did nothing—including help.

Adult shifters in varying states of undress entered the circle, each treading carefully over the pine. June had never seen so many bare bottoms in her life. Some walked past her. All ignored her. Many regarded Gavin with open hostility, lots of crossed arms and angry expressions.

Two rangy, black wolves darted into the clearing from the bridge. They halted outside the pine and barked.

"No wolves in the circle," Gavin yelled.

Both shimmered into nude bipedal forms. Neither appeared to be cowed by his outrage.

"That's better." He thrust out his chest. June recognized one of the men—Lionel. He crossed the ring and whispered to Bianca, who glanced at Gavin.

"What's going on?" Gavin demanded.

"Lionel was the last adult on the bridge. The juveniles are at their posts." Bianca tossed another baggie into the fire, this one sending up sparks and pops. "We can begin."

What happened to stalling? June had to get loose. Now.

The herbalist rang the triangle again. Shifters filtered around the circumference, linking by touch. They began to jockey for positions in a pecking order June couldn't decipher, but one that would eventually snake its way to her.

She made another desperate effort to pitch free and get her hands on the mountain laurel. The pine. Dirt. Anything. Her heart thudded so hard it felt unhealthy. She half rose and pushed with her toes, throwing herself back at the same time.

The chair legs caught on something, and the seat lurched. Tilted. June found herself falling until she came to an abrupt halt before her face had an unpleasant encounter with the ground.

She'd been caught by someone—someone strong and quick who didn't want her to hurt herself.

Her heart leaped. Was it…

No. The hands were smaller, the arms delicate, the scent flowery.

"Careful." Susan righted June. The woman was dressed like Bianca, in exercise apparel. Her exposed skin was pale, tinged orange by the light of the enormous bonfire. Her short curls matched the pale coat of the wolf June had been seeing all night. "You don't want to cut that pretty face."

The other woman didn't seem to be mocking her. She regarded June with kind eyes, her face unhappy. June couldn't blame her—the new alpha had assaulted her with a log.

"Get me out of here," she begged, one unhappy woman to another. "I'm a juvenile. I don't want to take this risk."

"I'm not the alpha." Susan's jaw firmed. "I don't get to make those decisions."

While they did monitor the wolves, covens interacted with local pack members as little as possible to cut down on the chance of recognition. Packs weren't attracted to covens like indie wolves, which made avoidance easier. June couldn't remember ever conversing with Susan, but her voice sounded familiar. So did the disappointment in it.

"Bianca doesn't want to include me," she told

Susan. "She wouldn't be mad if you sort of nudged me out of the circle."

"Bianca is only half the equation. Too bad Harry won't be the other half. He was perfect."

Harry was perfect. Where had she heard that phrase recently?

This morning—when Donna Manns telephoned her house looking for a mechanic.

That hadn't been Donna Manns. It had been Susan. How that knowledge could help June, she had no idea, so she asked, "How is Harry perfect?"

Susan gazed toward the bonfire. "Perfect for what we needed."

Susan too? There were hundreds of candidates all over. They weren't all Bert. Some were progressive, intelligent. Why did Millington's pack want Harry when he didn't want them?

"Don't you have any recessives in the pack?" June asked. Gavin wouldn't have been able to eliminate them like he had the candidates.

"No male recessives," Susan said, her voice dry. She pulled June's nightshirt down her thighs, covering her. "Not that it matters."

Before June could reflect on that, somebody grabbed her upper arm, linking her into the circle. Violet, irritation pouring from her like a heater. She didn't seem to care that her fingers bit into the flesh of June's arm.

On her other side, Susan placed a warm hand on her neck. There had to be some reason Bianca's lieutenants had picked spots on either side of her. She felt nothing magical—yet.

What would happen to her? Would they sense she was different? Would she wind up bonded to the pack as a witch? Or would she wind up an inconvenient dead body?

The herbalists began to pass Dixie cups around the circle. June struggled, but the shifters kept her in place. A few pine needles stuck to her clothes, nothing touching her skin, nothing she could use.

The only ones who looked happy were Gavin, some of his men and...Bianca.

Bianca?

"Welcome, my kith and kin," the female alpha said with a smirk. She waved away the cup offered to her. "Tonight we renew our commitment and connection. We cleanse the old. We welcome the new. Circle of life, blah blah blah. You know why we're here."

"I like the new speech," Violet whispered. "Pithy."

"Who wants to commemorate this?" Susan answered over June's head. "I'm sure next year will be as tedious as ever."

Violet's grip on June eased. "Don't give up yet, Sue. He's around here somewhere."

"Who?" June asked, but they ignored her.

While Gavin paced, Bianca strolled around the ring, making eye contact with each person. The cups progressed faster than she did until Susan held two of them, the green smell of peppermint reaching June's nose.

She twisted her arms, and one of her hands slid out of the restraint. Finally. She kept it hidden. Bianca reached Susan, June and Violet, touching Susan's hand where it rested against June's neck, before continuing onward.

"Enough," Gavin ordered. "The one-on-one crap comes later. Instate me."

Bianca returned to his side. Some might view her as obedient. Those people hadn't seen her face. Or her hands, curled into claws. "I suppose we have to do this. Is there anyone here who challenges Gavin Householder for the position of Millington pack alpha?"

Amid a sudden murmur of voices, a large gray wolf padded out of the shadows and into the firelight. He shimmered, stretching upward, until he solidified into a man. A lean, familiar man with a head of dark, shaggy hair and a smile that dared anyone to question his presence at the ceremony.

"I do."

CHAPTER EIGHTEEN

GAVIN RAMMED INTO Harry before he had a chance to aim the gun. The pistol flew out of his hand, skidding across the dirt into the pine boughs. Harry landed on his back, the other shifter's hands around his throat.

The bridge had been guarded by heavily armed young men when he'd reached it, and they hadn't so much as blinked when he trotted past. He'd crossed the swaying suspension bridge and approached the circle unchallenged.

Was it the spell or was his timing exquisite?

When he got to the ring, the two-legs parted to let him pass. Even though he was a wolf, even though he was breaking pack law, no one stopped him. Several had stroked his fur. Many had smiled. One woman had whispered, "Thank God."

But none could help him, and he'd just lost his primary advantage. His only advantage. He'd planned to force Gavin to stand down and take his place in the ceremony. Vern had been right about one thing. What did Harry care about the pack's opinion of him using a gun if it meant June was safe?

Being pack alpha would have been tricky enough,

but now it seemed he'd be lucky to survive the encounter.

Harry yanked at Gavin's wrists, and the other man squeezed harder. The packer's strength cut off his wind.

"Stop him," a woman screamed. "He'll kill Harry."

June. Was she all right? Harry had scented her but hadn't seen her. He dug his nails into Gavin's fingers, craning his head in her direction.

Not enough range of vision. All he accomplished was letting Gavin get a better grip.

"You dumbass." Gavin shook Harry, banging his head against the dirt. "I'm pack. I'm alpha. You're nobody. Your mother couldn't take me and neither can you."

Harry whipped up his knees, pounding Gavin in the back. The other man lurched forward. Harry slammed his skull into Gavin's face.

Bone crunched. Blood splattered.

"First blood to Smith," someone cheered.

Gavin let go of Harry long enough to punch him. Pain splintered through his head and he struck back, scrambling. He couldn't gain purchase in the blood streaking Gavin's arms.

Gavin, blood drizzling from his nose, got his hands back around Harry's neck and tightened. Spots appeared in Harry's vision, sparks of firelight. Was this going to be over before it started?

No time to be squeamish. Or sportsmanlike.

Harry was taller than Gavin. He went for the eyes.

Gavin howled and released his hold, protecting his face. Harry's instincts told him to shift to a wolf, fight with tooth and claw, but he wasn't the feral here.

Despite the shifters' worship of the wolf, the contest to rule a pack was between men. A gun Harry would risk. A shift would mark him for death—as if Gavin hadn't already done so.

Harry heaved the other man up and over, rolling toward the bonfire. The ring of mesmerized two-legs broke when Gavin tumbled near, none allowed to interfere once the challenge had begun.

Gavin grabbed a large branch from the circle, his muscles bulging as he ripped off limbs. Blood oozed from his nose and his eye was beginning to swell shut. Harry's throat and face ached with bruises. No doubt he looked as rough as Gavin.

No doubt he'd look a lot rougher after two more minutes of this.

They circled each other, Gavin thrusting with the wood. Harry spotted June, tossing a chair into the circle as if she hoped he could use it as a weapon, and ducked under a swing. Another. And another.

Barely.

He was not going to win a contest of strength. He had no idea where the gun was. Nor could he reach the chair June had thrown. He had to come up with something to stall so the coven could move into position. They'd told him they didn't have the power to put the pack to sleep, yet they promised they'd extract June if he played his part. It was all he had.

So he played.

"What the hell are you wearing, a rabbit?" he asked Gavin. His voice was gravelly. If he could make the other man angry, perhaps he'd become careless.

Gavin growled and advanced. Harry skidded to one side, nearly colliding with Bianca.

She didn't budge from her spot near the bonfire, a delighted smile stretching across her face.

"Chicken shit." Gavin bared his teeth. "You're going to die tonight, Lapin. Finally."

How could anyone say Harry was chicken when he'd challenged a shifter who was the odds-on favorite? Indie versus packer? He was surprised he'd lasted as long as he had.

Harry danced away from the branch, letting it smack his hands. He tried to yank it free, but Gavin had momentum. The flesh on Harry's palms ripped on the sharp wood.

"I love it when men fight over me," Bianca taunted.

Harry wasn't sure if she intended to rile him or Gavin. The other man knew Harry was the pack's choice—knew he wasn't wanted. Why was Bianca so pleased by this unbalanced fight? What did she know that Harry didn't?

Gavin threw the log at Harry and used the distraction to close on him. His fist caught Harry in the gut.

Air whooshed out of his lungs. Harry threw himself sideways to avoid an uppercut to the jaw. The blow glanced off his shoulder. Gavin swung again, missed and caught Harry's arm when he attempted to reciprocate.

He wrenched it upward, trying to twist it behind Harry's back. Harry dropped instead and pitched Gavin over his shoulder.

When Gavin landed, it was Harry's turn to pin him to the ground, hands around the other man's throat. Gavin gagged and clawed. Harry felt a burst of triumph, a primal urge to squeeze the life out of his opponent. The flesh, the bones of the throat, compressed beneath his fingers.

But Gavin was pack, and Harry was not. The other man threw Harry off. Blows rained on his head and shoulders, savage blows. The fists stopped, Harry caught his breath, and suddenly Gavin was flying through the air feet first like a ninja.

Harry didn't duck in time. The unexpected attack snapped his head back. Felled him like a tree. Nausea rose in his gorge and he remembered Vern's advice to shift. But shifting would mean failure, maybe death, if he couldn't outrun Gavin and the pack.

He wouldn't run. He couldn't see June anywhere and hoped she'd escaped to the coven, who should be here. Yet there was no sign of them.

He struggled to rise. Gavin's body slammed him to the dirt. The move was showy but effective.

Harry's head thwacked the ground. Gavin squashed his stomach all the way to his spine. He doubled up like a pretzel, and Gavin punched him back.

Harry hit the ground. Again. Blackness tunneled his

vision. Gavin's leering face and crimson scar loomed over him as hands closed around his head. Lifted.

He was going to snap Harry's neck. Harry focused on the scar and thought about how good it must have felt to his mother to put it there. It would be the final sight he'd take to his grave.

"No!" A body pelted into Gavin, knocking him off Harry.

"What the hell?" Gavin tried to sling June aside, but she clung to him like a furious cat and jabbed him in the face with a twig.

What the hell? She shouldn't have come back. Harry crawled to his feet, gasping. There was damage to his windpipe. He couldn't suck a full breath. Hot pokers of agony seared his lungs—broken ribs.

"No interference from the pack." Gavin whirled, trying to rip June off his back.

"I'm not pack, I can do whatever I want," she yelled.

Gavin grabbed her hair and she squealed. "Somebody get this crazy bitch off me."

Her cry energized Harry. He darted in and punched Gavin in the mouth so hard it cut his hand.

Gavin's head whipped sideways. He remained standing, occupied now with fending Harry off instead of pulling June's hair.

She jabbed Gavin's good eye with her stick.

"This bitch is dead. They're both dead." He wrestled away from Harry toward the fire. "Get her off me, Bianca."

"Hell no, this is the best ceremony ever." Bianca

tossed a baggie of herbs into the flames while June shoved a leaf into Gavin's mouth.

The air around Harry bulged with shouts and sound, pushing him from every side. Then came a pop. The bonfire flared.

Gavin bit June and she cried out, snatching her hand free. Blood dripped from her fingers. He threw her off. She skidded across the dirt toward Harry. He tried to pick her up, but pain lanced him so sharply he nearly blacked out.

She was flat on her back, her blue eyes huge. Furious. A bruise darkened one side of her face and she clutched her hand. "Drink one of the Dixie cups."

Harry spotted a white cup in the hand of a shifter and ran. Gavin slammed into him from behind before he got to the edge of the circle.

The two of them stumbled forward, crashing into the shifters who didn't get out of the way fast enough. The coveted cup flew through the air, its contents spilling in an arc. Harry fell face-first into the pine. Branches scattered.

Gavin kicked him in the side, breaking another rib. Harry curled up to protect himself and flexed his hands, intending to grab Gavin's foot on the next blow.

It landed in the center of his back instead.

Something snapped. An agony so intense it whitened Harry's vision swept over him. When he could see, when he could breathe again, he realized he couldn't feel his legs.

Gavin grabbed his hair and yanked his head up.

"Something wrong, Johnny boy?" Then he let Harry's head drop into the pine. "Choices, choices. Do I break his neck? Rip his guts out?"

Murmurs, growls, rose around them, but the pack continued to obey custom.

And again, June felt no such restrictions.

She darted between Gavin and Harry, limping. Behind her back, she held a small cup, which she poured in Harry's face. The minty liquid trickled into his mouth. He licked and swallowed, the taste more pleasant than blood and anguish.

June, posture stiff, pointed at Gavin and Bianca both. "It doesn't have to be like this. You choose to be savages."

She crouched beside Harry and put her hand on his chest. He felt another surge of magic. His whole body seemed to inflate like a balloon before it sank, back into a world of pain. Did the other shifters feel the magic? Did they realize what she'd done?

Speaking of which, what had she done? He still hurt. He still had no sensation in his lower half.

"It will be like this because I want it to be." Gavin faked a lunge at her, laughing when she gasped. She still had on the nightshirt from this morning. No shoes. Her calves were scraped, dirty. Harry wanted to tell her that he loved her, that he was sorry he couldn't save her, but no words came out of his mouth.

The numbness in his legs crept up his body.

"You can have the pack." June stumbled away from Gavin. The ring of shifters watched. Waited. "Take it. Harry and I will go far away and never bother you again."

"But I want him dead, and what I want, I get." Gavin spread his arms. "I'll let you live. Maybe."

"Don't touch him," June warned.

"How about I touch you?" He lunged again, this time with greater intent.

She didn't have a chance. Harry couldn't get up. Gavin ripped June's nightshirt and threw her onto the ground in front of Harry. He could smell her blood, even through his own.

He could sense her pain, her determination.

"It's okay. They're here. I know what to do," she whispered before Gavin dragged her across the dirt, her fingers raking the surface.

Harry couldn't tear his gaze away. Gavin kneeled and hoisted June's hips into the air even as she fought him. He leaned over her body and grabbed her neck. "How do you want him to see it, bitch? You want to suck it or take it up the ass?"

Harry felt his hackles stir and anger twist through his body. A different anger. A protective one. His nails bit into his flesh as he fisted his hands. The ground rumbled. He realized he was growling so deeply it hurt his throat.

Why was no one helping her? This wasn't part of the challenge.

"Let go of me." June glanced at Harry, her face pale. Almost greenish.

Gavin shook her. Her hair tumbled around her face

as she bounced forward, hiding her expression. "No can do. Johnny needs to understand who's in charge here before I kill him." He raised his voice. "This whole pack needs to understand I make the rules now."

Voices buzzed in Harry's ears. He snarled—at Gavin, at all the shifters standing around, letting this happen. His wrath intensified when no one intervened.

Gavin bent over June's struggling form, one hand securing her hair. His scar blazed like fire, twisting his face into a demonic mask. "You think you can save her? Well, get up. Come on. Save her. Fate worse than death. I'm going to pound her so hard she bleeds."

Harry tried. Shards of agony lanced down his legs. He welcomed it. He'd figured they would stay numb until he shifted—if he ever shifted again.

Gavin unlaced his breechclout, his dick popping free. "How's her hole, loser? Is she tight and hot or is she a flappy whore?"

"Oh, Goddess. That's just… I'm going to be sick." June convulsed and vomited, greenish liquid spewing from her mouth.

Raising his head, and thankful he had the mobility to do it, Harry glanced around. The pack was transfixed. Many appeared uneasy or angry. Was it standard procedure for their alpha to rape and murder as he pleased? He'd known the Millington pack was primitive, but not degenerate and evil.

"Somebody stop this," Harry managed.

Gavin cuffed June in the head. "Quit puking."

Whispers. Rustling. As the pack stared with growing revulsion at Gavin, no one except Harry noticed coven members dressed in camouflage snatching Dixie cups off the ground before disappearing into the shadows.

What was going on?

Harry's feet began to tingle. His next breath hurt less than the previous one.

June shuddered one last time before spitting on the ground. Gavin watched her with disgust on his face. "You make me sick."

"That's the idea," she croaked, a sly smile on her face.

Gavin smacked her thigh and grabbed her panties. "You think a little puke will stop me after you broke my pack rules?"

"Whoa now." Bianca, finally, approached. "It's not your pack yet."

Gavin glanced at her but kept a hold on June. "You're a lot of trouble, you know that, B? First I have to convince Pop to leave Roanoke so we can help your incompetent ass find the runner you lost. Then I find Harry when you can't, and I let him go because he's not worth crap. You need me."

"You didn't come to help with the lockdown. You came because you thought you had a chance at pack alpha." Behind Bianca, several figures broke rank and stood silhouetted against the flickering bonfire. "Douglas is desperate to get you out of his pack without banishing you. He had to be desperate, to come deep into my territory and pull this stunt with you. Don't pretend to be noble."

Gavin pushed June into the dirt and shoved his foot in her back. Harry caught her gaze. She didn't seem as horrified as he would have expected.

"That may be true," Gavin drawled, "but how about after I kill your precious Harry, I walk? You ran Dad off this morning, so I've got a day before I lose my juice. Mom would take me back, no matter what Pop wants. Then your whole pack will dissolve around you and you won't be able to do a thing about it."

Bianca startled, as if that hadn't occurred to her. "You wouldn't."

"Good God, B, do you think nobody knows you set Bert up? Like I want to be next on your hit list."

She paced out of Harry's view, her voice uncharacteristically tentative. "I don't know what you're talking about."

"You tipped off the cops when he was on the job."

"He was my husband. That's ridiculous." She returned to stand between the shifters who'd broken rank, her back to Gavin. The bonfire danced. An owl called. No one else in the circle so much as whispered.

Harry didn't think it sounded ridiculous. He just wondered why it hadn't occurred to him before.

"I overheard the cops talking when I was at that old bat's house. Not hard to put two and two together." Gavin noticed June raising her head and pushed her face back into the dirt.

Bianca conferred with the others, one grabbing her

shoulder urgently. They changed position enough that Harry could see it was Susan, which probably made the other one Violet.

While Gavin gloated, Harry bent his legs. His ribs tortured him, but the paralysis he'd feared seemed to be fading. He fingered his midsection, assessing the damage. Would he be able to attack Gavin one last time?

"It doesn't matter, anyway." Gavin smacked June's ass. Harry gathered himself to lunge. God, this was going to hurt. "I got me a new alpha bitch here. If you don't make me real happy, Bianca, you're not the only one who has a hit list."

Bianca stalked toward him. "I won't allow this."

"Heard that one before. You don't have a choice. I'm in charge unless you want to lose the pack, and I'm going to—" He paused, shutting his mouth with a deep frown. "I am going to—"

Vomit.

Gavin threw up green bile, and June scrambled out of the way, straight to Harry.

"Temporary," she murmured. "Be ready." She patted his hips, finding the pill bottle in his jeans pocket. She withdrew it and fed them both one.

Harry gagged it down, the dry swallow difficult.

"What the hell have you and June been eating?" Bianca asked.

"I haven't—" Gavin puked again, a third time, a fourth time. A lot more than June had. He clutched his stomach and moaned.

His misery invigorated Harry. That or the pill. Relief coursed through his tortured limbs. It was like...

Magic.

June tugged his hand. He rolled to his feet. Energy filled him, energy and power like he'd never felt before. The coven's restoratives were amazing.

He turned to the closest man wearing clothes. There weren't many. They all had to shift at the end of the ceremony, and clothes were a hindrance.

"Give her your shirt." He motioned toward June, who'd wrapped her arms around her bare breasts.

The man obeyed without question.

Gavin bent with his hands on his knees, heaving. Harry tested his ribs. The pain barely registered.

"You have to kill him," Bianca said to Harry conversationally. "It's what you came here to do."

"I came for June." He'd intended to sacrifice himself, one way or another, but June's safety was paramount.

Bianca shrugged. "Same difference."

"Not sure about that." Harry's heart thumped against his chest as he considered Gavin, weakened by whatever June had done. Did the pack realize there was a supernatural force involved in Gavin's condition?

It seemed unfair to defeat a man handicapped by magic. Of course it also seemed unfair to defeat him using a gun, but now Harry didn't need it. He didn't even need to shift to heal his injuries.

What was in that pill? Would it last? He had to free

June and get himself instated as alpha as quickly as possible.

Harry turned to Bianca. "She walks or I don't step up."

Bianca straightened. "She walks."

"You can't be pack alpha." June tugged his arm. "You and me, Harry, we'll go somewhere. Canada. South America. You don't want to be pack. This isn't fair."

He cupped her sweet face in his hands and kissed her forehead. Her breath smelled oddly of mountain laurel. "I promised your friends. This is the bargain I made. I'm taking Gavin's place."

"Harry's not going anywhere," Bianca said.

"You don't need my friends' help. I'll help you. Don't do this," June begged. Tears glistened on her eyelashes as she fought not to cry. "I'll lose you. We'll lose each other."

"Girl, can the melodrama," Bianca said with an exasperated sigh. "You can be with your boyfriend all you want. I don't care. I'm not going to marry him. I just need him to balance the pack."

"She's definitely not going to marry him," Susan added. She and Violet had followed Bianca from the fire to support their alpha.

No marriage, no argument, no issues with him having a girlfriend. Was the pack more modern than he realized? If so, why had they allowed the brutal pack challenge and Gavin's abuse of June to go on as long as it had?

The whole situation infuriated Harry. He was going to be a terrible alpha, but at least June and the witches would be safe. It was in the coven's best interest to have a sympathetic alpha in charge. One they could bend to their will, which he hoped was benign.

He trusted June and Annette, but Vern was another story.

"June won't be joining us," Harry informed everyone. "She is going to walk out of here and nobody is going to stop her." He eyed Gavin, gasping for air. Gavin would be confined until he got severed from his old pack and lost his powers. The men who'd planned to join up with him could get the hell back to Roanoke. In fact, they must have already sensed the tenor of the group, because they were no longer in the circle.

June shook her head. "I'm not leaving you."

"Yes, you are." Harry felt powerful enough to command a regiment. He allowed his alpha side free rein. Unfair advantage? He didn't care about that any more than he'd cared about running. Changing his name. Cultivating grannies in a tea room. Looking like a coward with a gun. The only thing that mattered was keeping her safe.

To his surprise, June turned on her heel and started walking, a stricken expression on her face. She didn't even hug him goodbye.

A pang struck his heart. He ignored it.

"Whoa. I noticed that a minute ago," Bianca commented, her eyebrows raised. She was actually surprised; he could smell it. "Spoken like you're already a pack alpha. You are independent, right?"

"You know I am." Harry watched June tiptoe through the ring, fighting every step—but stepping away from him. Another couple of feet. Another. Would he ever see her again?

"You haven't always been. According to Gavin your name's John Lapin."

"That doesn't change anything."

"True. But…" Taking him by surprise, Bianca swiped a finger through a rivulet of blood on his face and stuck it into her mouth.

"What are you doing?" Blood exchange was sometimes part of a bonding ritual. He hoped he didn't have to bite anyone. He'd tasted enough blood for one night.

In the corner of his eye, he noticed June struggling at the pine barrier. Her gaze was focused on something in the woods, something he couldn't see, even with vision that seemed preternaturally accurate.

Hearing that seemed exceptionally sharp.

The scents coming to him were as distinct as when he was in wolf form.

The coven surrounded them. When he concentrated, he could hear them. Smell them. Each one, familiar to him. Each one, almost a part of him, in some way he didn't understand.

His skin, everything inside him, sizzled with power. It flowed into him from his feet. From the air. From inside.

"You're not independent. You're too strong." Bianca

backed away, halting between her seconds. "What are you?"

"What am I?" Harry inhaled, exhaled. All the scent markers in the area were like beacons. He would never forget a single one of these people. "I'm your alpha-to-be, just like you wanted. Come over here and let's get this over with."

She lurched forward at his command, stopping herself with some effort. "This isn't right. I don't want someone who can—"

"Who can what?" Harry grasped her arm, not hard, but enough to keep her in place. "Why did you hunt me? The truth this time."

"Because you're weak," Bianca confessed through gritted teeth.

"You thought I was weak? Pathetic?" That might not have offended Harry a day ago, but it offended the hell out of him now. Strength flowed through him like ocean currents. "Surprise."

She cast her gaze at Susan, who radiated distress.

"Harry, you don't understand," Bianca continued, a bit desperately. "No one thinks you're pathetic. We picked you because you were our guarantee. We didn't want the risks involved in the application process, and we didn't want another Bert who expected to rule the pack. Me. Everything."

He stared at her, not sure he was hearing her right. This was a whole new level of canniness on Bianca's part. "You picked me because you wanted a figure-head?"

"Most male alphas are archaic, at least the ones who want to be pack alphas. We hoped you'd step back and let us handle things."

"You handled this great," he snapped. Even as a figurehead, he'd be tied to the pack in a way he loathed. The bond could only change so much about a shifter's psychological underpinnings, not to mention his likes and dislikes. "I guess it's a good thing you're making me take over. I could hardly do worse. Thanks for ruining both our lives."

"I don't want to—" Bianca clapped a hand over her mouth.

"What?" He couldn't believe how easy it was to force the words out of others now. It had never worked this way before. "Answer me."

"I don't want to be with you," she said finally.

"And I don't want to be with you, but you haven't given either of us a choice. Unless you want him." He pointed at Gavin, on his hands and knees now, his body shiny with sweat. His skin rippled as he dry heaved, almost like he was trying to change into his wolf.

He was no longer a threat.

"I'd rather be stuck with you," Bianca said. "Are you going to be an asshole?"

"Probably," he growled, because he was angry, and because he felt like an asshole. So what if he'd never been much of one before this?

"I don't care if you're stronger than me, I won't marry you. Don't expect me to." She regarded Harry warily. Harry, who was nothing but an independent. Harry, whom she claimed she'd wanted because he was weak and now didn't want because he was strong. "Him, on the other hand—he's a rapist. Kill him."

"No." Harry had to admit, he wouldn't mind if Gavin were dead, but murdering a man when it wasn't self-defense—no one could make him do that. "If he survives severance, get proof about the rapes and report him to the cops. That should be enough. I gather you're good at that."

She kind of smiled, her teeth sharp. "It was for the pack, Harry. You'll see."

He didn't want to see, and he didn't care why Bert was in prison. "Lock Gavin up until we have time to deal with him. Get him out of the circle."

Bianca's lips tightened into a white line. "We'll get the chains." She tilted her head at Susan, who dashed into the darkness.

"You there—reform the circle."

Shifters leaped to obey, reassembling the pine in an unbroken circumference. Surprised comments trickled past Harry's ears as several looked for their herb shots and couldn't find them. He had no idea what the coven had wanted them for, but they hadn't done anything since they'd taken the cups.

They were just out there. Waiting.

Waiting like June, outside the ring at the edge of the firelight, her huge eyes focused on him.

Bianca touched his shoulder. "You have to send her away if she's not going to join us."

"She can't join us." He closed his eyes so he couldn't see June's face. *I love you. Be well.*

CHAPTER NINETEEN

"HARRY," JUNE CALLED to him, her voice quivering, "you need me. It's wearing off."

"What is?" His energy level? His strength? Those were undiminished. He was buoyed by power. He didn't need his eyes to feel her fear. Waves of color and force swooshed behind his lids. He could sense the shifters around him, tension levels high; he could sense the coven, their essences an open book.

How had he never realized his friends were kin? Annette and Peter and Vern and so many others. He knew each of them, and it was obvious. They were his network. His group. His circle. He strained for comprehension just out of reach.

They were his pack. His strength was coming from them.

A heavy weight crashed into his back and sharp teeth ripped his skin. Harry twisted and fell.

Unlike before, when the violence had elicited nothing but heavy silence, several shifters screamed. Gavin, in wolf form, snarled and howled. His saliva, Harry's blood, splattered in all directions.

Bianca cursed and barked out orders. "Son of a

dog. He's feral. Hunters, find the Roanokers, make
sure they aren't tainted. The rest of you, protect the
children. I'll take care of this."

Adrenaline buzzed in Harry's hearing. He hit the
ground for the hundredth time that night. In wolf form,
Gavin savaged him, more powerful and bestial than
when he'd been a man.

Gavin had lost control. Lost his reason. Lost his
right to call himself a shifter. He would kill anyone
who got in his way now, starting with Harry.

It wasn't the first time. Harry knew that, even if no
one else here did.

The only thing he could do to defend against Gavin
was shift or he wouldn't last a minute. Didn't matter
how strong he was, how much power was in him. Four-
legs triumphed over two-legs every time in a fight.

In a fight without a gun.

Damn.

The change wasn't easy with Gavin tearing holes in
his flesh. Unlike a normal shift, it took too much time.
There was no instant flicker of transformation. He got
stuck halfway, healing, being hurt, healing—he was
losing his grip on the magic. Gavin closed giant teeth
on his throat and he knew it was too late.

Harry was form stuck as a man. He was dying,
breathing his last.

Until a surge of energy came from the coven, and
he pushed himself into his wolf.

Gavin's teeth snapped on his ruff. Harry scrambled
to his feet, his body sore, his wounds present but no

longer life-threatening. Vitality streamed into him, a Zen calm that allowed him to assess the situation and everything in it.

June and the coven members stepped into the ring, power rippling off them in waves Harry suspected no two-leg could see.

Bianca, in slow motion, ran for the exit.

Violet, near the bonfire, fed it…something. Then ran.

Susan, with a set of chains, crouched on her knees as if she were about to shift.

Adult shifters dashed into the shadows, away from Harry and Gavin, no longer frozen by tradition. No one wanted to be near a wolf who'd lost himself to rage. They would secure the juveniles first, deal with the feral second.

All this Harry absorbed in a split second, and he chose his course of action.

Dominate.

Failing that, eliminate.

His gaze locked with Gavin's, the other wolf's eyes white as snow and just as cold. He was a big animal, bigger than Harry, his coat rough and dark. The red flesh of his scar had transferred to his wolf.

Back off, Harry ordered.

Gavin shook his head, droplets of Harry's blood slinging free. He crouched, but not in submission. A menacing growl reverberated from him.

Harry hadn't interacted much with shifters in wolf form. Sometimes he ran with wolves, played. He'd never been in a four-leg confrontation, which wasn't unusual for an indie.

If he was an indie anymore. With the coven feeding him, he felt like something else.

Back off, he ordered again, accenting it with a deep, commanding bark.

Gavin's ears flattened against his head and his reddened muzzle wrinkled.

This time Harry lunged first.

He bowled the other wolf over, snapping and growling. Gavin's movements were fast, lightning fast, but Harry was faster.

He set his teeth in Gavin's throat. Blood spurted into his mouth.

He wasn't expecting the metallic burst, and he gagged. His jaw loosened enough that Gavin ripped himself free.

Only long enough to jump Harry again. Sharp claws raked his back. Gavin's teeth clamped on his muzzle, cutting him from lip to eye. Red blurred Harry's vision on one side. He contorted his body, flipping Gavin off.

Instead of giving Gavin a chance to regroup, Harry trounced him. He missed the throat, latched on to an ear.

Gavin yelped, his first sound of pain. His claws tore Harry's foreleg to the bone. He wrenched away, leaving part of his ear in Harry's mouth.

Gavin tried coming at him from the side. Harry twisted into the air and landed on him, biting his neck. From the top, the ruff was thinner. Harry's teeth sank in.

This time he was ready for the blood.

Gavin rolled. Harry slipped to the side but hung on to the skin, chewing and choking his opponent. He shook his head brutally, whipping Gavin back and forth. He wasn't bigger, but he was smarter. And he was, right now, stronger.

Gavin stumbled to the side but couldn't free himself. They crashed into a table, sending condiments in every direction. When he fell, Harry slashed his side. His claws scraped Gavin's ribs.

Gavin let out a series of yelps, frantic to escape. Harry bit harder. Salty, hot blood rushed into his mouth.

The other wolf coughed and whined. After one last attempt to lurch away, he rolled again, onto his back, as far as he could with Harry gripping his skin. Gavin's tail wrapped around his privates and he ceased to struggle.

It was over. Harry shook and released, leaping on the other wolf and poising over his underbelly. If he dug in, he could disembowel Gavin in seconds. He'd never done it before, but unlike in human form, fighting as a wolf was instinctive.

Blood matted them both. Harry could only see out of one eye, but the skin at Gavin's throat flapped open. Harry was clearly the victor.

He growled and affixed his teeth in Gavin's throat.

Gavin urinated on himself, the acrid stench filling

Harry's nostrils, cutting through the copper whang of blood. The other wolf made no move to fight back. His body shivered beneath Harry in fear. One crunch of Harry's jaws, and Gavin would be history.

And he, Harry, would be a killer.

With another growl, he hunkered away from Gavin, shaking his head. Blood dripped from numerous wounds. He stared at Susan, who still had the chains, and barked. Things might get dicey because he wouldn't be able to shift anytime soon. As he understood it, the upcoming ceremony required him to be on two legs.

After holding his gaze for a minute, Susan nodded. Harry didn't miss that she failed to lower her gaze in submission. A strong, quiet one, maybe a recessive. She began unlocking the thick, iron bindings in order to cuff the vanquished wolf.

Harry glanced around with his single eye. Besides Susan, the only people in the clearing were coven, but he could hear the shifters whispering, wondering, waiting. They'd return with guns if the alphas and their seconds couldn't handle the feral.

Good. That meant fewer people would notice the coven lending him strength. How had the witches known they were his pack and could give him power? Had they bonded to save him or was this one of their spells?

What would happen to them when he switched allegiances to the new pack?

Harry trotted to June, who stood between Annette

and Vern, and stared up at her. She kneeled in front of him. "You don't have to do this. Let the pack dissolve. They don't deserve you."

He couldn't answer her, so he licked her face. The smell of the other man's shirt nearly made him snap at the cloth. Her dried tears were saltier than Gavin's blood.

Beside them, he heard Susan advance on Gavin, still passively on his back. Harry hoped Gavin appreciated the fact he'd been spared. Other packs might have terminated him and Harry both for succumbing to the shift during a challenge, but Millington didn't have that luxury. They needed two alphas in place before this night was over.

"Since you're so good at shifting, it's time to shift back," Susan told Gavin coldly. "Or you can go in a woodshed. Your choice."

Instead of obeying, Gavin vaulted off the ground, straight for Susan's throat. She was a small woman. Gavin was a large, fast wolf.

Harry darted for them, but he was too late. Gavin landed on Susan and bit down. Her terrified keen faded quickly to a gurgle.

And then a succession of deafening cracks exploded through the clearing, sending Gavin tumbling to one side as if a sledgehammer had struck him.

It wasn't a sledgehammer. Bianca stood at the edge of the clearing with Harry's gun and a black expression.

Susan's body shimmered as she tried to shift away

her injuries. It was taking too long. Veils of color radiated over her body. She struggled for breath. Harry could smell death on the air, death on the wind. Gavin alone? Or would Susan join him?

June started forward, but Annette grabbed her arm, stopping her.

"We can't," Annette whispered. "I'm sorry, honey, we can't."

Bianca glared at Harry, her scent marker fierce and wild. Susan's body finally collapsed into a small, pale wolf, her coat wavy and her throat bloody.

"You did this," Bianca spat. "I told you to kill him. We know how to deal with dead bodies. Is that what stopped you or are you missing your balls?"

Harry lowered his head but felt no guilt for his mercy. He'd do the same thing again. He was, indeed, going to make a terrible pack alpha. These weren't decisions he wanted on his shoulders. They weren't decisions he felt equipped to make. But here he was.

Bianca cursed him, stroking the side of the small wolf. "You could have prevented this. Now she's dying. Oh, God, she can't die! Susan, no. Susan, don't die."

Tears streamed down Bianca's face. Harry had no urge to submit to her, but because he wasn't slave to his instincts, slave to a pack—yet; because he knew it was the right thing to do, he crept to her side, sank to the ground and whined.

Bianca waved him off. "Stuff it, Harry. I know you're faking."

"You love her," June said to Bianca. "She's your mate."

"You're a genius." Bianca wiped tears off her face, her movements abrupt. "Sorry we won't be adding your vast IQ to the betterment of the pack. Who are these people, more indies? Just what I need in my territory. Organized indies. We're not city wolves. We're not sharing our space. I will tell you right now, I have no problem killing people who get in my way."

What Harry could smell belied that. Her scent was pungent with grief but also horror. She had wanted him to kill Gavin so she didn't have to do it herself. Just like she hadn't been able to arrange an unfortunate accident for Bert, so she'd arranged something less deadly.

"If she dies, I will never forgive you," Bianca told Harry, her voice cracking. "I will never obey you. I will never support you. I will never rest until you suffer. I will never—"

"You will never shut up." Vern squatted on the other side of the small wolf. "Who wants to live with that? Give her this." He held out a large brown pill.

Bianca glared at him. "Why would I do that?"

"Because you don't want your girlfriend to kick it?"

She sniffed, eyes narrow. "You're the busboy at the tea room."

"And you're a bitch. If you won't do it, I will." He pried at Susan's slender muzzle, shoving the large pill into the back of her throat. Her ribcage heaved up once and her body stiffened.

And then nothing.

Bianca vaulted over Susan's body and flattened Vern quicker than Harry had ever seen anyone move in his life. "I just killed one bastard. I don't even know you and I can tell you're a bastard."

"Erk," Vern said. "I hef to..." He coughed and gasped. Bianca growled in his face. If she'd been in wolf form, Vern might already be dead.

"I can do it," June offered.

"Save your strength, sugar." Annette rolled up her sleeves. "Vern, I swan. Two hundred years old, and you're still an impulsive idiot. Pete and I will handle this."

Annette and her husband sat by the wolf. Harry licked Susan's throat, wishing he could help. He couldn't even dial 9-1-1, and they wouldn't treat an animal anyway. He didn't know Susan well, but she tasted like someone who deserved to live.

Annette and Pete placed their hands on the wolf. A shrill whine pierced the air that none of the two-legs appeared to hear.

Harry howled in pain. June limped to his side, touching his fur. Then his ears popped.

Annette quirked an eyebrow at him. "You're sure sensitive. Okay, well, I'm fresh out. You out, Pete?"

"I'm more than out. That was close." Pete rose, knees creaking. He yawned and rubbed his eyes. "She'll be okay."

The wolf beneath their hands rolled stiffly into a sitting position. She nuzzled Bianca on the neck.

Bianca released Vern with a disgusted heave. "You're still a bastard." Then she hugged Susan, burying her face in the wolf's ruff.

Harry had felt the vigor of those pills himself, but this was incredible. Was it the pills, then, that made him feel so strong?

He didn't think so. His wounds were not all healed and he felt the same connection to the coven that had boosted him through his confrontation with Gavin.

He was right. They were his pack.

And he was about to leave them for another.

They smelled regretful, as he knew he did, but he sensed no worry from them. Not anymore.

When June straightened, Harry stuck to her, pressing her legs. If this was his last chance to be around her while knowing how he felt about her, he was going to touch her as much as he could. The coven wanted to make him forget after he joined the pack. He hadn't agreed, but he wasn't sure he could stop them.

Either way, it was time for him to uphold his end of the bargain and become alpha here. Time to say goodbye.

"Bianca," June said, "Susan's a recessive, isn't she?"

Bianca glanced up. "So?"

June picked up a Dixie cup and poked her finger into the contents, stirring it. "You need a partner to balance the energies of the pack. Does it have to be Harry?"

"Do you see any other candidates around here? I

just see a bunch of…I don't know what you people are
You obviously know about us."

"We do," June agreed. "We're not a risk to your
pack or to any shifters. I swear it. As long as you're
not a risk to…us."

"You're not lying." Bianca nibbled her lip as she
hugged Susan. "You're a juvenile, June, but the rest of
you don't smell right. I have a good nose."

"I know you do." June rubbed Harry's ears gently,
avoiding the sore spots. She exchanged a glance with
Annette. "Normally I don't adlib. I hate to adlib. But
I do have an idea."

CHAPTER TWENTY

AFTER HELPING BIANCA with a revised ceremony that instated Susan as the second alpha, June and Harry accepted a ride from Annette back to Millington. Or, June accepted it on their behalf. Harry was form stuck and cross about it, growling at everyone but her.

"I think that went well," Annette said as the mini-van trundled up a steep grade. "The poppy in June's spell should fuzz their memories enough that they think they came up with the bright idea to boost Susan themselves. They'll think Harry's indie friends rescued him, but they'll have a little trouble remembering faces and scent markers. It works out great."

"Should we talk about details in front of the dog?" Vern protested from the back.

Harry gruffed at him, and June wished she could too. Vern was not only a coven elder but a region elder; he just didn't behave like one.

"He already knows everything," she reminded them. She and Harry rode in the middle seat, his big, hairy body pressed against her like a winter coat. "Sorry to talk about you like you're not here, Harry."

His skin twitched, the lupine equivalent of a shrug.

"Whatever." Vern clicked the buckle on his seat belt repeatedly. "As you say, he is sitting right here. We'll talk about this when he's not."

"There's no need to talk because we're not going to erase him." June poured some alpha into the announcement. It didn't seem fair to force her and Harry back to status quo—her as Sandie, Harry as her friend.

Nothing but friends.

There weren't enough libido-dampening spells in the world to counteract her love for him now that she'd taken the final step. If she and Harry ended up on the lam, their progress was going to be hindered by the fact that, between the two of them, they owned no functional vehicles.

No one responded to June's assertion for a long, awkward moment. Vern continued to snick his seat belt, and Harry growled irritably, but he'd been doing that so much they ignored him.

Pete changed the subject to distract them from the growing tension. "I didn't know you could do that with lavender and parsley. Convince people to do things they wouldn't normally do."

"*We* can't. June can." Annette patted her husband on the shoulder. "I wonder if it's connected to her being an alpha? She's always been stronger than the rest of us."

Vern's seat belt rat-a-tat halted. "Not stronger than me."

"I didn't force them to do it. They were willing to take the risk."

"Sure they were." He laughed. "They thought you

were crazy when you suggested it. You mind-wham-mied them into submission."

June shook her head. "I gave them the confidence it would work and lowered everyone's resistance to change. Bianca told me a willing heart helps a cer-emony succeed."

"That's touchy-feely B.S. I have a theory."

"About what I did?" June asked sharply. Usually she took Vern's competitiveness in stride, but right now she wanted to lavender and parsley *him*. Unlike the mountain laurel she'd used on Gavin, the con-fidence spell hadn't rebounded, which indicated it wasn't harmful.

"No, about you in general." Vern leaned on the seat-back between June and Harry. "If you're strong be-cause you're alpha, I bet the alpha gene makes you resistant. How can I find out if I'm an alpha?"

"Great," Annette grumbled. "Casanova thinks he's going to get himself a shifter girlfriend."

"You live as long as I have," he said, "you'll try anything once."

Harry sniffed Vern in the head and sneezed.

"Bark three times if I'm da man," Vern said to him. "Do you think Bianca and Susan would be interested in a hottie sandwich?"

Harry snapped at Vern, and the witch slung himself back into his seat. "Does he bite?"

"Yes," June said.

"Does he have rabies?"

"Vernon, would you act your age?" Annette

snapped. "You're worse than a teenager fighting the change."

They finally reached the main road in Cranberry Jetty. The other coven members had departed before them, so they were the only ones on the highway at this hour. They would all go home for some much-needed sleep except for Pete, who had to conclude the investigation into Sandie's disappearance before his comrades on the force discovered anything revealing. June would stay hidden until she could muster the strength for her Sandie disguise.

Unless she didn't need it anymore. She was considering sending Sandie to a retirement community in Florida—a time-honored choice for coven members ready to be young again—and starting her second pass-through as June Travis, Sandie's granddaughter.

And girlfriend of local mechanic Harry Smith.

Assuming he was interested in something that serious. The past several days had been so hectic, there had been no discussion of what would happen when they returned to their real lives.

A knot formed in her stomach. Harry might not be interested. She'd never known him to date anybody longer than a couple months. As if sensing her worries, he snuffled her neck, his whiskers tickling her skin.

Pete swiveled in his seat, his arm around the headrest. "The thing with Gavin isn't going to cause a pack war, is it? The ugliness that went down in the 1970s is not something I'd care to repeat."

The covens did what they could to neutralize violence in their home territories; the worst incidents had been in urban areas as shifters adjusted to modern society and cramped quarters. Packs had become so thick on the ground up north that territories overlapped—part of the inevitable modernization of shifter social structure. So were a rise in the number of indies and a rise in the number of covens who interacted with indies, along with the complications that created.

"I don't see why they'd go to war over this," June said. "Gavin challenged. He lost. It's a risk any candidate takes. There's more danger in how the packs will react to the fact Millington's anchors are both female."

"Millington has two mommies," Vern said with a snicker. "You think they'd have figured it out already. Eh, they're sexist bastards, the lot of them."

What June had suggested wasn't radical—for witches. The shifter community had only just begun to consider that alphas didn't have to be married. They had to be savvy leaders and sound foundations for the pack's bonding magic. Two male or female alphas was as logical as a male-female combination for that purpose.

"When Harry can vocalize," she said, "I'm sure he'll shed more light on the subject. Won't it be convenient to have our own trustworthy shifter consultant?"

Harry settled into the seat and laid his head in her lap. She stifled a yawn. The treetops had begun to bleed red with dawn.

"I'm not against Harry keeping some of his memories, necessarily." Pete braced his hands on the dashboard as the minivan sped into Millington's valley. "The other covens won't like it."

"They won't like anything that happened here the past several days." June yawned again, followed by Harry. "Most of all they won't like the fact we seem to have created the first ever coven alpha."

Since a pack bond was magical, the coven had used the pack's herbs to augment the linking spell on themselves, funneling their energies into Harry to sustain him through the confrontation. It was based partly on their group work when they pre-charged spell components and partly on the pack's ritual.

And it was wholly experimental, hence the unexpected results.

"We think it will wear off," Pete said gruffly. "Nobody realized the depth of Harry's connection to us until yesterday. But it did give us the idea for the spell."

"The way indies flock to covens, I'm surprised this has never come up," June said. Witches had always known indies were drawn to them because of the shifter desire for a network, but had never experimented with the relationship beyond how to avoid the sex.

At least, none of the covens had publicized any experiments.

"He wasn't functionally our anchor until the spell," Annette said. "The coven voted in favor of it, knowing there could be consequences. You're not the only one who's fond of Harry."

"All the more reason for him to retain his memories. If he keeps the power, do you really want him to forget what we are and what he can do?" June patted his side, her fingers twined in his fur. "He'll realize something is up immediately. His strength and senses are enhanced, and he'll have undue influence over others. Including us."

He'd have more influence over her too, but she no longer cared. He wouldn't hurt her or push her. Not if he knew the truth.

"If he's here to stay, packs need two alphas to balance that undue influence," Vern said. "I should be the other one."

"Goddess save us," Annette muttered. Bars of glaring sunlight slanted across the blacktop as they reached Millington. She slowed the minivan when they approached the turnoff for Harry's driveway.

Harry hopped up and barked in Annette's ear.

She flinched, jerking the vehicle halfway off the road. "If you would change your hairy butt back, we wouldn't have communication issues. We don't care if you're naked."

Vern coughed in the back of the van. "Speak for yourself."

"I think..." June's cheeks heated. "I think he wants to come home with me."

Harry sat back and panted.

"I suppose he can't let himself into his house." Pete cracked his window. "How long will he be in wolf form?"

"I'm not sure." If being form stuck was like being drained of magic, it could be as long as a day.

Vern snickered. "He needs a doggie door."

Harry growled. June patted him and wished they could drop Vern off somewhere. When a witch put on a young face after decades in an old one, sometimes they got to feeling their oats.

Again.

She certainly felt liberated in her natural face, one of the reasons she'd like to keep it. Fewer daily spells. More...fun. She wouldn't start at eighteen, like Vern, but witches could begin and end their pass-throughs wherever it was logistically convenient for them and the fake identifications the coven in D.C. fashioned.

"That's not why he's going to June's house." Annette met her gaze in the mirror with a thoughtful expression. "Is this a good idea, Junie?"

Annette might mean, if the coven planned to erase Harry's memories, spending more time with him would only increase June's heartbreak. And she might be concerned about something else. Well, Harry already knew about witch genetics, and June was pretty sure she and Harry had had enough sex to certify her resistance.

"Is there a rule against it?" She wouldn't be so crass as to mention details, but they were all adults here.

"We're breaking so many other rules, it hardly matters," Annette said with a sigh.

"There's no rule against it." Pete waved to the cop car parked on the corner in town. "There's no rule against it in other circumstances, either. It's just not recommended."

At June's house, June and Harry hopped out of the vehicle. He padded onto the porch and waited by the screen door, but she stayed behind to lean in Annette's window.

Witches didn't have to belong to covens, the same as shifters didn't have to belong to packs. It was just that most preferred it. Since it wasn't as deep a commitment as being in a pack, coven membership was easier to try on for size.

The Millington coven was perfectly June's size, but if they erased Harry's memories, she wouldn't be able to handle being near him, unable to love him. Any future intimate relationship between them would never work because he'd sense her genetics, starting the cycle all over again. There was simply no precedent for a witch-and-werewolf relationship that didn't involve the witch turning tail. Literally.

Like Millington's double-female alphas, she wanted to set a new precedent with Harry.

"I want you to know," she said, "if you decide to erase him, I'm leaving."

Annette's face crumpled. "You would leave us for him?"

"I would." If June could act before the coven did, she'd ask him to come with her, but a life on the run was nowhere near as appealing as a life in Millington with Harry. "He's not a risk. He'll never join a pack, so the compulsion of a pack bond is a nonissue."

Pete leaned across Annette to speak. "Nothing is decided."

June had as much of a vote as anyone in her coven, but she was one voice. The rest might not go for the Harry experiment, no matter his accidental status as their alpha. "I just thought I should warn you."

"You're blackmailing us," Annette said in a testy voice. "Your strength is half the reason we've been able to specialize in pre-charged components. Before you we had nothing going for us but ginseng."

June shrugged. Coven specialization wasn't her concern right now. "Will you let me know when the board is going to meet so we can argue our case?"

"There's no reason to postpone. Everyone knows what's going on," Pete said. "Let's set the table for later today. Five-fifteen at the tea room?"

"I'll be there."

It would have to do. Now she needed to prepare a speech for the coven meeting that would knock everyone's conventional socks off.

If the Millington pack could buck tradition, so could its coven.

A LARGE WEIGHT bounced on the end of June's bed, waking her from the light slumber she'd fallen into after a bleary trip to the restroom. Aches and pains had stiffened her limbs during her rest. The bright blast of light when she opened her eyes stabbed her in the brain. She threw the blankets over her head and groaned.

"Harry," she warned, "I told you I draw the line at a wolf in the bed."

"That's too bad." The weight shifted above her, pinning her under the blankets. "Have I mentioned your couch sucks?"

He wriggled the covers past her chin. While she was relieved to see his human face peering down at her, she couldn't drag her arms free to rub her eyes. "If you shed all over my new sofa, there's a lint roller in the second drawer in the kitchen."

"Werewolves don't really shed, thank you very much." He kissed her nose, his bare shoulders flexing. "How long are you going to sleep? I'm starving."

"Are you serious?" She bumped her knees, jouncing him in the behind. He had on boxers, nothing else. "You've been in my house a million times and suddenly you can't feed yourself lunch?"

"Dinner," he corrected cheerfully. "It's five in the afternoon."

"What?" June tried to sit up but he was too heavy. "Harry, get up, quit fooling around. We have to go. The coven is scheduled to meet at five-fifteen. We haven't discussed anything. Planned what to say. This is a disaster."

"Yesterday was the disaster." He propped himself on his elbows and adjusted his lower half atop her more comfortably. "Today is tomorrow."

Her stomach lurched. She'd slept for thirty hours? It could happen when a witch overextended herself, but what terrible timing! "Oh my gosh, they already met?

Why didn't you wake me? I didn't have a chance to get my speech ready and talk to them and—"

He pressed a finger to her lips. "I took care of it."

"You?" She stopped wriggling to gaze at him in amazement.

"Don't look so surprised." His golden-brown eyes twinkled. "I can be pretty convincing when I put my mind to it."

A pack alpha wouldn't hesitate to mold the reactions of people around him. Douglas Householder, who'd seemed like a nice guy, had done it to two car crash victims merely because they wanted to wait for the cops and he didn't agree.

The coven wouldn't respond like a pack afterward, though. They wouldn't take it in stride, part and parcel of the pack experience. They would neutralize anyone who tried to steer them quicker than a cat would pounce on a bug.

Surely Harry hadn't pulled a stunt like that.

"Don't tell me," June said, "that you pressured them as an alpha."

He grinned, dimples creasing his cheeks. "Okay, I won't tell you that."

She loved his dimples, loved the way he smiled at her when he was being naughty. Loved the way he was smiling down at her, loved that he was in her bed, loved how her body was responding even though they needed to have an important discussion about their future.

Loved him.

None of which addressed the matter at hand.

"But did you?" she asked. "Did you lean on them through the bond?"

"Relax." He inched the blankets down until her neck and chest were free. "There was no need."

"Why not?" He clearly had his memories, but that wasn't the whole story. What had happened?

"I don't think they had any intention of erasing my memories. They wanted to intimidate me." He kissed her temple, her cheek and her lips. "I have to subject myself to humiliating magical experiments, though. And I'm not allowed to order anybody around."

"What does this mean?" She didn't add "for us" because it seemed presumptuous.

"I don't know yet."

"Should we talk about it?" They'd been friends for years, but they'd only been like this a few days. Sure, she'd told him she loved him when she thought they might never see each other again, but he hadn't said it back.

He didn't say it now, either. Instead of answering, he kissed her, his tongue as sweet as pie and ice cream. June responded with enthusiasm, though she'd rather affirm their relationship verbally than physically.

First, anyway. The physical part could come soon after.

He nuzzled her throat, his lips on the pulse. His tongue flicked out to taste her, and June squirmed beneath him.

She meant to distract him, but her movement

rubbed their hips together in a way that left no doubt in her mind where his thoughts had strayed. If they'd strayed. He might have intended to have sex with her from the moment he'd woken her up.

His lips blazed a trail of fire down her chest, teasing her skin at the edge of her nightgown. Slowly he unbuttoned one, then two, then three pearls until her breasts were nearly exposed. His breath tickled her skin.

"Harry," she protested weakly, "I asked you a question."

"Mmm." He closed his lips on her nipple through the thin cotton fabric.

Her headache, even the soreness in her limbs, faded as desire rushed through her. Harry's kisses were superior to willow bark. His teeth scraped her hardened nipple, surprising a moan out of her. He responded by yanking the neckline of the gown aside and closing his hot mouth on her skin.

June's passion soared at the moist suction, as did her temperature. By the time he turned his attention to her other breast, she'd broken out in a sweat.

"It's too hot." She wriggled until her arms popped free and tried to push the blankets out of the way.

He raised his head. "No such thing."

She fanned her face. "I've got on a sheet, a blanket, a bedspread, a nightgown and a werewolf. I am melting under here."

"We can't have that." In the next ten seconds, Harry remedied her complaints. He hovered over her, both of them naked, a gleam in his eyes.

She trained her gaze on his face, though his body against hers tempted her to look. Touch. Feel. But she gave it one last shot. "Shouldn't we, uh, talk first?"

"I love you too." Harry smiled. "Now what?"

"I guess we have sex," she said, content. For now. "Then I'll cook dinner. I think I have steaks in the freezer."

His lips pressed together and his eyes closed for a moment, as if savoring something delicious. "You are the perfect woman, June. I can hardly express how perfect. I never thought I would find someone like you, or that if I did, you'd love someone like me. You're funny, you're smart, you taste like dessert, you have interesting hobbies and you make me clean up my language. My act. Everything. You're my best friend. When I'm with you, I never feel alone. But I confess, though I've always been a little bit in love with your cooking, I got us some take-out. We just have to heat it up. I thought it would leave us more time for sex."

And it did. When they finished, their limbs still entwined, their hearts racing, their stomachs growling, she asked, "So what happened at the meeting yesterday? This time I want all the details. What did they say?"

He grinned.

She didn't trust that grin. That grin had just incited a two-hour sexual romp, and she truly didn't have the energy for two more hours of…that.

"They said we should set the date for June."

"Set what date?" The date they planned to erase his

memories? Her memories? Why give her and Harry
months to fall deeper in love only to take it away?

He laughed. "The date for our wedding. Don't you
think someone named June should get married in
June?"

They got married in September.

* * * * *

ABOUT THE AUTHOR

JODY WALLACE GREW up in the South in a very rural area. She went to school a long time because she couldn't find a job and ended up with a master's degree in creative writing. Her résumé includes author, college English instructor, technical documents editor, market analyst, web designer and general all-around pain in the butt. She lives in Tennessee with her husband, kids and world-famous cat, Meankitty (from www.meankitty.com). One of her several alter egos is the Grammar Wench, which should give you an indication as to her character. Ms. Wallace publishes fantasy romances as herself and hotter romances as Ellie Marvel.